Twin sisters Allie and Zen have always shared everything: including an unconventional upbringing at Pagan Spirits Farms. They even fall in love at the same time. Pagan priestess Allie thinks she's met the man of her dreams in her buttoned-down lawyer fiancé, Paul Phillip. But is he everything he seems? Zen, a witch gifted with the sixth sense, falls for Orlando. But there's a catch: Orlando is married to someone else. As the celebration of Beltane nears, the sisters seem destined to be unlucky in love. But the Goddess moves in mysterious ways, and May Day may turn out to be magic for them after all.

Chapter One

Zenobia Van Zandt consumed her usual tall macchiato, but felt more than a caffeine buzz as she packed her suitcase. She could hardly believe it: Allegra, about to have a baby. Becoming an auntie for the first time was exciting enough, but Zen also had some news for Allie: she'd enrolled in nursing school and would be a nurse-midwife. Zen's participation in Allie's childbirth would be her first practice. She couldn't wait to get to Indianapolis and see her sister.

She could hardly contain her own feelings. Ramesh sitting at the end of the bed didn't help. He looked far too good, dressed for the Milwaukee winter in black corduroys, a thick, gray cashmere sweater, and a beige scarf. His black hair, pulled back into a ponytail, showed off his deep brown eyes and handsome face. Ramesh's slight smile might have told an average woman his thoughts. Zen, however, was not an average woman. At times like these she wished she didn't have the gift of empathy, the power to feel what other people feel.

Ramesh Sudhra felt lust. He wanted Zen so badly, all thoughts of manners and civility got pushed from his mind. He knew she could sense his purely animalistic longing, which only made the lust all the more acute. Zen could easily picture the two of them stripping out of their winter

Midsummer Night
Pagan Spirits, Book Two

Erin O'Riordan

All rights reserved. No part of this book may be reproduced or transmitted in any form or by any means, electronic or mechanical, including photocopying, recording, or by any information storage and retrieval system, without permission in writing from the publisher.

This book is for sale to adult audiences only. It contains substantial sexually explicit scenes and graphic language which may be considered offensive by some readers. All sexually active characters in this work are 18 years of age or older.

This is a work of fiction. Names, characters, places and incidents are solely the product of the author's imagination and/or are used fictitiously, though reference may be made to actual historical events or existing locations. Any resemblance to actual persons, living or dead, business establishments, events or locales is entirely coincidental.

Midsummer Night
© April 2011 Erin O'Riordan
All rights reserved

clothes and spending the whole day keeping each other very, very warm underneath her sheets.

"No," Zen said out loud, steeling her resolve, despite the sensations Ramesh was provoking in her body. "Duty calls. I have to leave for my sister's now."

"But it might be a week or more before I see you again. What am I supposed to do until then?"

Zen had hoped she could put off this conversation until after the baby's birth, but she couldn't hold back now. "Ramesh, we have to talk." She put down the long skirt she'd been folding and sat beside him. "Remember when I told you I'm going back to school?"

He narrowed his eyes. "Can this wait until after I get you out of those pants?"

"That's the thing; you and I aren't going to make love. Not for a while. We're not even going to kiss. We probably shouldn't even hold hands, or sit too close together on the couch when we watch TV."

He looked dumbfounded. His lust wilted. "What are you talking about, Zen?"

"I'm talking about a vow of celibacy," she said. "I talked to Kameko on the phone last night. Choosing my calling as a midwife is my first step on the way to becoming a Pagan priestess. My new tattoos are the second step. Now Kameko tells me if I'm really going to commit myself to being a living representation of the Goddess, then I need to spend some time focusing all my energy on Her."

"Son of a bitch," Ramesh said. "That's like giving a kid a new bike and then taking it away. So, how long are we talking about here? A long weekend? A couple of weeks, maybe?"

She shook her head. "A full four seasons."

"A year?" His utter disbelief coupled with anger and a deep disappointment. "I've already waited for you once, Zen. After you and I were the queen and king of Beltane, I came back to Kameko's farm every year, hoping to see you again. It was three years before I saw you again, Zen."

"Well, how was I supposed to know? We had this amazing, sensual, mystical experience that night in Kameko's wheat field. Great sex, yes, but also—I don't know, cosmic oneness, or something. When I woke up the next morning, you were just gone. Disappeared. How was I supposed to know you wanted a repeat performance?"

"That's not the point," he said. "The point is, you and I finally found each other again last summer. Now you want me to wait another year before I can even hold you again. Are you out of your fucking mind, Zen? Do you even know what you're asking?"

She was silent for a moment. He was right, after all. So early in their relationship, she asked for a huge sacrifice from him. She considered her response, then said, "I'm asking you to love me, Ramesh. I'm asking you to care about me so deeply, you'll endure this great, great sacrifice for me. I'm asking you to do this because I know you and I are meant to be together. I'm asking you to do this because I'm willing to wait for you."

He still felt angry, still confused, and still deeply disappointed. He also still wanted her. "Fine," he said. "I'm a big boy; I can handle it. Just tell me one thing: did you already make this vow of celibacy to the Goddess?"

Zen smiled. "No," she said. "I didn't technically make the vow yet. I just told Kameko I would. But I have to…"

He completed the thought with a kiss. Zen resisted at first, then let the sensations take over.

"Okay," she said. "One last ride before we put the bike away for a year."

Ramesh's anger and disappointment faded fast, and his lust returned as strong as ever. Stronger, she sensed, since he knew this would be their last time for a long time. As they kissed, Ramesh unbuttoned Zen's sweater and threw it onto Zen's favorite leather chair in the corner.

"It's a little chilly in here," she said, reaching out to unwrap the scarf from around his neck.

"Don't worry about that," Ramesh said, taking off his boots. He and Zen worked their way under her ivory-colored quilt and her flannel sheets. Zen slipped out of her thick socks. She took off her undershirt and reached behind her back for her bra, but he stopped her. "Slowly, now," he said. "This has to last us an entire year."

"Don't remind me." She leaned in for another kiss. He kissed her softly, keeping his lips pressed together, resisting her attempts to slip her tongue past them. She gave in, touching his arm lightly.

Zen's tongue pressed against the soft expanse of Ramesh's full lips. But no matter how many times she tried, he would not part them for her. So he was serious about them taking their time. In theory, she thought this was the most romantic gesture any lover had ever made for her. In practice, though, she grew increasingly frustrated. Ramesh's gentle kisses never failed to light the fire within her, a fire burning out of control as the kisses grew hotter, more intimate, more desperate. She expected the heat. Instead of tearing off her clothes and devouring her, he lay beside her, taking polite nibbles, metaphorically. Zen would have killed for literal nibble, especially on her earlobe.

As if he read her mind, Ramesh pulled Zen in closer to him, ran his tongue up her neck, and nibbled her earlobe. He sucked the lobe in, then out of his mouth, playfully running the tip of his tongue over her stud earring. She nestled against him, loving his mouth, its warmth and its wetness, and even the sounds he made in her ear. Adding fuel to the fire, he reached down and stroked her clit through her pants as she lay against him. She wanted more of this sensation, but not too soon. Ramesh pulled away, his fingertips now barely touching Zen's forearm.

"What's wrong, Ramesh?"

"Nothing," he said. "Nothing at all. I only wanted to keep things from going too fast."

He kissed her again, this time allowing the tip of his tongue past her lips, sending shivers of anticipation through her body. The shivers lasted the long minutes it took before the two of them lay, face to face, fully undressed. Zen had forgotten all about the chill in the air. She didn't give a thought to her pregnant sister. At this moment, the universe consisted of one bed, one man, and one woman who loved this man as if he were her very soul. At last the woman and her love would be united.

She looked into his eyes, so full of love. She felt the love penetrate her skin and seep into her bones. Love was a physical, palpable thing to her, waiting for her. Waiting for the next move.

Ramesh laid his head on Zen's pillow, staring up at the blanket covering them. His face looked serene, but Zen knew he was as eager as she was—not only because of her gift of empathy, but also because of his cock, erect and waiting for her.

With measured care, Zen crawled on top of him and straddled him. The heat radiated from where their bodies came together.

By then, Zen had caught on to the game of taking her time. She planned to sit here, gently running her fingers over his chest, taking him inside her slowly only once she could no longer bear the ache in her slick, waiting pussy.

Then Ramesh changed all the rules of the game on her.

With gentle urgency, he put both hands on Zen's hips, pulling her onto his solid shaft all at once. She cried out, not from pain but from surprise.

She caught her breath. "What gives? I thought we were taking our time!"

He laughed, the deep, throaty laugh of a satisfied man about to become even more so. "You're in control now," he said. "You set the pace. I'm yours; do with me what you will."

Zen smiled. She decided then she would give him her slowest, sexiest thrust, the one designed to make every inch of his cock feel her in all her might. Ramesh loved the slow stroke, and she could feel the pleasure she was giving him.

She decided she would bring him right to the edge of losing control. Soon she could hear it in his breathing, and see it in the look in his eyes.

Abruptly, she stopped, holding her body stock-still. Ramesh's eyes shot open. Zen laughed. She gave him a moment to regain his composure before she started the whole erotic slow-dance over again.

When Zen had her second orgasm, she knew Ramesh was close to coming with her. She couldn't let that happen. Not yet, anyway. She forced herself to be still, denying herself the pleasure of those delicious aftershocks to deny Ramesh the pleasure of his own earthquake. It was the same way with her third orgasm.

The fourth one crept up on her, striking with immense power at the base of her spine, traveling up into her throat and coming out as a rather pathetic squeak, followed by a howl. She lay her fingertips over Ramesh's heart. Its beat was steady, unmoved by her pleasure. She opened her eyes; Ramesh looked almost bored. He must, she thought, be rather numb by now.

Ramesh counted on the element of surprise.

In an acrobatic move, atypical of his usually mellow lovemaking style, he wrestled Zen onto her back. She laughed with delight at the chaotic moment of flailing, intertwining limbs, the intimate *coup d'etat*.

A dot of sweat fell from his face onto Zen's breast. She wiped the drop away. "I thought I was in control. I thought you were mine to do with what I will."

"Admit it," he said, running the back of his hand across his perspiring forehead, "this is what you want."

She bit her lip; she couldn't argue. He dove into her, covering her body with his, making her skin tingle with the intensity of this long-delayed pleasure. She breathed in, taking in the scent of his skin. Her brain barely had time to process its sweetness before she found herself on the verge of another orgasm.

"Try to stop me now," he said softly into her ear, challenging her.

Zen could do nothing, however, except hold onto him more tightly. As she did, the walls of her pussy clenched around him, drawing him deeper inside her. Zen sucked in her breath. She couldn't hold out any longer. In seconds, they came together. She could feel the immense satisfaction of his release, making hers all the more intense.

Time once again slowed to a crawl as they rode out the aftershocks of their mutual earthquake. Hours seemed to pass before they separated, becoming two again.

Ramesh rolled onto his side, took the gasping Zen in his arms, and held her against him. They lay there, paralyzed by the intense pleasure. Zen started to fall asleep, but was suddenly struck with a pang of guilt: her sister was waiting for her in Indiana.

"I'm sorry," Zen said into Ramesh's chest. "I have to go."

"I know," he said, letting go of her. "We should shower."

They took a moment to gather up the courage to brave the cold, to leave behind the intimate embrace of the covers. They sprinted to Zen's bathroom, holding hands, getting under the hot water as quickly as possible. Standing in the narrow shower, struggling to share the hot water equally, Zen and Ramesh held onto one another.

"I can't believe this was be the last time we'll make love for an entire year, Zen. Are you sure I can't talk you out of it?"

"Think of it this way: one year from now, I'm going to fuck your brains out," she said. As she did, she turned to watch him rinsing the last soap suds from the front of his belly. Soon he grew hard again. Zen let Ramesh finish washing, then dropped to her knees. She couldn't believe how quickly he came in her mouth. She stroked him only a few times, and he unloaded his cum.

"God, I'll miss the taste of you," she said.

He struggled to catch his breath. "Thanks," he said. "After all the times you got to come, I'm glad I at least got a second one in. How many times *did* you come, anyway?"

She held up five fingers. "The fifth one was amazing."

The last of the hot water ran down the drain, and Zen and Ramesh scrambled for their bath robes, hanging on the back of the bathroom door. They dried themselves quickly. Ramesh, who didn't have any other clothes with him, rushed to put on the clothes he'd shed under the covers. Zen flung open her lingerie drawer and quickly shimmied into a pair of lavender panties and a matching bra. She pulled on a pair of black jeans, a long-sleeved tee and her red sweater, a Winter Solstice gift from Ramesh. She dressed in record time.

"Did you remember to pack your camera?" Ramesh asked her as he zipped his black cords.

"No," she said. "Thank you." She got the camera case from its drawer, but realized how much she would miss him. She suppressed a tear as she snapped a photo of him, one last remembrance of their last night together as lovers for a long time.

Ramesh was quiet as he helped Zen carry her bag down the stairs.

"Oh, I almost forgot," Ramesh said, zipping his parka. He took his backpack off his shoulder, opened it, and pulled out a brightly colored tin. He offered it to Zen.

"What's this?"

"*Gajar barfi*."

"Sounds disgusting."

Ramesh opened the tin, filled with a lightly orange-colored fudge, with big chunks of pistachio. She caught a whiff of cardamom, and Zen's mouth watered. "You tell me," he said. "My mom makes too much of it. You know me; I don't have a sweet tooth for anything except you." He kissed her cheek. "My God, I'm going to miss you, Zen."

"I never said this would be easy," she said, picking up her heavy suitcase. "This may be the hardest thing I've ever had to do. But I have to do it, Ramesh."

"I know."

As she walked through the snow to Ramesh's car, Zen avoided stepping in Ramesh's footprints. She wanted to see them there when she returned from her sister's house.

He drove her to the airport.

Before she got out of the car, he touched her cheek and pulled Zen in for one more long, lingering kiss. Then he said his goodbyes and drove off.

The snow wasn't as deep in Indy as it had been in Milwaukee. When the taxi driver let her out in front of Allie's, Zen found the walkway nicely shoveled, and the porch lights on for her. She hadn't even reached the door when it opened. Allie's baby's daddy, Orlando Parisi, stood in the doorway in all of his winter gear.

"Let me help you with your bags," he said. "Allie's taking a little nap, but I'm sure she won't mind if you wake her."

"Thanks." As she stepped inside, Zen felt relieved despite the ever-present possibility things would feel awkward between her and Orlando. He'd been her lover before he met Allie. She felt relieved to find Orlando didn't feel any of his former attraction to her. He felt happy to see her, but only because they'd become friends. He felt completely in love with Allie, if a little worried about her.

Zen went upstairs to her sister's bedroom. Through the open door she could see Allie lying on her side, her eyes closed. Zen hesitated to disturb her. Allie had always been thin, and after battling morning sickness for several months, she looked more fragile than ever, despite her very-pregnant belly.

"It must be weird, looking at her like that."

Zen turned around. Orlando stood at the top of the stairs. She hadn't heard him come up.

"What do you mean?" Like Orlando, Zen kept her voice low.

"Because she looks like you, except pregnant. Isn't that like seeing yourself pregnant?"

She watched Allie breathing, her sister's chest rising and falling. "I hadn't thought of that." She looked down and imagined what it would be like to see her own belly so swollen, to feel a child kicking inside of her. Only two springtimes ago, Zen would have imagined herself in Allie's position, pregnant with a baby who had Orlando's bright hazel eyes. Now she thought of Ramesh, and what it would be like to be a mother to his baby. The thought barely crossed Zen's mind before she felt a stab of longing. That particular joy seemed so far off in the future, it felt as if the day would never come. If it ever came at all. Maybe Ramesh would get tired of waiting for Zen and find someone new...

Orlando set Zen's suitcase down by the door. "You know, you don't really look *exactly* like her," he said, studying Zen for a moment. She felt a slight hesitation on his part, a kind of mental blush. "You're blonde, and Allie's the vegetarian, no-alcohol, always-doing-yoga one. She doesn't have your curves." He said *curves* admiringly, and she sensed briefly that some part of him still missed the feel of her body. "I've tried getting your sister to put on a little more weight, but it hasn't happened."

"It would help if you could cook," she said.

He smiled. "Sure I can. You don't know good Italian food when you taste it. You don't know your *melanzana* from your *carciofini*."

Allie sat up. As she turned toward Zen and Orlando, her face glowed with a wide smile. "Hey, Sis," she said. "When did you get here?"

Zen knelt on the bed, hugging and kissing her sister. "Goddesses above, Allie! The last time I saw you, you were just starting to show. Now you're as big as Auntie Kameko's barn."

Zen could tell Allie was not amused. Fortunately, Orlando distracted Allie with a full-mouthed kiss.

"Are you leaving now?" Allie asked Orlando.

"Not yet," he said. "Two more hours. I think I'll watch the weather channel for a few more minutes, make sure there isn't a winter storm coming this way. I wouldn't want the two of you trapped in the house together."

"What's that supposed to mean?" Zen asked. "Why not?"

"Help me up," Allie interjected, holding out her arms. Zen and Orlando each took one of her hands, and Allie scrambled to her feet.

"Only a couple more weeks of this, honey," Orlando said. He was still holding Allie's hand. Zen felt peace and contentment between them as Orlando added, "The baby's almost here."

"Why shouldn't we be trapped in the house together, Orlando?" Zen pressed. "Allie and I get along fine."

"Always have," Allie said with a somewhat tired smile.

"It's not that," Orlando said. "It's—well, even though Allie's planned for a home birth, and I'm sure she and the baby will be fine, I'll still feel better if Kameko and the midwife can get here when the time comes." He kissed Allie's forehead and went downstairs.

Zen almost spilled her news right then and there. Before she could say anything, though, Allie hit her upside the head with, "Think about it, Zen—if things had worked out a little bit differently, you could have been the one pregnant with Orlando's baby."

Zen choked on her own spit. "Thank Goddess that didn't happen. You and Orlando were destined to be together, and you know it." Okay, so Zen had been thinking the same thing only moments before. Still, it was odd to hear it coming from Allie's mouth. Zen always hoped Allie had a selective memory when it came to their past.

Allie smiled sweetly, resting her hand on her belly. "Ooh, I felt a couple of kicks there. He really hasn't been kicking too much lately. Melissa says it's because he's getting so big, there's no room for him to move anymore." Zen sensed Allie felt excited, but also scared about the birth. Zen reached out and put her arms around her sister.

"You'll do fine," Zen said. "You're going to make a great mom."

"I know," Allie said. Zen felt her trying to push the anxiety out of her head. "Now come on. The pregnant lady's hungry, and maybe the pregnant lady's sister will help her make a grilled provolone sandwich for her and the baby."

"Anything you want." The sisters went into the kitchen. Zen let Allie monopolize the conversation as they got out the sandwich maker, bread, olive oil, and cheese. Orlando came in, asked Zen for a sandwich for the road, kissed Allie profusely, and left for his overnight trip to Chicago.

Only after he left did Zen reveal her plans for nursing school, and a career as a midwife, to her sister. Allie seemed impressed. "I'll be proud to have my only sister assisting with the birth," Allie said. "I'm going to need all the help I can get."

The guest bedroom had already been sacrificed to make the nursery, so the sisters shared Allie's bed. As Zen laid her head on what would normally be Orlando's pillow, she breathed in the all-too-familiar scent of his floral, unisex cologne. For more than a year, it had been the scent of the man Zen loved. Now that smell belonged to Allie.

So, too, did another familiar scent, this one less pleasant. "Allie?"

"What?"

"I know you have this quirk about sleeping with Orlando's dirty laundry." She reached under Allie's pillow and, sure enough, pulled out a white cotton undershirt. From the smell of it, Orlando had worn it through a morning workout. Or two. "But do you think you could find something a little less funky? A button-down, maybe?"

Allie snatched the t-shirt from her sister. "I like this smell," she said. "So did you, at one time. There was a time when you wouldn't have minded his sweat rubbed all over your naked body…"

"You disgust me," Zen said.

Allie lay back down, clutching Orlando's sweaty V-neck like a teddy bear. "Oh, please," Allie said. Zen waited for her to say more, but within moments, Allie snored softly.

Zen lay her head back on the floral-scented pillow. She closed her eyes and willed herself not to have any memories of Orlando. Her mind obliged, focusing on Ramesh instead. She thought of him, alone in his apartment near the campus where he studied biology. If he wasn't already asleep, he would be studying, reading some thick textbook about polypeptide sequences. Zen dreaded the day when she herself would be struggling through organic chemistry, or some other subject she needed for her nursing degree. Ramesh would be a great help to her then. They could study human sex hormones together—but no, she didn't mean it like that. There wouldn't be any of *that* kind of studying for a long while.

No more of the hungry kisses Ramesh would greet her with when they hadn't seen each other in a week or more.

No more of his sweet kisses on her eyelids right before she fell asleep in his arms.

No more of those wonderful things that led up to sleep: the way he'd flick the inside of her ear with his tongue, then trail tongue-flicks down her neck, over her breasts, down to her navel, not stopping until he'd reached the innermost part of her, her pussy wet and begging for more, and then more than his tongue.

Zen peeled off the first of two blankets covering her and her sister. She felt hot, but also lonely. Already. She hadn't even taken the dreaded vow yet. She couldn't stop thinking about Ramesh. Somehow she made herself think about the tattoo the experienced midwife, Melissa

Stargazer, had painstakingly inked on Zen's back. Imitating the art of ancient Greek pottery, it portrayed the huntress-goddess Artemis in the moonlight, hunting a white stag with her hounds. It reminded Zen she belonged, body, mind and soul, to the Dark Lady, her spiritual mother. Soon she would be a priestess, her whole life—including her lovemaking with Ramesh—set apart as sacred. The vow of sexual purity would cleanse her for the moment when her dedication became complete.

That moment, however, seemed so far off in the distance, Zen hoped she would not lose sight of it. Goddess give me strength, she prayed.

Zen and Allie got a few hours of sleep. Some time after midnight, Allie shook Zen awake. Zen knew right away she'd be practicing her midwifery skills a little earlier than expected.

Chapter Two

In the almost-perfect darkness, Zen helped her sister sit up. She hunted under the bed for Allie's slippers, found them, and put them on her sister's feet. "What does it feel like?" Zen asked as she helped Allie out of bed.

"Right now, it feels like I have to pee," Allie said, following with a short laugh. "But everything in that area feels kind of tight."

"Like you have cramps?"

Allie shook her head. "Like I had cramps, but I took something for them. The pressure, but not the pain." She lumbered over to the bathroom and turned on the light before closing the door. Zen blinked.

"I'm not an expert yet," Zen said loudly through the door, "but I bet it's just Braxton Hicks contractions. It's probably a false alarm." She'd already told Allie this, when Allie had first awakened her, but Zen figured she had to keep her sister as calm as possible.

"Probably," Allie answered.

Zen picked up the phone from Allie's bedside table. "I'm calling Auntie Kameko."

Allie answered with the sound of a toilet flushing. Zen dialed. She knew Kameko disliked the telephone. She had one phone in her house, kept where it had always been, in the kitchen hallway next to the cellar door. It was an old rotary-dial phone mounted to the wall. Zen would have to let it ring and ring.

When Auntie Kameko finally answered, she sounded out of breath and slightly suspicious, as if this might be a prank. "Hello?"

"Auntie Kameko, it's Zen. I'm at Allie's house."

Kameko took a deep breath. "What's going on?"

"Allie doesn't feel good. She and I agree it's probably Braxton Hicks, but I think you and Melissa should get here, if you can."

"What did Allie's doctor say?"

"I haven't called the doctor or Melissa yet. We haven't even called Orlando. Only you."

Kameko took a moment, Zen guessed, to be flattered she was the first one on the phone list. Then she said, "Orlando? Where's he?"

"Staying with his mother in Highland Park," Zen answered. "He had some stupid board meeting in Chicago."

"I thought he sold the lumber company?"

The bathroom door opened. Zen looked over at Allie, who stood in the doorway with a vague half-smile on her face, rubbing her belly. "He did, and I'll be happy to fill you in on all the details as soon as you get here."

Kameko got the message. "Call Melissa," she said. "I heard the snow plow out on the main road earlier, so I should be at her door in half an hour. But it might be another four hours before we can make it to Indy."

"We've got time," Zen said. "Even if she is in labor, it's going to take forever, right? Because this is her first one."

"Don't say that," Allie said from across the room.

"Hand the phone to your sister," Kameko said. "I want to talk to her while I get ready."

Zen couldn't hear what Kameko said to Allie; something soothing, because she could feel Allie relaxing. Allie crossed the room and handed the phone back to Zen. Zen heard a dial tone. "Call Melissa," Allie said.

Although Melissa was a close friend of the Kitatani-Van Zandt clan, and had recently become Zen's mentor, Zen still had to look up Melissa's cell phone number in her address book. She dialed the digits, and before long Zen heard Melissa's voice. "Melissa?" Zen said. "Were you already up?"

"I'm seventy-six years old," Melissa said, sounding perfectly alert. "I don't need much sleep anymore. What's going on, my dear? Do you have needs in matters spiritual, or temporal?"

"Gynecological and obstetrical," Zen said. "Hey, where are you going?" She directed the question at Allie.

"Kitchen," Allie said. "Is there any of that Indian carrot fudge left?"

Zen shook her head. "We ate it all."

"Go make your sister something to eat and a cup of tea," Melissa said. "And relax. She's probably not even in labor yet. Even if she is, we have time. I was in labor with my oldest for thirty-two hours."

"Auntie Kameko is on her way to your house now," Zen said. "We'll see you when you get here."

"Think pleasant thoughts," Melissa added. "Be positive. Encourage her. "

"I will," Zen said.

"Don't panic."

"I won't. See you in a little while." She ran after Allie, helping her down the stairs, carrying the mobile phone in one hand. They settled at the kitchen table, where Zen washed a bunch of purple grapes for Allie while Allie called Orlando.

Zen set the bowl of grapes on the table and started some water for tea. "Is he coming home?"

"Of course," Allie said. "He's bringing Bojana with him."

Zen opened the cabinet where Allie kept a selection of herbal teas. She spun the lazy Susan slowly, contemplating each colorful box of tea as it spun past her. Allie noticed.

"What's wrong?" Allie said. "Aren't you eager to finally meet Orlando's mama?"

"Honestly, no. Bojana knows perfectly well Orlando was still married to Catherine when he and I started seeing each other."

"He was never married to Catherine, technically. That marriage was annulled. Besides, it's ancient history."

"Ancient history or not, I'm still going to feel like she's judging me. I'm still going to feel like the hell-bound slut who was boinking her little boy."

Allie laughed. "I'm the one who's having his illegitimate child here, okay? No offense, but I don't think you're going to be the center of attention tonight, Zen. I'm the hell-bound slut now. I'll have the licorice."

"Oh, yeah." Though she still spun the lazy Susan, Zen almost forgot about her sister's tea. She grabbed the black licorice tea box. She closed the cabinet and shut off the boiling water, then reached for one of Allie's mugs. "You know, I should probably consult my herb guide before I give you anything. Maybe licorice induces labor."

Allie picked a handful of grapes from their stems and popped them all into her mouth at once. "I'm going to lie down on the couch. I'll put in a movie, and maybe I can get back to sleep before everybody gets here and tells me I made them travel in the middle of a January night for no reason."

"February," Zen said, looking at the clock. "It's after midnight; it's the first of February now."

Allie started to get out of her wooden kitchen chair, and Zen ran to help her. "February first?" she said, reaching for the grapes. "It's Imbolc. I have to light the candles—"

"I'll bring them to you," Zen said. "Just take your grapes and sit down. I'll bring the candles, your tea, the herb guide, something yellow to wear, and whatever else you need. You go be a pregnant woman."

Allie half smiled and half frowned. "Thank you for being here with me, Zen," she said. "I'd be lost without you."

"You'd be fine. A little lonely, maybe."

Allie gave her sister a quick kiss on the cheek before making her way to the front room. Zen dashed upstairs, leaving Allie's licorice tea to cool on the counter. She went to the bedroom, where she flung open a drawer and grabbed the first yellow thing she could find: a pair of socks. When Allie had taken her vows as a priestess, she'd dedicated herself to the goddesses of light, of sun and fire. She probably thought it was cute, then, to own a long pair of yellow-and-gold striped socks with smiling, cartoon suns on them. Zen laughed as she slung the pair of socks over her shoulder.

Next Zen went for her suitcase. She slammed it onto the bed and threw it open, tossing bras and panties out as she searched for the small stack of paperbacks she'd brought with her. At last she found her herb guide and stuck it under her arm.

She grabbed the three-branched candelabra from the top of Allie's dresser, with its white, red and black candles. She carried it into the master bath.

Zen sighed. "Why does she have to have so many candles in here?" she said out loud to herself. She did the best she could to scoop up all the scented candles from the natural-stone ledge of Allie's huge, custom-made bathtub. She couldn't carry them all in one armload, so she juggled as many as she could. She hurried to get back downstairs, letting the book and candles fall onto Allie's beige leather couch.

Allie sat in the matching armchair, with her favorite beige-and-gray afghan spread across her legs. Zen held out the socks to her. "Here."

Allie laughed as she took them. "Perfect," she said. "You have to wear something yellow, too."

"I didn't bring anything yellow," Zen said. "Besides, you're the sun-worshiper. I'm about to be dedicated to the dark aspects of the Goddess; I'm a strictly moon-goddess type of a girl."

Allie shook her head. "All priestesses traditionally wear yellow on Imbolc," she said. She handed one of the socks back to Zen.

Reluctantly, Zen sat and put one yellow sock on her own foot. Allie stuck hers on her hand, reminding Zen of a sock puppet. "I can't reach my feet anymore. The Goddess will have to deal."

"She'll understand. How are you doing?" Zen asked.

Allie patted her belly. "I'm fine," she said. "I feel a little twinge, every once in a while. This isn't all the candles, is it? Where's my pumpkin spice candle? It's the big, orange one."

"I couldn't carry them all," Zen said. "I'll have to make another trip."

"Where's my tea?"

"I'll bring it." She picked up the herb book and flipped through the pages as she walked to the kitchen. She didn't see anything about labor or childbirth under the licorice listing, so she supposed it was safe to give Allie the tea. In moments, she'd delivered the tea to her sister, run back upstairs for the rest of the candles in Allie's bathroom, grabbed the lighter, and returned with them. Zen felt frantic after running all over the house. She was amazed at how calm Allie was, talking to her belly with the sock puppet hand.

"If I were you," Zen said, "I'd be more than a little bit nervous right now."

"I forgot today was Imbolc," Allie said. "Ever since you reminded me, I've been a little bit excited. I want to be in labor, Zen. I hope my son is born today."

"You're kidding, right? Because you know that's not going to happen. You're not even due for two more weeks."

"It's going to happen if it was meant to happen. I think it was, Zen. It's been nine months since Beltane, and Orlando and I were meant to get pregnant at Beltane."

Zen didn't dare say out loud what she thought: Allie had forgotten about her little fling with her ex-husband, Paul Phillip, the day after Beltane. Allie still wasn't entirely sure whether Orlando or Paul Phillip was the baby's biological father. Since Paul Phillip now lived in Saugituck, Michigan, with his boyfriend, Zen and Allie both had their fingers crossed, hoping the baby looked like Orlando.

"I think this baby was meant to be born on Imbolc, Zen. I think he's going to be a child of the fire-goddess, like his mom." Moving the sock on her hand like a mouth again, she said to her belly, "You're ready to come out, aren't you? Well, you need to wait a little bit longer. At least wait until Daddy gets home."

"I hope so," Zen said. She knew how lame it sounded, but she didn't want to rain on Allie's parade. She gathered all of Allie's candles onto the coffee table in front of the leather sofa and arranged them in a large circle.

"Careful, Zen. We don't want to set any of the new furniture on fire."

Zen laughed. "We've been doing this since we were teenagers, and Auntie Kameko was doing it even before then. We've never set anything on fire." As she arranged the candles around Allie's chair, she added, "You're turning into such a mom."

"Let's hope so," Allie said, rubbing her belly. "I wish Orlando was here already. I'll feel better when he gets here."

Zen completed the circle of candles around the two of them. She held up the candelabra with the white, red and black candles in front of Allie. She offered Allie the lighter in her other hand. "Would you like to do the honors, oh daughter of Brigid, goddess of fire?"

Allie nodded her head graciously and took the lighter. She lit the white candle as she composed an impromptu prayer. "Oh Brigid, our mother, goddess of fire, we dedicate this sacred feast of Imbolc to you. At this dark and gloomy time of year, when it seems winter will never end, we know the days are actually getting longer and warmer, and spring is coming soon, thanks to you. Care for us, mother, and do not neglect to give us your light and your heat so we may live. Give your light and your heat to the earth so the springtime crops grow so we may have food to sustain ourselves and our children. Let the young be birthed and plants renewed so that fresh breath is given to life. So let it be."

"So let it be," Zen echoed her. She set the lighter aside and placed the candelabra in the circle. She used its black candle to light the candle next to it, and then used that candle to light the next, until she had gone all the way around the circle. As she did, she added her own prayer. "Goddess, if it is your will for Allie's son to be born today, on your sacred day, then please grant that she and the baby be safe in childbirth. And please don't let us fall asleep and burn the house down. So let it be."

"So let it be," Allie said. "Now, what do you want to watch?"

"Since it's just the two of us, how about *Thelma and Louise*?"

Allie shook her head. "How about something a little less tragic?"

"*Romeo and Juliet*? The Leonardo and Claire version?"

"Zen, that movie is tragic in every sense of the word. Since you want to be all Shakespearean, how about *A Midsummer Night's Dream*, the Rupert and Michelle version? There's nothing like Midsummer to get your mind off a long winter's night."

"Good call. Romance, magic, fairies, and a young Christian Bale. Yummy."

"Down, girl!" Allie laughed. "Is it possible my pregnancy estrogen is screwing with your brain?"

"It's almost certain, and yet knowing this does nothing to diminish Christian Bale's deliciousness." She gave Allie a satisfied smile, then went to the entertainment center and looked through her sister's movie collection until she found the right disc.

The costumed fantasy, with its star-crossed lovers and mischievous fairies, distracted them from Allie's discomfort. When the movie ended, they started it up again.

The candle light aided the mood, and soon Zen almost forgot they were waiting for Kameko and Melissa. The headlights of Melissa's ancient, battered Volkswagen outside of Allie's house snapped Zen back to reality. She got up and opened the door for them.

"Hey!" Allie complained. "You're letting all the cold air in!"

"I'm letting the experienced midwife, and the baby's grandma, in!" Zen countered. Kameko, wearing a long red coat with a fake fur collar and matching mittens, came in carrying a large plastic bowl with a lid. Stepping carefully over the ring of candles, she set the bowl on the coffee table and wrapped her arms around Allie.

"How are you feeling?" Kameko said.

"I'm okay. I feel—well, it's like a boa constrictor is squeezing my belly. But just every now and then. It's not too bad. Is this what Braxton Hicks contractions are like?"

Melissa stepped out of her black parka; Zen took it from her and hung it in the coat closet. Underneath, she wore a yellow t-shirt, a white scrub top, and white pants. "Well, yeah," she said. "And it's also what labor is like. How far apart are the contractions?"

She looked at Allie, but Zen answered. "Thirty to forty minutes."

"Plenty of time, then," Melissa said. "I'll check you in a little while to see if you're dilated yet."

"What's in the bowl?" Allie asked Kameko, unfazed by what Melissa had said.

"Lobster fried rice. I know Imbolc isn't usually one of the feasts you'd eat meat for, but you need your strength. So I brought you a little protein."

"I didn't know you could make lobster fried rice," Zen said, taking Kameko's coat. "You never made lobster fried rice for me."

"You've never had a baby, either. You have a baby and I'll make you whatever you want."

"She made it for Naoko when Naoko gave birth to Dakota. Remember, Kameko? When Naoko and Steve came down from Seattle for the birth?"

Kameko laughed at she settled into the sofa, near Allie's chair. "How could I forget the birth of my first grandchild?"

"That was also the first time you saw me in action," Melissa said proudly.

"Not exactly, Melissa. I was there when you gave birth to Daphne, and again when you had Ariadne."

"Wait a minute," Zen said. "You were the midwife for your own children's births?"

Melissa and Kameko laughed. "That would be pretty much impossible," Melissa said. "But I did give birth to the last three of my seven without any outside help, other than Kameko, a few of our other girlfriends, and my Santiago." She sighed. "I miss him, Kameko."

"I know," Kameko said. "I miss Eric, too."

Allie let out a cry, clearly in pain. Zen felt it from across the room. Allie felt sore and anxious.

"Relax," Zen said. "You're in very capable hands, whether you're actually in labor now or practicing."

Allie managed a smile. "Can I have some fried rice now, or do I need to wait until Melissa examines me?"

"It's up to you," Melissa said. " Zen and I are here to help you, not try to dictate this birth to you. The only 'must' in childbirth is, eventually, the baby must come out. But if you want to know the truth, it usually happens anyway, even if we don't do anything at all."

Allie laughed. "I hope he's going to be born today. I want an Imbolc baby. I hope he can wait until Orlando gets here, though." She looked at the clock. "It's pretty much a straight shot south from Michigan, but Orlando might not be here for another hour or two. You all had better help me keep this puppy in here a little while longer."

"Don't worry," Kameko said. "There's plenty of time. Have some fried rice. Zen, why don't you make your sister another cup of tea?"

"Raspberry, if you can find it," Melissa said. "Raspberry is good for menstrual cramps and women in labor."

Zen made a mental note of it as she stepped around the ring of candles and went into the kitchen. Kameko followed her. When they were alone, Kameko put her hand on Zen's shoulder. "I didn't tell your sister this, because I wasn't quite sure how to bring it up, but I called Paul Phillip and let him know what was going on."

Zen almost dropped the water kettle. "Paul Phillip? What did he say?"

"Don't worry; he's not coming down here. But he said he would call Allie in a few hours and see how she's doing."

"Why?" Zen asked. "What was he concerned about, Kameko? I know he still cares about Allie, even if he isn't in love with her anymore. But you can't tell me all of the sudden, after nine months of totally avoiding her, he's suddenly interested in being a father."

Kameko shook her head. "I don't think he wants to be a father, but he at least wants to know if the baby is his."

"It doesn't make any difference. Orlando's a good man. He hasn't treated Armin any different since finding out Catherine cheated on him and someone else is Armin's biological dad. He'll do the same thing with Allie's baby. Paul Phillip will not be the daddy, whether he's the father or not."

"I understand how you feel," Kameko said, "but this is between Allie and Paul Phillip. Don't you think your sister should get to make the choice?"

"She did make a choice. She and Orlando may not have known each other well when they made this baby, but they're in love now. She chose Orlando, and he chose her. Auntie Kameko, I wish you could feel what I feel when they're together. As much as it pains me to say this, Kameko, he loves her much more than he ever loved me, and they haven't even been together for a year yet."

Kameko looked into Zen's eyes. Zen felt how excited she was to be having another grandchild, how much she loved her two foster daughters, and how stubbornly she wanted to stand up for her ex-son-in-law. The water kettle whistled, and Zen turned off the flame. She pointed to the cabinet behind Kameko's head.

"Allie keeps the tea in there."

Kameko obliged, opening the cabinet and spinning the lazy Susan until she found the magenta-colored box with the big raspberry on the front of it. Zen had neglected to bring Allie's used mug with her, so she got out a clean cup and poured the water over the tea bag. Kameko watched her, saying nothing before she went back into the front room.

"I still prefer the classic film adaptation of *A Midsummer Night's Dream*," Melissa was saying to Allie as Allie ate the cold lobster fried rice directly from the bowl, with a spoon Kameko had provided. "Have you seen in? It has James Cagney."

"Who?" Allie said, slightly irritating Melissa.

"Never mind," Melissa said. "This guy they've got playing Oberon is really pretty. What's his name again?"

"Rupert Everett," Kameko said. "Don't get your hopes up, Melissa. He's as gay as—"

"—As Paul Phillip," Zen said pointedly, staring Kameko down.

Allie groaned.

"What's the matter?" Melissa asked her. "Is the raspberry tea already taking effect?"

"No," Allie said, "I'd forgotten all about a certain gay ex until Zen said something. I kept thinking this birth would be a nice little family affair, just me and Orlando, his mom, and the three of you. I forgot there was another horse in the race. Or should I say another stud?"

"Don't think about it," Melissa said. "Your son's DNA is not the issue today, not at all. All we have to do today is welcome him into the world, if he's ready to come into it. Oh, and you!" She pointed at Zen. "Before you're ready to attend to the sacred duty of the priestess-midwife, we need to carry out the next stage of your initiation."

Zen's stomach lurched. She was *so* not looking forward to making her vow of celibacy official.

Allie set the bowl of fried rice aside. "I think I'm ready for my check-up now."

Melissa nodded at Zen, then looked back at Allie. "Where will you be more comfortable: out here on the couch, or on your bed?"

"Bed," Allie said. "Do I have to wear one of those shorty hospital gowns that don't close in the back?"

Melissa laughed. "Not in your own house, sweetie. You wear whatever you want. Walk around naked if you want to. Your pajama top looks fine. Get rid of the bottoms and make yourself comfortable under the blankets."

"As comfortable as I can be with my mom's best friend and my sister about to look up my bum," Allie muttered to herself as Kameko helped her out of the chair. She finished her raspberry tea while it was still hot and went upstairs with Kameko.

Melissa looked at Zen. "This is an important day, Zen. What I'm about to teach you is a sacred tradition, passed down from woman to woman through all of the generations, ever since Goddess created woman and gave birth to her from her own sacred womb."

"Yes, Priestess." Zen didn't take all of Melissa's Goddess mythology literally, but then, neither did Melissa. They both knew their deeds were more important than their words, though words had very powerful magical significance.

"When I marked your body with symbols of Her, the Goddess of the Underworld, the Earth's womb, that was the first stage of your initiation. Your life is marked to be dedicated to Diana, Goddess of the moon, to her sisters Selene and Hecate and Persephone, and to all the world's Goddesses of dark, of night, of underworld. This is a great responsibility. Do you take it freely?"

"Yes, Priestess. I am proud and happy to serve Her."

Melissa smiled as she reached out and put her hand on Zen's shoulder. "As a symbol of your devotion to Her, your strength and willingness to serve Her, will you, Zenobia Van Zandt, vow to remain as a virgin for one year?"

As a virgin. The words sounded so impossible. It was as if Melissa had asked Zen to turn back time and be a little girl again. Zen's sexuality played such an important part in her life. It had led her into her relationship with Orlando, which had blossomed into a friendship and his being a worthy companion for her sister. It had led her to Ramesh, whom she loved, and wished she could be with even as she stood inside the ring of candles, getting ready to take her vow. It seemed impossible for her to live for a year without his touch, his kisses, making love to him all night. It seemed to Zen that three years before, when she and Ramesh had been strangers, meeting one another for the first time as the queen and king of Beltane, bodily worshiping the Goddess of Fertility without even knowing one another's names, her adult life had truly begun. Now she would subsume that life into the worship of the same Goddess with a different face. Melissa had mentioned strength. Was there really so much strength in Zen? Could she truly be the master of her own desires long enough to learn to serve?

Melissa waited patiently for Zen's answer. As she did, the ring of candles grew more and more dim until it seemed all the candles had burned out, leaving only puddles of cooling wax in Allie's candle containers. But no, the three candles in the candelabra, the first ones to be lit, still burned. Zen watched them flicker until, before her eyes, the black candle signifying the underworld aspect of Goddess and woman burned out. The red candle, signifying the sexual woman and the mother, burned out next. That left only one candle, the white. The color of innocence, childhood, and virginity.

"Yes, Priestess," Zen said at last. "I accept the vow of celibacy and purity for one year. During that time, I will study the sacred art of the priestess-midwife and dedicate myself to serving Goddess and woman. So let it be."

"So let it be," Melissa responded. "Now, let's go have a look at Allie."

"Can you tell whether she's in labor or having Braxton Hicks contractions?"

"We can tell by looking at her cervix," Melissa said. "When it gets ready for delivery, the signs are unmistakable. I'll show you."

"I never imagined I'd want to look at my sister's cervix," Zen said.

After performing the examination, guiding Zen through the process, Melissa told Allie it seemed clear she was in labor. "Don't worry, though. You've still got a long way to go before you're ready to give birth. There's still plenty of time for Orlando to get here."

Zen felt the wave of anxiety washing over Allie. "I knew this day would come sooner or later," Allie said, grabbing Kameko's hand and stroking it. "I tried to be ready, but how can you be ready to have a baby for the first time? I don't know how to do it."

"You may not know how, but you'll be able," Melissa said with confidence. "The knowledge is there. It's a very natural thing, like losing your baby teeth. You're in good shape, you've taken care of yourself, and you'll do fine."

"Of course you will," Kameko said. "And Orlando will help you. He'll be here soon, I'm sure."

Allie's phone rang. Zen and Kameko looked at each other. "I'll get it," Zen said.

"Let me get it!" Allie protested. "It's my phone!"

"I'll pass it right off to you," Zen assured her. "You sit and rest. You never did get very much sleep tonight."

"Rest," Melissa reiterated, patting Allie on the shoulder. Zen had already gone to get the phone.

Zen could tell from the caller i.d. Orlando was calling from his cell phone. She answered the phone, "Where are you?"

"We're on our way, Allie."

"I'm Zen."

He paused for a moment. "Zen, we'll be there in about an hour. How's Allie doing? Is she still having contractions?"

"Yes. Definitely." She looked over at her sister, who lay on her side on the bed, wincing with pain. "Don't worry about her, though. She'll be fine until you get here."

"Is the midwife there yet?"

"Yes," Zen said. "I'm handing the phone to Allie now. See you soon."

" 'Bye, Zen."

She handed the phone to her sister, and Melissa, Kameko and Zen went downstairs to give Allie some privacy. The older women settled onto the couch, where Melissa took out her midwife's kit and spread its contents out onto the table. Zen picked up candles. She went upstairs to put them back in the bathroom. As she passed

Allie's bedroom door, she couldn't help but overhear a snippet of the conversation.

"I don't understand," Allie said. "Why now, all of the sudden?" Allie had gotten out of bed and paced the floor, the way she always did when she had to take an emotional phone call.

Zen felt Allie's dismay, her confusion. She couldn't imagine what Orlando would have said to cause it. What did he propose, that he stop for fast food on his way home? But no, that wouldn't explain what had gotten Allie so upset. Zen's heart sank. What was Orlando doing to Allie?

"You and I talked about this months ago, Paul Phillip," Allie said. Zen felt relieved, but also angry. What right did Paul Phillip have to be bothering Allie now, now that she belonged with Orlando? Clearly Allie felt the same way. "I told you there wasn't a place for you in this, and you agreed. If you and that—that blond caterer of yours want a baby so badly, you're going to have to have your own. Yes, I know it's physically impossible, Paul Phillip. Can't you check the classifieds in your local gay newspaper, under 'Surrogate Mothers?' I'm sure you could find a hag who'd—come on now, Paul Phillip, that was not a gay slur. Was not. Paul Phillip, I am not going to argue with you today. I'm trying to bring a person into the world here, and I need to stay calm. I will send you the results of the DNA test. Yes, I will e-mail you pictures. Goodbye, Paul Phillip." Allie clicked the phone off and sat back down on the edge of the bed. "I know you're in the hall, Zen. You might as well come in here."

Zen sat beside her sister. "Tell me Paul Phillip is not talking about wanting to be a daddy now."

"Yeah, that's exactly what he's doing. I guess Kameko called him and told him what was going on."

"He's got a lot of nerve trying to get back in the picture now."

Allie shook her head. "That was my gut reaction, too, but you can't really blame him, Zen. Becoming a parent is a very powerful thing. A few hours from now, I'm going to have this little person who totally depends on me for his every need. He's going to scream at me, throw up on me, and quite possibly piss on me, and I'm going to love him as much as I love you. I already do, and I can't even put my arms around the little guy yet. Wanting to be a parent is a good impulse. Paul Phillip's setting himself up for disappointment, though. I know Orlando's the father. I can feel it in my heart. The Goddess wouldn't let it happen any other way, after all the trouble Orlando and I went through to get together."

"I really hope you're right, Allie."

"Zen, promise me if Paul Phillip and Chris ask you to have their baby, you'll say no."

Zen laughed. "I don't know, Al. Chris catering a gay baby shower could be a lot of fun. He's really awesome at baking cakes, and I bet they'll get a lot of really stylish gifts."

"Oh, shut up," Allie said. "Paul Phillip called me right as I was saying goodbye to Orlando. He was the last person I wanted to hear from tonight."

"I know, but Kameko's heart was in the right place. He does have a right to know. He still cares about you."

"Divorcing me and moving in with another man is a funny way to show he cares," Allie said.

Zen thought about throwing out a line like, "Well, sleeping with him the day after Beltane was a funny way to show you're divorced," but she decided against it.

"Let's go back downstairs," Allie said. "Walking around like I did with the phone felt good, and I think I want a little more of Kameko's fried rice."

"You're going to have to fight me for it," Zen said.

Allie ate a little more, walked a little more, and then decided to take a bath. As she got into the soothing warm water, her contractions got a little closer together. Melissa showed Zen the technique for giving Allie a back massage. She used a lavender scented oil, which helped Allie relax. Allie then asked Zen for another cup of raspberry tea, so Zen went to boil water while Melissa carried on with the massage. Zen and Kameko stood in the kitchen, making tea for everyone, when Orlando and his mother finally arrived.

No one would get to drink tea, though. What followed happened so quickly, Zen barely had time to process it. Orlando went straight up the stairs, where he took over rubbing Allie's back from Melissa. Melissa gave them some time to be alone together, but soon, Orlando came downstairs to get Melissa and Zen. Allie's water had broken, and in what seemed like no time at all, Allie's contractions went from ten minutes apart to almost one right after the other. Melissa told Zen, "I've never seen a first-time mom go through the stages of labor so quickly before. It's like as soon as Orlando got here, she was ready to go."

Zen ran out to Melissa's Volkswagen and got one of Melissa's soft, padded birthing mats. Melissa laid it in the bathtub, after she'd drained out most of the water, and Allie crouched on it on all fours, supported by Orlando. His clothes were soaked from holding Allie's wet body, so he stripped down to his boxer shorts.

"That's better," Allie announced as Orlando took his place beside her again. "I like the way your skin feels."

Orlando continued rubbing her back, and Zen could feel he was keeping her calm. Surprisingly, Allie now felt confident and happy, so happy she was almost elated. She felt very little pain. When one of the contractions hit her, she would make a feral growling sound, reminding Zen of a tiger getting ready to birth a cub.

"Whatever you have to do," Melissa said close to Allie's ear. "Don't you worry at all about how you look, how you sound, how you smell. You can't shock me, Allie; I've been doing this for forty years. At the hospital, they won't let you have anything but ice chips. Here at home, you get lobster fried rice and all the tea you can drink. Piss yourself, shit yourself, I don't care. The only thing we care about is a healthy baby and a healthy mama."

Allie began to cry, more from joy than from pain. "You're doing great, Allie," Orlando told her. He leaned in and kissed her shoulder.

Zen sensed Kameko and Bojana, the baby's grandmothers, standing outside the bathroom door in the bedroom. They talked very quietly about their own birthing experiences, but Zen couldn't hear most of the words. Melissa called her name, and the next thing she knew, she saw the top of her nephew's head, covered with the same dark hair as Allie (and Zen, when she went natural). He seemed to come out quickly after that. Melissa showed Orlando how to cut the cord, and Zen how to clean out the baby's nose and mouth, and his loud first cries filled the air. Everyone, except Allie and Orlando, cheered. Allie simply collapsed against Orlando.

"The birth went very well," Melissa announced to everyone, examining baby Antonio. "The baby is a good color, has good lungs, and appears to be healthy." He appeared a little on the small side, Zen noticed, but Melissa's judgment that he was healthy was all that mattered. "Now, Allie, you're going to pass the placenta soon. Nature's way of helping the process along is for you to offer him your breast. Don't worry about actually feeding him. Your milk will come when it's ready to come, and he won't be hungry yet anyway. You've been feeding him perfectly well through the placenta up until now. There, like that. Hold him against you, let him know he can still feel your heart beating. That's all you have to do. He'll suck if he wants to; if he doesn't, it's okay. Zen?"

Melissa prepared Zen for the delivery of the placenta. Zen was a little grossed out, but she did much better than she'd thought she would. "Now what?" she asked Melissa.

Melissa produced a length of red cloth, something like a wide, thick scarf, and wrapped the afterbirth in it. She then placed the cloth inside a large freezer bag.

"Oh no," Zen said as Melissa handed her the plastic bag. "You don't really want me to—"

"In the freezer," Melissa said.

"Not next to the ice cubes, please," Allie added. "Put it in the back with last summer's rhubarb."

"Isn't that, like, against some kind of health code or something?" Zen asked, wrinkling her nose at the sack of bloody tissue she held in her hands.

"Zen, the placenta is a beautiful thing," Melissa said. "It kept your nephew alive for nine months, and when spring comes, it will be help fertilize Allie's garden."

"We're planting a tree next to it," Allie said. She sounded nearly exhausted. "The tree and Antonio will grow together."

If Melissa had been afraid of discouraging Allie from breast-feeding the baby, she had nothing to worry about. Antonio Milan Parisi Van Zandt latched on to his mother's breast. Allie relaxed, overcome with happiness, and her pre-milk fluids flowed naturally. When the baby had finished sucking, Zen felt another, fresh wave of happiness from the new parents. She looked over and saw Antonio's eyes wide open. He had the same bright hazel eyes as Orlando and Bojana.

Zen let all of the happiness in the room cascade over her, crying tears of happiness. She hadn't had time to wonder if Bojana liked her, if Ramesh missed her, or if her sister thought she was doing a good job as an assistant midwife. She'd been so gloriously wrapped up in the moment. These were Zen's favorite days, the days when she could fling herself, body and soul, into her work. As the other women helped Allie to her bed, and Orlando sat staring at Antonio, enraptured by the infant's face,

"He's got my nose," Orlando said, almost to himself. "But he has Allie's hair color. Yes, you do." He beamed at the tiny boy in his lap.

Zen offered a prayer of thanks to the Goddess. She couldn't imagine herself happier. At that moment, she didn't regret her vow one bit.

Chapter Three

Gillian tied the last ice-blue ribbon, hanging the last of the cardboard-and-silver glitter snowflakes from the sprinkler pipe running the length of the shop. The ladder wobbled slightly, but Gillian no longer minded. She'd been decorating since before the shop opened. Even Zen would have to admit the shop's cheerfully cantaloupe-colored walls looked a little better trimmed with some (fake) evergreens and poinsettia blooms. Zen had allowed Gillian to tape her glittering snowflakes to the shop's front window and the glass door, but nixed Gillian's plans to spray everything in the shop with canned pine tree scent and fake canned snow.

During a rare break between customers, Zen sat in a stuffed black chair near the front register, engrossed in her studies. She looked up to see Gillian teetering at the top of the ladder.

"Oh my goddesses, Gilly! You're going to fall and break your neck!"

"Put that book down," Gillian said, looking down at her. "This ladder is perfectly safe." She jumped, and the ladder hopped with her. To further demonstrate its stability, she stuck out one leg acrobatically. "My dad's a painter; I'm an old pro at ladders. I'm more worried about what's going to happen to you if you don't stop spending all your free time studying." She came down from the ladder with a flourish.

Zen lowered her biology textbook and stared her assistant in the face. "You know I have finals next week, and if I don't know the difference between DNA and RNA, I'm going to fail. I can't screw this up. I've already come too far with it."

"I'd say," Gillian said, rolling her eyes for emphasis. "If I had a boyfriend as fine as Ramesh, I'd be all over him like warts on a frog. I'd—"

"Frogs don't really have warts," Zen interrupted. "That's just an old husbands' tale. Don't you ever read any of these books we sell, Gilly?"

"Sometimes," Gillian said. "When things are slow. I don't know if you've had time to look up from those books long enough to notice this, Zen, but it's our busiest season."

Zen nodded her head. "I know. I've left you and Corey alone here too often, and you're working your asses off for me. Don't think I don't appreciate it. But I've got enough on my mind without thinking about Ramesh."

"He never even comes around here anymore," Gillian said. "I miss him. I miss his jokes, and the way he used to get coffee and sandwiches for us."

"Corey gets sandwiches for us!"

"Not anymore. He and Riley broke up again two weeks ago. I think it might be permanent this time. The last time I went into the sandwich shop, Barry told me he may have to fire Riley if Riley doesn't stop moping around all the time. He even drives slower now. Barry says it took him forty-five minutes to get back from those new condos the other day."

"What new condos?"

Gillian sighed and sunk into the other chair behind the counter. "Exactly. Those condos are blocks from your apartment, Zen. They started building them in June, and people are moving in now. But you didn't notice the construction, or the ups and downs of the Corey-Riley saga."

"Oh, I wouldn't worry about Corey and Riley," Zen said. "They break up every couple of months, and every time, you say it's going to be permanent this time. Those two can't stay away from each other, and you know it."

"That's so not the point," Gillian said. "The point is, you're no fun anymore, Zen. We never hang out at O'Connor's anymore. We never go out for brunch. I can't remember the last time you invited me up to your apartment to watch a movie. We never even sit around the shop and bullshit like we used to, because you're always studying for some nursing exam."

Finally, Zen put her book down on the counter. "I do miss the bullshit," she said.

"Let's do something fun," Gillian insisted. "Let me do a tarot card reading on you. I'm getting good at it."

Zen shook her head. "We already know what the future holds for me: two more months of celibacy, followed by endless studying, followed by helping babies get born. Let *me* do a reading on *you*."

Gillian agreed. She followed Zen from behind the counter, patting the shop's eerie-eyed gargoyle mascot on the head as she went. They went down the shop's center aisle, through the gold door, into the reading room. Zen stopped to hang the "Reading in Progress, Please Do Not Disturb" sign on the golden doorknob. They sat opposite one another across the round table, which was covered in a dark blue celestial-patterned tablecloth. Gillian took the cards in her left hand and shuffled them, then handed them back to Zen. Zen laid out the array in a Celtic cross pattern.

She studied the cards. The eight of cups, the eight of swords. The three of swords. The five of pentacles. Gillian's major arcana were even more interesting: the high priestess, the lovers, the sun and the moon. She studied them carefully; the cards seemed contradict themselves. After some thought, Zen announced, "I think you're going to fall in love."

Gillian looked at the array. "It doesn't say that."

"It never says anything," Zen reminded her. "It suggests things. You have to put two and two together to come up with four. I think it says four. Love."

Gillian laughed. "Who am I going to fall in love with, Zen? A mysterious stranger? Am I going to meet a knight in shining armor?"

"Stop mocking the cards, Gilly. It's bad form. No, I think what the cards suggest is that someone you already know will appear to you in a whole new light, and you'll fall in love."

Gillian shuffled the cards back together. "Hey, what are you doing?" Zen protested. "I worked very hard on that array."

"You're doing it wrong," Gillian insisted. "You must be. You know I don't know any single men in Milwaukee. Well, except Corey, and he's a female impersonator half the time. All the guys I know are back home in Kenosha, and Goddess help me, I am never, ever going back there again."

"Hey, what about your friend Mike?"

Gillian froze. "What about him?"

"Weren't you asking me a few days ago what you should get Mike as a Winter Solstice gift?"

"I ordered him a bottle of cherry wine off the Pagan Spirits website," Gillian said casually.

"Exactly," Zen said. She sounded like a detective who'd come up with a big break in a case. "You know what Mike likes to drink. You've been friends for years, and Mike is a single guy who lives in Milwaukee. Are you ready to see him a whole new light, or what?"

Gillian laughed off the suggestion. "I am *not* going to fall in love with Mike Lubeck, okay? So get that notion out of your head right now. I don't care what the cards told you."

"We'll see," Zen said, smiling in the know-it-all way that always irritated Gillian.

Gillian seemed about to respond when the door chimed, announcing a visitor at the front of the store. Both women went up front to see.

She stood in the center aisle, browsing the vegan cookbooks. Gillian had never seen this woman before, but she was impossible not to notice. She at least six inches taller than Zen and a good ten inches taller than Gillian. Black fishnet stockings and a knee-high pair of fur-trimmed black boots covered her long legs. The stockings had old-fashioned seams up the back, with black star-shaped rhinestones spaced evenly up and down the seams. She wore a short black denim skirt, artfully torn, which exposed a bit of her red satin panties. Over this she wore a heavy black turtleneck sweater, but no coat, even in the below-freezing weather. She ran her fingers over the spines of the books.

She had a thin face. Her neck looked pale, but her face seemed even more pale with her translucent powder. Her lips were blood-red, with a hint of a wet shine. Her eyelids looked heavy with metallic-gray, green, and blue eye shadow, and as much black mascara and eyeliner. Her steely-blue eyes looked intelligent as she scanned the book titles. A wisp of her dishwater-blonde hair, streaked with mint green, fell in front of them, and she brushed it away.

"Hi," Gillian said, breaking the spell of silence that seemed to fall as the women observed this striking new customer. "I'm Gillian. Is there anything I can help you find?"

The woman laughed. Her teeth were milk-white beneath her lipstick.

"If we don't have it in stock, we can still get it before the Solstice," Gillian continued.

"I'm getting ready to do a little entertaining. Do you have a favorite cookbook, maybe something with lots of appetizers and party ideas?"

The door chimed again, and a group of wide-eyed women, their arms loaded down with shopping bags, came in. Zen went to help them.

"I like *Nectar of the Goddesses*," Gillian said, pulling a copy down from the shelf to show the green-haired woman. "It has a lot of good drink recipes, both alcoholic and non-alcoholic. Take a look."

The woman didn't look at the book. Instead, she seemed to study Gillian. Gillian cleared her throat, suddenly uncomfortable.

"I'm sorry," the woman said. "I don't mean to stare. You look very familiar to me. Have I seen you before?"

"If you've been in here before, probably," Gillian said. "I'm here a lot, or at the sandwich shop next door."

"No, that's not it. This is the first time I've been here. Do you go to the Unitarian church?"

Gillian smiled, though the suggestion brought up another bad memory of her hometown. "I haven't been inside a church in years," she said. "You may have seen me at one of the bonfires, though. I am very active in the Pagan community. In fact, up until this year I was one of the organizers of the Solstice celebrations in the park."

"Oh, that must be it," the woman said. "But you're not involved this year?"

"I'm going with my boss, Zen, to her mother's house in Michigan." Gillian wondered what it was about this woman that made her want to open up and reveal so much.

"Too bad," the woman said. "I'll be at the park this Solstice, and I'm always trying to make friends with new witches."

"Well, you know where to find me," Gillian said. "I'll be here at Light and Shadow if you want to talk." That sounded lame, and she knew it. Gillian couldn't quite put her finger on why she wanted this "new witch," as the customer put it, to like her so badly. Was it that she still felt like the geeky kid in school, and this was obviously one of the popular girls?

That must be it, Gillian thought. She's so much cooler than me.

The green-haired witch giggled slightly and nodded. "I suppose I do. I'll take the cookbook. Do you have a business card? Maybe I should stick one in the book so I can find this place again. I never know when I might need more magical assistance."

"Yeah," Gillian said, walking over to the register, where she kept a small stack of Light and Shadow business cards shaped like cauldrons. Gillian attached one of Light and Shadow's pens, too, shaped like a broomstick. She held them out for the woman. "That's me, Gillian Kramer."

The woman took the business card, then held out her hand for Gillian to shake. Gillian noticed her mint-green fingernails. Each of them was decorated with the same black, star-shaped rhinestones gracing the back of her stockings. Wow, Gillian thought, she really knows how to coordinate an outfit.

"Astrid Dejonghe," the woman—Astrid—said. "It's been a pleasure meeting you, Gillian. I'll see you again some time."

Astrid turned to go, then seemed to remember she hadn't yet paid for *Nectar of the Goddesses*. She let Gillian ring up her purchase before striding out of the shop, past the line of shoppers waiting for their turn in the reading room with Zen.

The gold door opened, and the first of the women emerged, her eyes wider than ever. "Oh my God," she said breathlessly. "It was like she's known me my whole, entire life." The other women laughed and chatted amongst themselves until one of them stepped up to go next.

"I love Winter Solstice season," Zen said, winking at Gillian.

Gillian smiled back. "Me, too." As Zen disappeared behind the golden door with her second client of the evening, Gillian took Zen's biology textbook and hid it behind a cluster of evergreen boughs.

* * * *

Zen was on sensory overload. She'd gotten the results of her biology exam back that morning. She had passed, and by a wider margin than she'd even thought possible, even after all the hours of studying she'd put into it. She'd gotten a 96 out of 100, and rewarded herself with an extra macchiato.

Now Ramesh arrived. He stood in the doorway, wearing his gray cashmere sweater, the one she loved so much. Zen bit her lip. The temptation was going to be awfully hard to resist, especially with Ramesh holding the mistletoe up in the air, over his beautiful head of gorgeous, long, curly, black hair.

"Oh cruel Fate, why do you mock me?" Zen said, running to the door to greet him.

Ramesh smiled, and Zen could feel both his happiness and his frustration. "One kiss isn't going to undo almost eleven months of celibacy, Miss Van Zandt."

She put her arms around him and held him close, reveling in the familiar smell of the cashmere, mixed with Ramesh's aftershave. Oh, Goddesses above, aftershave meant he'd just shaved, and his skin would be so smooth...she couldn't resist. She kissed him first on his soft, smooth cheek, and then on the lips. She let the kiss go on until she began to feel guilty, then pulled her lips away.

"I missed you," she said, still refusing to let him go. "You have no idea how much I missed you."

"I have some idea," he said. "It must be something like the way I've missed you. This is almost killing me, Zen, but I have to admit, I really admire you. You're doing so well in nursing school, and keeping your vow on top of that must add to the stress."

She nodded sadly. "I'm sure it adds to your stress, too, not being able to get any relief."

"You forget—unlike you, I didn't take a vow not to *relieve* myself," he said. "As far as I'm concerned, every night you've made me lie in bed thinking about touching you instead of touching you is an IOU, and as soon as the first of February comes around, you're going to pay them all back. With interest."

"I like the way you think," Zen said, leaning in for one more quick kiss. "Are you ready to go?"

Not trusting Ramesh's aging Dodge Dart, they took Zen's Toyota Celica. They each brought an overnight bag. Kameko's invitation to spend Winter Solstice with her had two parts. On the evening of the twentieth, Zen and Ramesh would spend a cozy evening alone with Kameko, Allie, Orlando, Orlando's son Armin, and Antonio. The next day, Kameko would open her barn and her land to her Pagan Spirits employees, the local Pagan community, and anyone else who wanted to come out and celebrate the Solstice.

As they started south, Zen got the conversation rolling. "So, Ramesh, does your family celebrate a winter holiday?"

"Sure," he said. "We do Christmas, like everybody else."

"Not *everybody* else," she said.

"Okay, like *almost* everybody else. We always have a tree covered in ornaments, tinsel, and garland, with an angel on top and way more presents than we need underneath. My sister and I used to leave cookies and milk out for Santa Claus until I turned six. That was the year Priya told me there was no such thing as Santa and made me cry. Basically, I had everything except the manger scene and the mandatory Midnight Mass. Oh, and instead of a ham or a Christmas goose, we ate lamb biryani. Otherwise, it was the traditional American secular commercialized Christmas. What did you have?"

Zen shrugged. "I can't remember having Christmas with my birth mom. I'm sure I did, but since I don't have any photo albums or anything from her, I may never remember it. Before Kameko, my foster moms always had a gift or two for Allie and me, but those foster moms were old ladies, and the gifts were usually things like new school clothes. If Allie and I were lucky, we had a Christmas party at school, and maybe there would be cupcakes. One of the foster moms—I think it was Mrs. Bensen, when we were eleven and twelve—made us go to church on Christmas and Easter. I didn't understand what was going on, and I always got mad when I couldn't have bread and grape juice like everybody else. After Kameko took us in, she said we were welcome to celebrate Christmas if we wanted to, but the Kitatanis always had Winter Solstice instead." She paused to take a sip of her hazelnut cappuccino. They'd stopped at Zen's favorite chain coffee store on their way to the toll road. "I thought your family was Hindu."

"They are," he said. "Well, Mom and Priya are, mostly. Dad is whatever Mom tells him he is." He laughed. "Do you know why Hindus believe in reincarnation? Because it takes way more than one lifetime to understand Hinduism. It seems like every day is a festival or a holiday. Of course we observed Diwali, but Dad also wanted us to—you know, blend in with the other kids at school, be an American family."

"But you and I spent Christmas day together last year," she said. "If your family celebrates Christmas, why didn't you go home to have it with them?"

"That's a long story, Zen."

"Well, tell it to me, Ramesh. We've got a lot of time to kill between Milwaukee and Michigan."

"All right," he said. "I suppose you're going to find out sooner or later, so I might as well tell you now."

"Tell me what?" Zen was sensing only mild disappointment from him, so she didn't believe he would tell her anything earth-shattering.

"I haven't spoken to my family in a while. In a long while. That's why you haven't met them, Zen. My mom's disappointed I didn't turn out to be a devout Hindu like Priya. She never liked me experimenting with European Paganism—those are her words. I tried to tell her about the amazing experience you and I had when we met, but she didn't want to hear it. She said Beltane was a coarse peasant's holiday, and I was wasting my time trying to find you again."

"Why didn't you tell me any of this before, Ramesh?"

"Because they can all kiss my ass, Zen. It doesn't matter what my mother and sister think of you, or about our life together. All that matters is, I knew I loved you from our very first night, and now we're together again. Can you understand, Zen?"

"Yes and no," Zen said. "Ramesh, I'm flattered you're so loyal to me. I feel the same way about you. I can't imagine my life without you now. You can't turn your back on your family, either. I know what I'm talking about here, Ramesh. As much as I love Kameko, I would give almost anything to have my birth mom back, and to know anything about my father. You have to treasure your family, Ramesh, because you never know when you might lose them. You're lucky if you get to know them at all."

He shifted in his seat. "Hey, it's not like I cut off all ties with them. They haven't disowned me or anything."

"But you're having a family argument. An argument over me," she said.

"It started long before I met you, Zen. I'm not going to lose you, Zen, so don't even suggest it." He reached over and took her hand. "You are my family, Zen. You are my future. If I didn't believe that, then I wouldn't have bothered to wait for you to fulfill your vow. I'd be out there fucking everything in a skirt."

She smiled, but said nothing. After a long moment of silence, Ramesh turned up the radio and scanned through the channels until he found a Chicago alternative rock station.

Halfway through "My Name Is Jonas," Zen turned the radio back down. "Wait a minute," she said. "Your mom makes carrot fudge for me. Why would she make me fudge if she didn't like me?"

"She doesn't make fudge for you. She makes it for me."

"Well, why would she make fudge for you if you're having some big argument with her?"

"Because deep down, she believes her cooking plants a seed in my mind. If I eat her *gajar barfi*, then I start to miss her, and then I realize what a terrible son I am and come back to her on my hands and knees, begging her for forgiveness. So she sends me food. It's sick and twisted, but that's the way my mother is."

He turned the radio back up, in case Zen didn't get the message he didn't want to talk about it anymore. Zen was left to wonder whether there was anything she could do to get Mrs. Sudhra to like her.

The journey seemed extra long this year, and not only because of the tense silence between Zen and Ramesh. Snow had recently fallen, and the roads weren't in the best condition through Wisconsin and Illinois. A few miles before the expressway leading them around Chicago, traffic slowed to a crawl. A semi was rolled over in a ditch. Zen and Ramesh both prayed no one was hurt even as they cursed the slow-moving traffic and the icy roads.

Things seemed to improve as they drove through Indiana. Crossing the Michigan border, though, was like crossing some magical threshold. The roads suddenly cleared, the wind seemed to die down, and the snow lay placidly without a drift in sight.

"Look at the fruit trees," Ramesh said, pointing out Kameko's neighbors' cherry trees as Zen drove. "It's kind of depressing, isn't it?"

"Why?"

"Because they look dead. And it isn't even officially the first day of winter yet."

"I don't know," Zen said. "It looks kind of dreary now, but the fruit always comes back."

"Does it?" he said, turning to her with a sly look on his face. "Because if I know anything about Beltane, it's you and I getting it on in the wheat field is a prayer ensuring the fertility of the farm for the year to come. But you and I weren't at Beltane this year, were we?"

"Of course not," she said. "It would rather defeat my vow of celibacy."

"So how do you know the ritual was carried out? Maybe the wheat fields, the barley, the apples, the cherries...maybe they're not coming back. Maybe the earth isn't properly blessed."

She laughed. "Oh, it's blessed," she said. "Allie and Orlando were there. I'm sure they did enough blessing for all of us."

After the cherry trees, Zen recognized the familiar apple trees of Kameko's farm. She turned into the driveway, and found Orlando's black Audi parked in front of the barn. The two pine trees in front of Kameko's farmhouse were decorated with twinkling white lights, but the front of the house was dark. Zen pictured her family deep inside the house, in front of the fireplace, and the deep comfort of being home filled her.

Ramesh got out into the nearly knee-deep snow and took the bags from the back seat. "Why is your bag so heavy?" he asked Zen.

"Presents for everyone," she replied.

"I'm not going to get what I want from you," he said under his breath as they went up the shoveled path to the farmhouse.

Zen didn't knock, and the door wasn't locked. Kameko and Allie stood inside the door, waiting for them, smiling from ear to ear. Zen hugged and kissed her foster mother first, and then her sister.

"Oh, man, I missed you," Zen said to Allie. "I haven't seen you and the boys since before you left for Slovenia."

"That's right," Ramesh said as he and Allie shook hands. "That's where Orlando's mom is originally from, isn't it?"

"Orlando was born there, too," Zen said.

"Baptized there, too" Allie added. "That's why Bojana wanted Antonio baptized there. I agreed to it because, well, I guess I've been agreeing to a lot of Catholic ceremonies lately." She held up her left hand, and Zen noticed for the first time Allie was wearing a diamond solitaire ring.

"No!" a stunned Zen said. "Are you serious? You and Orlando got engaged?"

"At Lake Bled," Allie said, nodding. "I didn't want to tell you over the phone, so I decided to wait until now and surprise you."

"Congratulations," Ramesh said. He went to shake Allie's hand again, but she put her arms around him and hugged him.

Zen threw her arms around Allie, locking Ramesh in between them. "Oh, that's great news, sis. I'm happy for you. But wait—did you say you're having a Catholic wedding? You, my Pagan priestess sister?"

"The legal ceremony will be in the Catholic church, yes."

"And you're allowed in there, tattooed and all?"

Allie laughed. "Of course. Orlando and I have to take marriage classes with the priest first, and so far, the priest and I have only gotten into one serious argument."

"Yeah," Orlando said, appearing in the doorway. "Crucifixes and pentagrams were flying everywhere like ninja stars. Luckily I got in between them before they started throwing punches or pulling hair." He stood beside Allie and kissed her on the cheek.

"Congratulations to both of you," Ramesh said.

"Thanks," Orlando said. Allie pulled herself out of the group hug and clung to Orlando.

"How's the baby?" Allie asked her husband-to-be.

"Finally asleep. Out for the night, knock on wood."

"Where's Armin?" Zen asked.

Kameko gestured toward the kitchen. "I gave him a plate of my famous almond cookies. He's eating them in front of the fireplace. Why don't we join him?"

After Zen and Ramesh had a chance to take off their winter gear and put down their bags, they followed Kameko into the family room. As they went, Allie caught hold of the back of Zen's shirt. "Hey, we're having a Pagan wedding, too," she said.

"That sounds more like the Allie I know."

"Orlando wants to get married before the little guy turns one, so we're getting the church thing out of the way. Then, this summer, we're planning a moonlight ceremony at Lake Michigan."

"What, is there a one-year grace period before having a child outside of marriage is considered a sin?" Zen teased.

As they entered the family room, Armin got up from his cozy spot in front of the fireplace, abandoning the last two cookies on a paper plate strewn with crumbs. He ran to Orlando's side and said, rather shyly, "Hi, Aunt Zen. Hi, Mr. Sudhra." Armin was ten years old, a tall, thin child with dark hair and blue eyes. Zen had never met Catherine, but she knew from pictures in Orlando's old house (before he moved in with Allie) that Armin resembled his mother.

"It's very nice to see you again, Armin," Ramesh said. He and Zen had met Armin at Winter Solstice the year before. Orlando had always been careful to keep his relationship with Zen separate from Armin while they were dating.

"Hey, kid," Orlando said to Armin, "are Auntie Kameko's cookies good?"

Armin nodded. "Really good, dad. Want one?"

"No thanks, big guy. Those are your cookies."

"I'll bring the tray," Kameko said. "There's enough for everyone. I'll bring some hot glögg, too."

"Some hot *what*?" Ramesh said.

"A seasonal favorite from Pagan Spirits," Zen said, sounding like a commercial. "Red wine, mulled with honey, cinnamon and cardamom. Kameko boils the alcohol off so all of us can drink it."

"Is it good?" Ramesh asked skeptically.

"Taste it for yourself when I bring the tray," Kameko said.

"I'll help you," Allie volunteered. She and Kameko went into the kitchen. Armin sat back down, and the others joined him near the fire.

"How did you propose to Allie?" Zen asked Orlando. "Did you make some grand romantic gesture?"

He shook his head. "After we had little Tony baptized, while we were in the middle of Lake Bled, Allie said she wanted another baby. I told her she had to marry me first. That's pretty much it."

"Way to keep it simple," Ramesh said, smiling.

After a round of Kameko's light, flaky almond cookies and some glögg, the six of them got started on the preparations for the Winter Solstice celebration. This involved leaving the warmth and comfort of the fireplace and moving to the mud room off the kitchen. There, Kameko had set out a five-gallon bucket, filled part of the way with good, stiff pine cones, another bucket filled with bird seed, and six empty pie tins. From the kitchen she brought butter knives and an extra-large jar of peanut butter.

"Does everyone remember how to do this?" Allie asked.

"Sure," Armin said. "It's easy. Put peanut butter on the pine cone, spread some bird seed at the bottom of the pie plate, and roll the pine cone in the bird seed until it sticks."

"Don't forget to tie some fishing line to the top," Kameko said. "Otherwise they won't hang." She took a spool of fishing line and small scissors down from a shelf and handed them to Armin.

Everyone got busy, and soon they had six serviceable winter bird feeders. Only once did things threaten to get out of hand, when Orlando "accidentally" got peanut butter on Allie's nose.

"Let me lick that off for you," he said, close to Allie's ear.

She wiped the peanut butter away. "Save it for later," she said.

Ramesh dipped his finger in the peanut butter and touched Zen's cheek. "Oops," he said. She leaned in, and he kissed it away. Orlando glared at them, and Zen felt a flash of jealousy from him. Somehow, Allie sensed it too. She responded by kissing Orlando full on the lips.

Armin helped Kameko tie the fishing line onto the end of her pinecone. Kameko stood and wiped a few stray seeds from her lap. "Tomorrow night is the longest night of the entire year," she said. "The most darkness. After that, even though it seems as if winter will drag on and on forever, the days will actually be getting a little longer all throughout the winter and the springtime. That, my friends, is a small miracle. So, to say thank you to the earth for allowing us, once again, a little closer to the sun, and bringing us the sun's light and warmth, we do something kind for the earth. Anyone want to guess what that is?"

"Feed the birds," Armin said.

"That's right," Kameko said. "And not just the birds, but..."

"We're going to leave food out for all the wild animals," Allie said. "Apple and orange slices, brown rice, and peanuts."

Kameko nodded. "We also leave out a pomegranate, the symbol for the dark part of the year in Greek mythology. Don't forget, everyone has to eat at least one of its seeds."

"Let's not forget, we're going to sing to the apple trees," Zen added.

"Right. Now, let's get in the kitchen and get our munchies together."

They left the bird feeders sitting in the pie tins. Kameko wasn't satisfied to simply leave out the food for the animals; she had to make a worthy tribute from it. This meant using her large, melamine party platter. It was Kameko's favorite dish, bought on a trip to see her relatives in Japan in the 1970s. Its cherry blossom pattern was still beautiful.

Zen and Allie got some kale leaves from the fridge and covered the tray with them for garnish. Ramesh and Orlando cored and sliced the apples and then pulled the oranges apart into segments. Kameko showed Armin how to cut the pomegranate and let him have the first taste. They passed the two halves of the fruit around until everyone had eaten some of the sweet, tart seeds.

"Here," Allie said next, handing Armin the bag of peanuts. "You can help me and Aunt Zen arrange the food on the tray."

They laid a bed of brown rice on top of the kale, then made two rice "hills" on the back of the tray. With a little bit of good-natured arguing, they'd soon made a pretty arrangement of fruit, rice and peanuts. When they'd finished, Kameko added a final garnish of two sprigs of mint from her indoor herb garden.

"Beautiful," Kameko pronounced. "Now, everybody get your winter gear back on."

Allie and Orlando had just finished zipping their coats and tugging on mittens when the baby began to cry. Orlando started to take his coat back off, but Kameko laid her hand on his arm. "You go," she said. "I'll stay inside with the baby."

"Are you sure?" Allie said. "You're the matriarch, Kameko. You should be leading the festivities, not stuck in here changing diapers."

Orlando shook his head. "Doesn't sound like a wet diaper to me. I think he's hungry."

"He is not," Allie said. "I fed him right before you put him down to sleep. He's either wet or lonely."

"Hungry, wet, tired, lonely, bored," Kameko said. "Whatever he is, I'll take care of him. You two go outside and have some fun." She handed Zen a lighter to get the bonfire started; Zen tucked it into the front pocket of her coat.

Allie kissed Kameko's cheek, then pulled on a ski mask. "Don't laugh," she told Orlando. "It's cold out there, and you're going to wish you had one of these."

"I'm not laughing," he said, pulling his hood over his head.

Armin was chosen to carry the tray and lay it down in the grass between the two pine trees. Next to the tray, Zen set up two white candles and took out the lighter. She tried her best to light them, but between the wind and her gloved hands, it took a moment. With the candles finally lit, Allie said a brief prayer. Zen gave everyone a stick, which they lit from the candle. They hung the bird feeders in the pine trees.

Having fed the wild things, they trudged through the snow, out to the apple field. Kameko had cleared out an area for a small bonfire. Everyone threw their lit sticks onto it. The flame started off small. The wood had gotten slightly wet, and smoked, but didn't seem to want to burn.

"Throw some paper on it," Allie suggested.

Zen looked back at the farm house and sighed; the walk there and back was daunting. Then she remembered she'd shoved a handful of napkins from the coffee shop into her coat pocket earlier in the day. She threw the brown paper napkins on the fire, and suddenly they had a decent-sized flame. Allie, Zen, Orlando, Ramesh and Armin made a circle around the fire pit, holding hands, trying to shield the fire from the wind with their bodies. Zen's toes grew numb by this time, and she knew everyone else felt as chilled as she did. A roaring fire seemed so crucial then, and they protected it with all their might.

"I forgot the words to the song," Armin said.

"Then I'll start it," Orlando said, squeezing Armin's hand. He began to sing "Oh Apple Trees" to the tune of "Oh Christmas Tree," the way he'd learned first from Zen, and then from Allie. The sisters had started this lighthearted take on the tradition of singing the fruit trees into life while they were still teens. The others joined in, and when they were starting to warm up and confident of their singing, they began a simple circle dance around the fire. Soon they had worn a round path in the snow.

Armin broke away first. He seized the opportunity to make a snowball, which he hurled at Orlando's back.

"Oh, yeah?" Orlando said, bending down to make an even bigger snowball. "I'm gonna get you back for that, little man."

"Catch me!" Armin yelled, taking off in the direction of the apple trees.

Ramesh, still holding onto Zen's hand, fell backwards and pulled her along with him. She laughed. "I haven't made snow angels in years!" she said.

Allie fell backwards in the snow beside them. "I'm going to make a snow *goddess*," she said.

"Snow goddess," Zen repeated. "I like that." She stretched out her arms and legs and joined her sister.

Moments later, Armin and Orlando ran through the two linked snow goddesses and ruined the image. Allie threw a big snowball at Orlando, hitting him in the face. He dove and tackled her, and they wrestled in the snow. Armin continued to pelt them with snowballs all the while. So Ramesh couldn't resist tossing a snowball at Zen. Unfortunately for him, some of the snow went down her back. She screamed hysterically and then pummeled him with snowballs as fast as she could make them. He fought back with snowballs of his own.

About the time that no one could feel their fingertips anymore, they gathered around the fire and told stories and caught up on the details of each other's lives. Soon, Kameko turned on the back porch light and appeared at the door. "Hot chocolate!" she shouted, and they all ran for the door. At the kitchen counter, she had six mugs of cocoa and another pile of cookies, warmed up in the microwave, waiting. When Armin finished his cocoa and cookies, Orlando sent him to bed.

"Dad, do I have to sleep in the same room as you and the baby?"

"Yes," Orlando said. "You, Allie, Antonio and I are a family. We can share a room for one night."

"But Antonio cries too much. And you'll try to kiss Allie."

"Armin, you're a big brother now, and Allie's going to be your stepmom. You'll have to get used to the crying *and* the kissing."

Reluctantly, Armin went off to brush his teeth.

The five adults stayed up for another two hours, drinking mulled wine and finishing the conversation they'd started in the snow. Allie described exactly the way Orlando had proposed to her, and Kameko filled them in on all the details of Atsuko's and Naoko's families. "Naoko, her husband, and the kids will be here for Winter Solstice next year," she said. "We're trying to get Atsuko and her family to come, too, but it's much easier to coordinate a trip from Seattle than a trip from Tokyo," Kameko said.

"That's too bad," Zen said. "It's been years since you've had your two sets of twins together."

"Tell me about it," Kameko said.

Zen told them all about school, and Ramesh told them about his research. To Zen's pleasant surprise, no one brought up Zen's vow. That is, until she and Ramesh were getting ready to go to bed that night. He'd agreed to let Zen sleep in her old room, while he would take the couch in the front room. As Zen said goodnight, Ramesh sat at the end of the couch in his black pajama pants and a long-sleeved t-shirt. He patted the seat beside him, motioning for Zen to join him.

"I shouldn't," she said. "This is already hard enough without the added temptation of being so near to you."

"Please," he said. "There's something I need to talk with you about."

Zen swallowed hard. This time, it really felt as if something was wrong. Ramesh felt anxious and guilty. "I'm not sure I want to hear this," she said.

"But you need to. Please."

She sat in the middle of the couch, but avoided looking at him. "Last winter, when I told you I was going to take this vow, I knew it was going to be hard for both of us. I didn't imagine it would be this hard. I didn't know then how much being next to you is a part of my life."

"Zen, stop. I don't blame you for taking your vow. I think you've shown a lot of strength in surrendering something that's such a part of your soul. If anything, the way you've been faithful to your vow has made me love you more."

"I sense a 'but' coming," she said, staring down at her fuzzy slippers on Kameko's Oriental rug.

"I've been spending a lot of time in the lab with an undergraduate student, a senior named Kara Sarveswaran. She had a boyfriend, but they broke up a couple of weeks ago. Her parents really didn't like her dating non-Asian guys. They kind of drove him away."

Zen nodded her head. "You have a lot in common with this girl, then."

"In a way, yes. She was pretty depressed about what happened, and since she and I spend so much time in the lab together, we've talked about it a lot."

Bad memories were coming back to Zen at that moment, memories of men who'd broken her heart before she met Ramesh. All the times they'd sat beside her, telling her how wonderful another girl was, flashed through her mind. Zen didn't like this at all. "You know, Ramesh, this is a really great bedtime story. I think I've heard this one before, but remind me one more time. How does it end?"

"It ends with, 'And Zen and Ramesh lived happily ever after,'" he said. "Nothing happened between me and Kara."

She looked him in the eyes. "You're not telling me the whole truth," she said. "Something happened. Do I want to know what it was?"

Ramesh looked down at the floor, deeply ashamed of himself. Zen felt it, as cold and painful as a slap in the face. "She tried to kiss me, and for a moment all I could think about was how long it's been since I've had sex, and how good it would be to have a warm female body pressed against me. She's a beautiful girl, Zen. Almost as beautiful as you. She was giving me one of those looks telling me she'd do anything I wanted her to. She was mine for the taking, Zen."

She wiped a tear from her eye with one finger. "What are you saying, Ramesh?"

"Zen, look at me." He put his hand under her chin and tried to turn her face toward him, but she pulled away. "You can feel what I'm feeling, Zen."

Her own heart was beating so hard, she hadn't thought to calm herself down and try to pick through all of Ramesh's feelings. It hurt too much.

"I could have been with Kara, Zen, but I didn't. She kissed me, and I—I didn't resist. But that's all it was, Zen. Just a kiss. Can you forgive me?"

She stood up. "When were you going to tell me all of this, Ramesh? Why am I finally hearing all these things you've been keeping inside of you? Why now?"

"You had your exams, I've been busy with the university, and we haven't seen each other much lately. And because there is no good time for me to tell the woman I love, the only one I want to be with, someone else kissed me."

She needed to get away from him. She considered quietly saying goodbye to Kameko and Allie, taking her car, and leaving Ramesh stranded here. She didn't want to face him again, at least not until she figured out what she was going to do. She certainly didn't feel like having a party. She was tired, so very tired. What she wanted most was simply to crawl into the bed she used to sleep in and cry herself to sleep.

Zen went up the back stairs, trying desperately not to break down in tears until Ramesh could no longer hear her. She passed Kameko's room, and then the room that used to be Allie's. The only sound she heard was Kameko gently snoring. She was about to go into her own teenage bedroom when she heard voices in Kameko's library. The voices, clearly recognizable as Allie and Orlando, sounded muffled, but very excited.

At least they're happy, Zen thought. She went into her bedroom. She avoided Kameko's old rowing machine. She went to bed without bothering to get undressed. Underneath the slightly-dusty black comforter, Zen let the tears flow down her cheeks. She laid her head back on the pillow and tried to think of nothing.

This was not easy with Allie and Orlando across the hall, failing at trying to make love without anyone hearing. Zen heard the old hardwood floor creaking in time to their motions. She heard Allie groaning, trying not to scream. Even at this distance, she could sense their passion for one another.

She thought of Ramesh's words. "She's a beautiful girl." "She'd do anything I wanted her to." "She was mine for the taking."

Zen couldn't stand it anymore. She threw off the black bedspread, crossed the hall, and pressed her face against the library door. She wouldn't scream; she didn't want to wake Kameko, Armin, or Antonio. She could not, however, resist saying, "Good Catholics don't do that before the wedding!"

The noises stopped abruptly. Allie and Orlando didn't answer, but were *much* quieter afterwards. Eventually, Zen slept.

The next morning, Zen awoke to Allie standing beside her bed, holding a smiling Antonio in her arms.

"He looks happy," Zen said, stretching. She wished she could say the same thing for herself.

"He should. I breast-fed him five minutes ago."

Antonio turned his head in his aunt's direction.

Zen sat up and held out her arms, and Allie transferred the baby to her. "That's right, little Tony, it's Auntie. Look how big you got since the last time Auntie saw you."

"Is everything all right, Zen?"

Zen thought for a moment. "Not exactly," she said. "The celibacy thing is getting to Ramesh...and me."

"I thought so," Allie said. "A man will put up with a lot of things from a woman he loves, but being totally cut off is not usually one of them. I was lucky I wasn't seriously seeing anyone when I decided to take my priestess vows."

"Allie, do you think it's possible Ramesh and I aren't meant to be together?"

Allie shook her head. "You were the king and queen of Beltane. That's a powerful experience. I couldn't have fallen in love with Orlando if it hadn't been for the Beltane ritual."

"You mean you couldn't have fallen in love with Orlando if he hadn't knocked you up," Zen said, stroking Antonio's hair. "Ramesh and I didn't have that particular set of circumstances. I wish I knew if he's really the one, because we're so close to drifting apart."

"If it was meant to be, then it will be. Listen, Zen, we came in here to check on you, and also to let you know Gillian's here." She let Zen kiss the baby a few times, then took him back from her. "She's in the kitchen, giving Kameko a break from cooking for everybody."

Zen straightened up in bed. "Ooh," she said, "Gillian's crepes!" To her surprise, she had a healthy appetite despite her sadness, perhaps because she was so eager to have Gillian's sympathetic ear to her problems with Ramesh.

"I believe she did mention something about crepes, yes." Allie turned and almost walked out the door. "By the way, your little comment really threw Orlando off his game last night. I'm not complaining, though. He lasted twice as long."

Zen got out of bed and changed into something presentable. "Ew, Allie, I don't want to hear about your sex life with my ex. Especially while I'm unable to do anything about my own sex life." For emphasis, she threw a pillow at her sister.

"Be patient, Zen. I know how hard the vow is, believe me. But the year is almost over now. Whatever problems you and Ramesh are having, you'll work them out. And when your vow is finally over, the sparks will fly."

Antonio began to babble, repeating something that might have been an attempt to say "cereal." "I'd better see what he wants," Allie said. She and Antonio went.

Zen headed for the kitchen. On the way, she found Ramesh, still in his pajamas, staring out the front window with Orlando. Orlando, wearing jeans and an open, white bathrobe matching Allie's, looked slightly embarrassed to see Zen, but Zen's gift of empathy told her he was also amused by the whole thing.

"Merry Solstice, Zen," Orlando said.

"For you and Allie, apparently," Zen said, raising her eyebrows. She looked out the window and saw what the men had been looking at: Kameko's cherry blossom platter was now nearly empty, and animal tracks in the snow surrounded it in all directions. The snow was deep, and the tracks were many, so it was a little hard to tell, but Zen thought she could make out rabbit, deer, raccoon, and coyote footprints.

Ramesh bent to give Zen a welcoming kiss on the cheek, but she stepped back out of his reach. "Maybe I should leave you two alone," Orlando said. He went off toward the kitchen.

"It's the shortest day of the year," she said, still staring out the window. "The darkest night, and not just because the calendar says so. I feel it in my heart, too, Ramesh."

He nodded. "But now the darkness is starting to wane. The light is coming back. Zen, please believe me when I tell you I never wanted to hurt you. I didn't have to tell you, but I couldn't live with the guilt of thinking I'd betrayed you in some way, even though you never would have found out."

She sat down on the old-fashioned, high-backed chair in front of the window. "Why did you leave me, Ramesh?"

"I never left you," he said. "It was just a kiss. Kara was upset about losing her boyfriend. That's all. There was one kiss, and then I thought about you, and I made my decision."

"That's not what I meant. The first night we met, the Beltane ritual. We made love, and then we laid down to sleep in the wheat field. You had your arm around me when we went to sleep, but when I woke up, you were gone. Why did you leave me?"

He didn't hesitate. "Because what we did felt so real, so good, so holy. I was afraid if I got to know the human woman behind my image of the Goddess, the whole thing would have been ruined. Now I know better, Zen. Now I know the woman and the Goddess are the same." He held out his hand to her. "I hope you forgive me."

Zen stood and took his hand. She kissed the top of his head, stroking his lovely dark curls. "Never, never, never," she said. "Never put peanut butter on my face again."

Ramesh laughed. "It's a deal," he said. "I don't really like peanut butter that much, but I'll lick anything that has you underneath it."

"Now, I understand Gillian is here, and really thin pancakes are in the works. This does not mean I'm not still upset you kissed that little bitch Kara Sarves-whatever. It does, however, mean I'm hungry, I want to see Gillian, and I still believe you and I are meant to be together."

"I love really thin pancakes," Ramesh said. "And you." He held out his arm in a proper gentlemanly fashion, and Zen took it.

Kameko was sitting at the breakfast bar, beside Armin. Allie was at the kitchen table, securing Antonio in his high chair. At the stove, using a spatula to remove a perfectly browned, fruit-filled crepe from the iron skillet, was Gillian. "Hey, Zenny Penny," she said, flashing a wide grin.

"Hey, Gilly Willy," Zen said back.

Allie narrowed her eyes. "I called you 'Zenny Penny' once," she said to her sister, "and you punched me in the shoulder."

"That was about twenty years ago," Zen said. "What kind of fruit is in those pancakes?"

"A delectable melange of strawberry, sweet black cherry, pomegranate, and passion fruit," Gillian said. "Get it while it's hot."

Zen helped Gillian put the crepes on plates and distribute them to the entire clan, while Allie made coffee and tea. Armin took one bite and said, "This is the best, best, best thing I've ever tasted. Ever!" He finished off the rest of his crepes without another word, then asked for seconds.

As Gillian sat down to her own breakfast, Allie said, "He's right, Gillian. These are wonderful." Orlando, Ramesh and Kameko nodded their heads in agreement.

"I wouldn't normally turn my kitchen over to anyone," Kameko said, locking Gillian in her gaze. "Zen talked me into it this time when she called to say you were coming the other day, but I'm glad she did. Goddess bless you, Gillian. I would almost swear you used a little of your magic to make these taste so spectacular."

Gillian blushed, feeling both proud and awkward at the high praise. "Well, my mom *is* a pastry chef. This is one of her favorite recipes. I always used to tell her she's a Wiccan even though she doesn't realize it yet. This breakfast is my Solstice gift to all of you, so I'm glad you enjoyed it."

"Speaking of gifts, can we open presents now?" Armin asked Orlando.

"Soon," Orlando said. "Why doesn't everybody get comfortable in front of the fire place?" He picked up the coffee pot. "I'll make sure all the grown-ups get our second cups."

"Pour me a second cup, too," Zen said. "I'll be there in a minute; I want to clean up, since Gillian was nice enough to cook for us."

"That's sweet," Gillian said, "but I'll help too."

"Bless you girls," Kameko said, kissing Zen and then Gillian on the cheeks. "Bless you, bless you."

Gillian put the heavy skillet into the sink and ran cold water over it. "Did you sing to the apple trees last night?" she asked Zen.

"Always," Zen said. "As usual, our lovely Winter Solstice tradition deteriorated into a snowball fight."

"Deteriorated, or got more interesting?" Gillian asked. Zen handed her a plate, and Gillian rinsed it off. They made a stack of pre-rinsed plates, and another of forks, before Zen loaded everything into the dishwasher. "I gave Mike his bottle of wine before I left last night. He opened it right there on the spot."

"Your place, or his?"

"His. Kameko makes the best cherry wine I've ever tasted."

"You'll have to say something to the Buckmans. Theresa Buckman actually owns the cherry orchard. Kameko owns the apple trees and the hops, barley and wheat fields." Zen stacked the last of the plates inside the dishwasher and reached for the detergent. "Have you started to see Mike in a whole new light yet?"

Gillian dried her hands on the nearest kitchen towel. "Nothing is going to happen between me and Mike, I assure you."

"You assure me? And why are you so sure, young lady?"

Gillian giggled. "If I tell you this, you have to promise not to tell anyone, all right? Not even Ramesh. Not even Allie."

She sensed Gillian's excitement, which was the fun kind and not the nervous kind. Gillian had a juicy secret, that was for sure. "I promise," Zen said. "Tell me."

Gillian dropped her voice very low. "Remember that customer who came in looking for a party cookbook a couple of weeks ago?"

"Sure," Zen said. "She had that whole Goth-punk look going for her. Green hair, fishnets, torn skirt. Kind of a 'high-dollar whore' look."

"Yeah, exactly," Gillian said. "Her name is Astrid. She came into the shop again that weekend, after you left to study for your exams. She bought one of our sex books—"

"Which one?" Zen interrupted.

Gillian thought for a moment. "Um, *The Sacred Mountains of Venus*, I think. I don't really remember exactly which one. Anyway, I struck up a conversation with her, and I found out she's a stripper."

"Why am I not surprised?" Zen said.

"I know, right? I should have guessed that from the matching fishnet-fingernail combination. She told me where she works, and I thought her act sounded kind of cool. Astrid's a Wiccan, and she said she tries to incorporate Wiccan principles into her routine. You know, not just a bump-and-grind to raunchy music, but stripper moves mixed with traditional belly dancing moves, to music that's woman-friendly."

"Is she serious? She makes a living at that?"

"Well, I was curious about that, too, so I wanted to check it out."

"No way," Zen said with quiet awe. "My sweet little Gilly Willy in a strip club?"

" I was afraid to go by myself, and you were busy. So I asked Mike."

"Oh-ho," Zen said, smiling devilishly. "So you have seen Mr. Lubeck in a whole new light! The tarot cards triumph once again!"

"Well, not exactly," Gillian continued. She leaned against the counter, while Zen took a seat at the table. She narrowly avoided sticking her elbow in a strawberry Antonio had mashed into the tablecloth. "Mike and I went in and sat down, and it was really awkward. We started watching the other women on stage. I didn't know what to think. There I was with a guy who's been my friend for years, watching this topless woman pole-dance."

Zen shrugged. "You and I pole-dance every year," she said. "Maypole dance, anyway."

"Yeah," Gillian said, "but you and I are allowed to be sexual at Beltane. At a strip club, you can get turned on, but all you can do is stare. It's this weirdly detached sexual experience."

"I get it," Zen said. "So what about Astrid? Was she bullshitting you with all her talk about the dance of the seven veils, or whatever it was?"

"No," Gillian said. "Not at all. She's totally for real. Her music was really different, and even in that environment, with the drunk guys hooting and hollering at her, wearing nothing but a G-string, she gives this impression the dancing is her spiritual calling. It's really moving."

"Seriously?" Zen said.

"Seriously," Gillian repeated. "She's a real artist. On top of which, her dancing got me really turned on."

"Did something happen between you and Mike?"

"He wished," Gillian said. "No, something happened between me and Astrid. I've never even thought about another woman like that before, but she took me back stage, and before I knew what was happening, we were kissing. It felt so right, Zen."

"Gillian, you know I love you no matter what, right?"

"I wouldn't expect any less from you, since I feel the same way about you."

"Good. Then you know you'll always be my best bud, other than Allie, of course. I would love you straight, lesbian or bi. But I think you should stop and think before you rush into something you might regret."

Gillian nodded. "Sure. Of course. I mean, it's not like Astrid and I are planning on moving in together or anything. But I'm not just experimenting with her."

"Are you sure?" Zen said. "You're still so young, Gilly. How old is Astrid, by the way?"

"I don't know," Gillian said. "I never asked her. When we get together—and it's been a few times now—we don't do a whole lot of talking. At least not with words. We do a *lot* of talking with our bodies."

Zen nodded. She sensed Gillian was very excited about this new relationship. She was happy. And if Gillian was happy, Zen wanted to be happy for her, even if she had her doubts.

"I really didn't see this one coming, Gilly."

"Maybe you need a little more practice reading tarot cards."

As Gillian said this, Allie appeared in the doorway. "We're ready to open gifts now," she said.

Zen leaned in and kissed Gillian's cheek. "We'd better get in there," she said. "Party time." With her best friend here, surrounded by her family, and well on her way to forgiving Ramesh for his moment of weakness, Zen finally felt as if Winter Solstice could begin. The light cleared away the darkness in her heart.

Chapter Four

Zen awoke and looked around. In the dark, she could barely make out an unfamiliar lamp on an unfamiliar bedside table. It took her a moment to remember she was staying in a hotel on the north side of Indianapolis, a few blocks from Allie's house.

She'd barely had time to orient herself before she heard a knock on the door. Not the locked, deadbolted and chained door leading out to the hall, but the unlocked door between her room and Ramesh's. "Come in," Zen said.

Ramesh came in, wearing most of the good suit he'd brought with him. Goddess above, he looked great in those pinstriped pants and that white shirt, unbuttoned over his ribbed white undershirt. She had a strong impulse to peel each of these articles of clothing off of him and lick what was underneath. Then she remembered her vow, and how near it was to completion.

"Why aren't you out of bed yet?" he asked her.

Zen looked at the alarm clock. "Shit! We're supposed to be in church in an hour!"

Ramesh nodded vigorously. "Allie's going to be pissed if you're late for her wedding."

"It'll be her own damn fault. Who gets married at ten o'clock in the morning in the middle of winter?"

She jumped out of bed and ran for the bathroom. She shut the door and did her business, opening it again while she brushed her teeth. "No time for breakfast," she said with the toothbrush sticking out of her mouth.

He stood behind her, staring at their reflection in the mirror. "You'd better not touch me," she said. "You're all nice and clean and shaved and everything, and I'm pretty sure my armpits stink." She spit a mouthful of toothpaste into the basin.

"I'd forgotten how absolutely gorgeous you are in the morning."

"You're kidding," she said, half-smiling at the reflection. "I haven't showered, I'm not wearing any makeup—"

"But you're going to shower now," he said. His eyes were full of eager anticipation. Zen scanned his emotions, and discovered some sensations she hadn't felt in a very long time. He was excited, almost giddy, and it had nothing to do with Allie and Orlando's wedding.

"Yes," she said, looking him up and down. "And you're, what? Going to watch?"

Ramesh smiled and nodded. "Will you let me?"

She thought for a moment. "Taking my clothes off in front of you isn't exactly modest," she said. "Doesn't it violate the spirit of the vow?"

"Not being able to touch you violates *my* spirit," he said. "And I'm not asking to touch you. I'm not asking you to touch me. I'm not even asking you to touch yourself. Just do what you'd normally do, and pretend I'm not here. Please."

She stared at him for a moment. He needed this so badly. Zen took off her camisole and stripped out of the sweatpants she liked to sleep in. She threw her panties on top of the clothes pile, trying very hard to ignore Ramesh as he leaned against the sink. She stepped behind the semi-transparent shower curtain.

"I can hardly see you," Zen called as she turned the water on. "Can you see me?"

"I can see enough." Even with the hot water running over her, she heard him unzip his pants. "I can smell you, Zen. I can smell your pussy. You're so delicious." She closed her eyes to wash her hair, but imagined him a few feet away from her, stroking his cock, the cock she missed, and dreamt of every night. In Zen's dreams, her vow of celibacy never existed.

With her hair rinsed, Zen opened her eyes. She told herself to focus on washing and not look at Ramesh, but she couldn't help stealing a glance. His eyes were focused on her, almost unblinkingly. The look on his face was one of purest pleasure. It was a look she saw often in her dreams. She felt her body reacting. Her nipples were hard points, sensitive to the touch of the water drops falling on them. She felt a surge of moisture between her legs that had nothing to do with the shower. She'd almost forgotten she could want a man like this.

She bent to wash one leg, all the way down to the ankle. Ramesh groaned. Zen straightened up again. She pulled back the shower curtain and looked at him.

"What are you doing?" Ramesh said hoarsely. His hand never stopped moving up and down his cock.

"Come here," she said.

He seemed to move automatically, standing directly in front of the shower curtain. A few stray drops of water fell onto his white shirt. She could hear how heavily he breathed. He must have been close to a climax when she'd interrupted him. She wasn't ready for him to come, not just yet. Zen was sure she wanted to do more than just stand there behind the curtain.

"I want to touch you," she said.

"I want that too, but you can't." It sounded as if the words were painful to pronounce, but he said them. "What about your vow?"

"Right now it's taking every ounce of strength and self-control I have not to grab your ass and impale myself on your cock," she said. "If I were doing this for myself, then I would be breaking my vow. But I'm standing here, every cell in my body wanting to press up against you, needing you to fill me up, needing you to come inside me, and denying myself each and every one of those desires. It's no disrespect to my vows, Ramesh, to serve Her by serving others. Right now, you need me, and I need to do this out of love for you."

Zen wasn't sure she believed half of the things she'd said. When Ramesh did nothing more to discourage her, she reached out and let the fingers of one hand lightly touch his cock. Ramesh shuddered. She angled her body away from him, letting only her fingers come near enough his body to feel his heat.

Zen was amazed at how hot his skin felt, and how right, how her fingers seemed to know they belonged here and were meant for this. She'd been wrong if she'd imagined all the pleasure would be his, even though her pussy ached to be filled as she began methodically stroking his cock.

Ramesh closed his eyes, and Zen's fingers worked faster. She watched his lips. It stung her to know she was still three weeks away from being able to kiss them whenever she liked, however she liked. Yet she could live with the deprivation, even as her body burned. It was worth the torment for the one moment when Ramesh's beautiful lips parted. She knew then there was no turning back. She was ready to receive his seed in her hand, welcoming the moment, in fact.

Instead, Ramesh pushed her hand away, taking a step back from her. He finished the job himself, coming in his own hand.

Instinctively, she understood why. She closed the curtain and finished washing herself, waiting patiently as Ramesh washed up, got his suit back in order, and checked himself in the mirror. She stepped from the shower and discreetly wrapped the bath towel around her body. He was still leaning against the sink as she reached for the hair dryer.

"Zen," he said, "we've already held out for eleven months. We're going to make it another three weeks."

She smiled. "I'll be a while with my hair, makeup, and dress. Now you get the hell out of here."

"Don't forget coat, boots, scarf, hat and gloves. They said on the news this morning the temperature would only get up into the teens."

"Okay, so I'll need some time to do the adorable-snow-bunny thing. You'd better go chill in your room before anything else happens."

"Like what?" he said. "Are you afraid I'll catch another glimpse of you naked, lose my mind, wrestle you to the bed and have my way with you?"

"No," she said, "more like I'll catch a glimpse of you putting on your tie, remember I haven't had an orgasm since January of last year, wrestle you to the bed and have *my* way with *you*. Hell, Ramesh, if I don't quit thinking about you soon, I might have my way with this hair brush."

She laughed. "Why don't I meet you in the lobby when I'm ready to go?"

"Good idea."

Zen sped up her usual grooming process, and in twenty minutes was ready to meet Ramesh in the lobby.

"Free continental breakfast," he said, holding out a Danish for her.

"No, thanks," she said. "I'll grab a coffee and a banana for the car, though."

After she'd finished the coffee on the way to the church, Zen was glad she'd remembered to put some sugarless gum in her tiny purse.

They got into her Celica and made it to the church moments before the ceremony was supposed to begin.

From the outside, The Church of the Holy Spirit looked like a modest two-story building, its stuccoed walls painted taupe and badly in need of a fresh coat. Tall stained-glass windows lined the east and west sides, made up of textured blue, green and purple glass suggesting the ocean at sunset. The church's north face looked bare except for a heavy, wooden door, propped open, giving Zen and Ramesh a view of its Gothic buttresses and high ceiling. The buttresses and the pews consisted of the same dark wood, perhaps oak.

Behind the simple altar hung a sculpture of the crucified Jesus, carved from white marble. Zen found it incredibly beautiful. Two smaller altars flanked the sanctuary, one dedicated to St. Joseph, whose image was also carved from white marble, and the other dedicated to Mary the mother of Jesus. Mary's sculpture stood the largest of the three, and the sculptor had obviously poured much of himself or herself into its making. On the folds of Mary's flowing gown, there was a vein of dark coloring in the marble, a vivid blue. Zen saw it not as a flaw, but a cleverly carved decoration on the Virgin's dress.

In the church's narrow vestibule, Kameko and Allie stood. Kameko looked elegant in a rose-colored pants suit, but Allie stole the show.

"No way," Zen said, throwing her arms around her sister. "No way you're getting married in *white*. Even the Virgin Mary isn't wearing pure white."

Allie laughed and shifted her bouquet of white English roses from one hand to the other. "This is what Orlando wanted," she said. "It's traditional."

Allie's gown, actually more the color of aged lace than white, had a tight bodice that covered her shoulders and three-quarters of her arms, effectively hiding her Pagan tattoos. The skirt had one layer of satin underneath several layers of tulle. She wore matching satin gloves with pearl buttons. Her dark brown hair, swept up on top of her head, had a much more simple style than she'd worn at her first wedding. Unlike the first time, she also wore a veil. It covered her face down to the nose, drawing attention to the shiny coat of clear gloss on Allie's full lips. Even her lips are dressed modestly, Zen thought.

"What ever happened to 'white is for little girls, red is for grown-up women'?"

"I'm wearing red to the Pagan ceremony," she said. "I can promise you that. I won't be covering up my face again, either. But for the Catholic wedding, I went the whole nine yards."

"She's even wearing panties," Kameko said, laughing. Over their heads, where Zen presumed the choir loft to be, Pachelbel's *Canon in D* played. "That's our cue. Ramesh, take Zen to your seats."

Ramesh nodded. He gave Kameko a quick kiss on the cheek, then took Allie's hand. "You look beautiful," he said.

"Thanks," Allie whispered as she and Kameko got into place.

Perhaps one hundred people could fit in the church, and all one hundred of them seemed to have turned out for Allie and Orlando's wedding. Zen didn't recognize many of them, but assumed they must have been people who worked with Orlando at his lumber company, or worked with Allie at the architecture firm. Zen recognized Allie's friend and co-worker Jane Schumann. She assumed the handsome black-haired man with his arm around Jane's waist was her new husband, Adam. In front of the Schumanns sat Orlando's mom, with Antonio on her lap.

The priest was a small man with pink skin, bright orange-red hair, and a goatee. Taking her seat beside Armin, Zen studied him briefly, then looked over at Orlando.

Orlando always had great taste in clothes. His blue suit, so dark it was almost black, was perfectly tailored to his long, muscular body. His shirt was the same shade as Allie's dress, and he wore a classic black tie with a silver tie bar. Armin stood beside him, wearing a pre-adolescent version of the same suit with a white shirt. He was turning a small black box—the rings, no doubt—over and over in his hands.

Zen and the other guests turned their heads as Allie came down the aisle, with Kameko right behind her. Zen smiled, but couldn't bear to keep her eyes open for very long. She could feel what Orlando felt; he broadcast his feelings loud and clear, and Zen could pick it up even with all the other souls around her. His happiness was almost overwhelming.

Against her will, Zen found herself suddenly jealous. She'd spent so many nights trying to make Orlando happy. Despite her skill and caring, though, she'd never succeeded the way Allie had—simply by showing up. Allie took Orlando's hand, and the ceremony began. The priest said a few words, and then gave the lectern over to a young lady, who gave a reading from the Song of Songs.

Ramesh began to get impatient right around the time of the third reading from the Bible, this one from the gospel of Matthew. Zen rested her hand on his arm, leaned in and whispered, "First Christian wedding?" He nodded. "This is the short version. They'll exchange vows soon."

Bojana looked over at them and smiled. Antonio reached for one of the hymnals on the pew, but Bojana didn't let him have it. Instead she distracted him by making funny faces. The priest seemed to be amused.

He finished the gospel reading. Catholic members of the congregation responded with a "Praise to you, Lord Jesus Christ," and sat down.

"You know," the priest said, "this is an unusual wedding for me, and not just because the bride and groom's not-quite-one-year-old son is sitting in the first pew." Everyone laughed, including the bride and groom. "As many of you know, Allie is not Catholic. Shortly after Orlando moved here from the Chicago area and began attending services here, he told me he planned to marry his pregnant girlfriend, who belonged to the Neo-Pagan faith, and I thought he was pulling my leg." Another big laugh. "It took a while for Allie to agree to marry Orlando, but when she finally did, and I met her, I was struck by her sincere desire to have her son raised as a Catholic. Why would she want Tony to be Catholic, I asked her, if she was so sincerely devoted to Neo-Paganism? Then she told me about the deal she and Orlando struck: any boys they have will be Catholic, and any girls they have will be Pagans."

That brought the biggest laugh of all, though Zen knew as well as Allie and Orlando did that Allie had every intention of holding Orlando to it. She suspected he secretly prayed they'd only have boys.

The priest continued with a short sermon about responsibility, family, and love. He then asked Orlando for his vows to Allie, and Allie for hers to Orlando. Armin fished the little black cube that held both rings out of his pants pocket. As Orlando took the ring to put on Allie's finger, he pulled Armin in for a tight hug. Armin blushed, but not nearly as brightly as he blushed when Allie hugged him. Allie slipped the ring on Orlando's finger, the priest pronounced them husband and wife, and they kissed as if none of their family members and friends were there at all, as if the world had simply disappeared around them.

Immediately after the ceremony, as many of the guests filed out of the church and began making their way to the reception hall, Allie and Orlando slipped into the first pew. Orlando got in on Bojana's side, taking Tony from his grandmother. Allie stood next to her sister. Zen couldn't resist the urge to wrap her arms around Allie once again.

"I wish I could give you my gift of empathy for twenty-four hours," Zen whispered in her sister's ear. "I wish you could feel how happy your new husband is."

"I can," Allie said. "I feel the same way." She looked down the row at him, and in the brief moment Allie's eyes met Orlando's, Zen felt electricity in the air. This was all so romantic. It made her want nothing more than to take Ramesh back to the hotel and pretend she was on her honeymoon with him. That was impossible, of course, without undoing nearly a year's worth of celibacy. But from the way he was looking at Zen, Ramesh could feel it, too. He took Zen's hand.

As the photographer took Allie and Orlando away to pose for pictures at the altar, Ramesh leaned in and said to Zen, "I'll bet you anything this marriage will be consummated before the reception begins."

Zen laughed. Her laughter echoed through the now-mostly-empty church.

The reception consisted of dancing and a vegetarian meal catered by no one who had even heard of Allie's ex-husband's caterer boyfriend. Zen would have called it boring if she hadn't been so engrossed in watching how

Allie, Orlando, and their boys loved one another. Tony fell asleep after the first hour, and stayed asleep with his cheek on Kameko's shoulder. When dinner ended, Zen and Ramesh practiced their ballroom dance moves (neither was particularly skilled at this) to romantic Classical and early 20th century American popular music.

Allie cut in as Ramesh and Zen were swaying in time to "Always." "I'm stealing my sister from you, okay?"

"Be my guest," Ramesh said. "By the way, you look even more beautiful now than before the ceremony." Behind Allie's head, he mouthed the words "they did it" to Zen. Zen laughed.

"So, who picked this music?" she asked Allie.

Allie shrugged. "Orlando invited a bunch of people from the church and business associates, so we decided this reception would be classy. We'll have all the real fun after the Pagan ceremony." She raised her eyebrows suggestively.

"When will that be? Please say not until after the snow melts."

Allie nodded. "That was my thought, too. I want to get married at the beach this time, so we're going to wait until around the first of June."

"Are you sure you still want a second ceremony? This one was really beautiful."

"The ceremony was beautiful, and now we're legal, and Orlando isn't living in sin according to his church anymore. But our marriage still hasn't been consecrated to the Goddess, and given what happened at Beltane"—she looked over at Tony, still sleeping on his grandmother—"that doesn't seem right."

The song ended, and the twins paused to clap for the small orchestra Orlando had hired for the evening.

"You're not pregnant again, are you?" Zen asked as the next song began.

Allie snorted. "No," she said. "Look, I know as well as anyone things happen sometimes, but as much as we can help it, we're trying to wait until this one's out of diapers before we have a second one. I love Tony, and Goddess knows Orlando does most of the work with him, but it's exhausting being a parent." She looked over at Ramesh. "You should try it sometime."

"I will when I'm ready," Zen said. "Until then, I stand by my birth control pills." Allie started to say something, but Zen cut her off. "You know, I really don't think this is the time or the place for your lecture about how artificial hormones are keeping me from experiencing my natural moon-cycle power."

"You ought to take that seriously, now that you're becoming a priestess."

"I do take it seriously," Zen said. "I seriously don't want to get pregnant accidentally."

Allie shrugged. "My diaphragm always worked for me." At that moment, Tony woke up and began to cry. She turned, ready to run to him, but looked back at Zen. "That wasn't a diaphragm problem. That was a trusting-the-Goddess situation."

Ramesh seemed to suddenly appear from behind Allie. "Why do I have the feeling I don't want to know what this conversation is about?"

"Excuse me," Allie said, smiling at him. She ran to her son, but Orlando had gotten to him first. Zen watched him head for the nearest bathroom with Tony in one arm and the diaper bag over the other. Briefly, Zen pictured Ramesh with a diaper bag slung over his shoulder. To her surprise, she was pleased by the image.

At the end of the night, Allie found Zen again. "I'll see you three weeks from tonight, right?"

"Of course not," Zen said. "Three weeks from now, my vow will have officially ended. After performing a brief ritual of dedication to my Goddesses, I will crawl into bed with Ramesh and not come out until he and I are half starved to death."

"Think for a moment, Zen. When did you take your vow?"

"Right before you gave birth to Tony."

Allie nodded. "Yes, on the day my son was born. Which means that one year later..." She let Zen put together the rest for herself.

"Shit," Zen said. "You're right. It's my nephew's first birthday."

"That's right. You'll come back down to Indy on Sunday morning, bring a present—doesn't have to be anything fancy; he won't remember it anyway—eat some cake and ice cream, watch the kid go nuts destroying his own little birthday cake. You'll take lots of pictures, and it will be adorable. Got it?"

"Allie?" Orlando said. He had two champagne glasses in his hand and a huge smile on his face. Bojana was holding the baby. "Oh, hi, Zen. Listen, I'm sorry I haven't seen a whole lot of you and Ramesh this evening."

"I understand," she said. "There are a lot of business acquaintances here. You've had a lot of catching up to do." She didn't say what they both were thinking: given their past relationship, the fact he was so desperate to get back in bed with her sister made her feel a bit awkward.

"Yeah. Hey, it's really good to see you." He put his arm around Allie, who took one of the champagne glasses from his hand. This was one of the few occasions on which Zen had ever seen Allie drink alcohol.

"You, too," Zen said. "You and Allie make a really good couple. I know you'll be happy together for a very long time."

He held Allie to him a little more tightly. "Forever," he said. "I meant it this time. I absolutely refuse to do anything to fuck this up."

Allie laughed and pressed her head into his chest. "Me, too," she said.

"I believe you," Zen said. As they walked away, she looked around for Ramesh.

* * * *

Ramesh looked down at his watch again. Twelve minutes after eleven p.m. He'd expected Zen by now. He looked out the window of his apartment once again, but didn't see her Toyota in the spot where she usually parked. He thought about doing something to distract himself. Maybe a book, or some TV. But he couldn't sit still long enough. He was simply restless, ready to crawl out of his skin.

More like all over hers.

The knock on the door finally came at the stroke of eleven thirty, after eighteen more minutes of torture. He hadn't even seen her car pull up. There she was nonetheless, looking incredibly hot in a tight maroon sweater and a short white skirt under her favorite green pea coat. He shut the door behind her, pulled her to him, and locked his mouth onto hers. She allowed him to run one hand down her back, landing on her ass, pressing her hips against his as he explored her mouth with his tongue.

"Not yet," she said, pulling away. "It's not midnight yet."

"Does the vow, technically, end at midnight on the anniversary of the date it was taken?" he said facetiously. "Or are you supposed to wait until the exact hour you took the vow? Or should this whole day still count as—"

"Ramesh," she said, "I have said a prayer to the Goddess, thanking her for providing me with purity and strength. I have made an offering of apples and wine to my household shrine and released myself of my vow at midnight. To show my words were heartfelt, I even offered Her a drop of my blood." She held up a finger with a small bandage on it. "You'll wait until midnight. No sooner, no later."

He smiled. He'd barely touched her and he got hard already. Ready to back her up against the door and take her standing up, in fact. "A technicality," he said.

"A spiritually important one, though," she said. "Until then..." She held up a tiny black flag; he now realized she'd had it in her hand the whole time. He laughed, thinking of pirates raising the skull and crossbones. He was well prepared to be boarded. Then she folded the thing in half, and in half again.

"Is that for me, or for you?"

"You," she said. "Sit down, let me put it on you." He wasn't much taller than her, but still, she needed his cooperation.

"What are you going to do to me, Zen?"

"You'll find out. You'll have to wait and not see."

He laughed, kneeling on the carpet. She put the blindfold over his eyes and tied it loosely behind his head. "I hope tying my hands behind my back won't be necessary."

"No," she said. "I didn't want you to see where we're going. Once we get there, though, tying your hands behind your back might be fun." She slapped him, hard, on the ass. He liked it. She wrapped his winter coat around him next, and he stuck his arms through the sleeves.

Ramesh found he also liked being led around, blind, by Zen. It didn't alarm him when she opened the door and took him outside the apartment. She had the decency to use the elevator rather than trying to lead him down the stairs. He wasn't bothered when she put him in her car; at least she buckled his seat belt.

"Do you want to give me a hint as to where we're going?" he asked her.

Zen was quiet for a moment. She'd turned off the radio; the only sounds he heard were the miles whizzing by and his own breathing. Then she said, "I'm not transporting you across state lines."

"Okay," he said. "So, not your place."

"Not my place," she echoed him, and then laughed. Wherever she was taking him, it wasn't far. He heard her shift the car into park and step out. As Zen opened the back passenger door, Ramesh realized they were probably on campus, only three miles from his apartment. He grinned, thinking of all the fun they could have in the lab. She took his arm and helped him from the car.

"You'll need my i.d. badge to get in," he said quietly.

"Very clever. You've figured out we're on campus. But we don't need your i.d badge, and we're *not* going to your lab. If I have to look at your little girlfriend, Kara Sarves-whatever, I might do something crazy."

"Good point." He looked down at his feet, trying to see if he could tell where they were going. He couldn't, until she walked him through a pair of glass doors and into a cool, quiet building. He recognized the faded, raveling red rug she marched him down, especially as they walked over the university's insignia.

"Thank the gods the library is open late on week nights," Ramesh said.

"I'm taking the blindfold off now. People are starting to stare."

As soon as he could see again, Ramesh followed Zen, who dashed for the elevator. His heart raced as he wondered exactly what time it was. Was she up for some antics between floors? Two students, each staring down at a cell phone text message while walking, came out of the elevator as Zen got in. Ramesh got in, hands shaking with anticipation as the doors began to close.

"I've been thinking about this moment ever since your sister's wedding," Ramesh said, backing Zen into the corner. "I haven't gotten a good night's sleep since then. I can't even take a shower without thinking about what we did in the hotel room."

He wanted to tell her more. Better still, he would have liked to kiss the breath from her, holding her tight to him with one hand and exploring the insides of her thighs inside that tight white skirt with the other.

At that moment, though, the doors opened, and in stepped a dour-looking security guard. Ramesh backed up against the handrail and held onto it with both hands behind his back.

"What floor?" the security guard asked them. It hadn't occurred to Ramesh to pick a floor. He was too wrapped up in Zen.

"Seven," Ramesh said. As the security guard pressed the buttons for seven, and then ten, Ramesh sighed. He said to Zen, "Earth Sciences floor. Virtually no chance of running into any undergraduates there." She nodded.

At the seventh floor, the security guard made a disapproving noise as Zen and Ramesh got out of the elevator.

Now Ramesh took charge. He led her through the stacks of dusty old earth science books, past the restrooms, the drinking fountains, and an unstaffed reference desk, to the back of the building where the semi-private study carrels stood. Zen took a seat on top of a desk, smiling wickedly. They hadn't seen a single person on their way back here.

"I've had dreams like this," Ramesh said. "Alone in a deserted wing of the library with a beautiful woman who wants me. I've been a student here for almost seven years now, and I've never seen a woman as beautiful as you here."

"In Earth Sciences?" She peeled off her sweater and draped it over the walls of the carrel. Underneath she wore a tight, lace camisole. He could see the hard peaks of her nipples underneath it.

He reached out to touch her bare shoulder. "On this planet."

She looked past him at something. Frustrated by the distraction, he turned to see what she was seeing. "What is it?"

"Clock," she said. "Making sure it's after midnight."

He looked at the clock: 12:09.

"Thank you, Goddess," Zen whispered before Ramesh filled the space between them with his body, crushing her against him as he kissed her hungrily. She opened her mouth, sucking on his tongue, and he moaned softly. How he'd missed her mouth! Three hundred sixty-five days and nights dreaming of how her mouth would feel on his again, and now he no longer had to dream. It felt sweeter than sweet, sublime as the night they'd met. At last he knew what they meant by "Absence makes the heart grow fonder."

His heart wasn't the only part of him glad to be reunited with Zen's body, though his heart hammered in his chest as if he'd run up all seven flights of stairs. His whole body seemed to respond to her. His hands shook. His skin crawled with an odd sensation.

She parted her knees to allow him even closer access to her, and suddenly Ramesh grew aware of his erection. Zen must have felt it, too. He heard her laugh, a wonderful welcoming sound in his ear that told him she'd been longing for this as he had.

"Oh, my," she said with another giggle.

He knew full well if the university president came by, giving a guided tour of the library to a group of nuns, he still couldn't pull himself away from Zen. It would take the combined efforts of the entire campus security force to pry them apart now.

He reached for her panties, barely concealed under her short skirt. "What other surprises do you have for me?"

She didn't stop him. "See for yourself." All that separated him from her soft, wet, pink pussy was the tiniest of white lace thongs.

"Damn, Zen," he said, coming up to kiss her lips again. At the same time, he pressed two fingers of one hand into the thin fabric of her panties, rubbing her hot clit through them.

Her head rolled back in ecstasy. "Damn, Ramesh!" For once, she didn't try to guide his fingers. His instincts were right on target.

His other hand held tightly to hers. Her skin was so much softer than he'd remembered, and she smelled maddeningly good, like the honey lotion she liked to use in the winter. Combined with the smell of her aroused sex, the delicious perfume made him sweat, even in the chilly library. Here she was, everything he'd been wanting for so long. Everything he'd been dreaming of during the long years when he'd gone to Kameko's farm to look for her on Beltane night, but hadn't found her there. Here she was, his Goddess, finally ready to make love to him again the way they'd done that first night.

He couldn't help it. In the quiet of the library, Ramesh let out a fierce, feral growl. Zen responded with an equally feral grunt, a sound that told him she wanted him. He fumbled with his jeans for a moment, but soon had his cock, hard and glistening with a drop of fluid, ready for her. She sighed, and spread her knees wider.

Ramesh didn't bother to take off Zen's thong. With his fingers, he tugged aside the thin piece of fabric that partially hid her pussy from him. Her pussy lips were swollen and slick; he ran his fingers over them appreciatively, drawing a moan from Zen.

"Come on," she said, reaching for his cock.

Ramesh pulled out of her grasp. "Look at you!" he teased her. "All impatient and shit. Take your time, Zen. We've got all night. Or, at least until the library closes." He leaned in and kissed her lips again, running his hands over her breasts.

"Ramesh, it's been a year," she said into his ear while he groped her. "I want you inside me. Now."

He bit his lip and stared at her for a moment. Then he acceded to her wishes, bringing the head of his cock up to the mouth of her pussy. For one sweet, torturous moment, he stood like this, unmoving, anticipating. Zen moaned again, louder this time. Her hands pulled him to her. Then her wetness allowed him easy access to the innermost part of her. He shivered with delight, feeling the inside of her moist-velvet pussy. He'd dreamt of this for the past twelve months. His woman. His Goddess. His fierce warrior-Goddess, destroyer of evil, the beloved Kali to his Shiva.

Soon, though, Ramesh's deep thoughts gave way to the simple, yet profound, joy of feeling his body against hers, inside hers. They kissed fiercely now, holding nothing back, as lost in one another as they had been in the darkness of Kameko's wheat field. Time lost its meaning. The library faded into nothingness, all except the wooden desk that supported Zen's beautiful ass.

Ramesh heard himself making odd noises, growls and coyote-like barks until his throat burned. Zen answered him in precisely the way he'd remembered, her pleasured moans coming as answers to his growls and barks, her fingernails digging into his shoulder blades through his loosely knit sweater. He loved the feel of those sharp points in his back, distracting him momentarily from his pleasure. Without them, he might have lost it before now, before Zen let go, throwing her head back, breathing like a marathon runner. Even if he hadn't felt the walls of her cunt contract around his cock, drawing him in deeper, clutching him as though they might not let go, he would have known she was coming.

"Zen," he said, "I can't hold out any more."

"Come for me. Come inside me."

She'd barely had time to say the words before he obeyed them, clenching his teeth to keep from shouting himself hoarse as he spilled his seed into her slick, violently contracting pussy.

They enjoyed only a moment more of the glorious feeling of oneness before they separated, eager to get dressed and return to the illusion they hadn't been doing anything wrong on the Earth Sciences floor. As she pulled her sweater back on, Zen said, "So, do you figure there are any security cameras up here?"

"Sure," he said. "Either security's not paying attention, or they liked watching us too much to try to stop us." She laughed. "I just hope we don't see the video on the Internet six months from now."

She put her arms around him. "I don't care. I don't care who knows I love you. I love you, Ramesh."

"I love you, too, Zen. I've loved you ever since I met you. I'm glad your vow is over, though. I'm still a guy. I do think about pussy every twenty seconds."

He took her hand as they walked back to the elevator. They shared a smile at their private joke, their breathing still not quite slowed to normal, drenched with sweat under their clothes and, he didn't doubt, smelling like sex.

At Zen's car, Ramesh said, "Are you going to put the blindfold back on me?"

"If you want me to."

"What's next? We go to the grocery store and do it in the produce aisle?"

She shook her head. "We'll duck inside some quiet little bar in your neighborhood, have a couple of drinks and maybe a sandwich to keep up our strength. Then we go back to your place, strip down to nothing but a smile, and fall into bed again. Or maybe onto the kitchen table first. I haven't settled on the order yet."

He leaned over and kissed her cheek. "Nobody on earth knows me like you do, Zen. I love that."

"I've really missed knowing you," she said, smiling. "I am going to know you until seven o'clock tomorrow morning."

He sat up straight. "What's at seven?"

"Driving back to Indiana for my nephew's first birthday party," she said. "Want to come?"

"Already did," he joked. "Are you serious? Our first full day of being able to make love again, and we're going to spend it at a baby's birthday party?"

"I didn't plan the timing of Tony's birth," Zen said. "Well, in a way I suppose I did, in the sense that I was the one who invited Orlando to the Beltane celebration, which ultimately resulted in Tony's conception—"

"Not the point," Ramesh said. "I had this fantasy all worked out, where we spent twenty-four straight hours in my apartment, only taking the occasional break from fucking like dogs in heat to eat, get an hour or two of sleep here and there, and maybe pee once or twice."

"Amend it," she said. "We have six more hours to fuck like dogs in heat."

Ramesh smiled. "Sounds good when you say it."

Even that plan didn't go quite as smoothly as expected, though. After their second round of lovemaking, Ramesh fell hard and fast asleep. He didn't wake up again until it was time to get ready for the party.

* * * *

Allie struggled to balance her canvas bag, full of last-minute groceries for Tony's party, in one hand while digging in her purse for her house keys with the other hand. Awkwardly, she opened the back door and let the canvas bag flop over onto the kitchen counter. A box of birthday candles tumbled out, and several of the candles cracked. Upstairs, she heard Tony crying.

"Orlando?" she called up the stairs. He didn't answer. Forgetting about the quart of raspberry gelatto in the bottom of her shopping bag, Allie went up to the nursery.

She found Orlando sitting in the rocking chair, gently rocking his pink-faced son. Tears flowed down Tony's cheeks. With his face contorted like that, Tony looked more like an irascible troll than her sweet little boy. As Allie came nearer, Tony seemed to calm down. His howling cries became a gentle, persistent sob. Orlando stretched out his arms to transfer Tony to Allie. He gave her his seat in the rocking chair, kissing her cheek as they changed positions.

"What's the matter with him?" Allie asked.

"He's tired, I think," Orlando said. "Poor kid. He needs a nap, but I can't seem to get him to go down for one."

Allie wiped the tears from Tony's cheeks with the corner of the soft blanket on the back of the rocking chair. "Oh, I see how you are," she said to the boy. "Won't go to sleep for Daddy. You need your nap today, little guy. I don't know if you realize this, but after nap time, you're going to have a big party. Cake, presents, everything."

"Cake," Tony said.

"Nap first," Allie said. She rocked gently in the chair, and Tony closed his eyes.

"Thank you," Orlando said. "You saved my life. I've been trying to get him to go to sleep since you left the house."

She smiled sympathetically. "I'm sorry. Listen, can you do me a quick favor? I left groceries on the counter, and my gelato's going to melt if you don't put it away. Then, if you want to lie down for a while before the party, I'll take care of Tony."

"Yeah, no problem." He kissed her lips. "Love you, baby. You, too, little baby." He kissed the top of Tony's head and went down the stairs. Moments later, Allie heard him come back up the stairs and close their bedroom door.

She rocked Tony, humming one of the Slovenian lullabies she'd picked up from Bojana. Eventually, when she knew he was asleep, Allie placed him on his back in his crib and covered his legs with a blanket. She kissed each of his cheeks and whispered, "Sleep tight."

Allie took off her shoes and left them by the nursery door. She crept into her own bedroom. Orlando lay stretched on the bed. He seemed to have fallen asleep without even bothering to take off his running shoes. Allie sat on the edge of the bed, untied his shoes, and took them off, one by one.

Orlando opened his eyes. "Hi."

Allie didn't say anything. Instead, she knelt on the bed. On her hands and knees, she crawled up Orlando's long legs, stopping to kneel beside his hips. "Am I bothering you?"

"Not at all," he said. "Please, carry on."

"Because maybe, I thought, what you really want is to rest."

He shook his head. "I like your idea better. What, exactly, is your idea, again?"

Allie showed him. She tugged at the waistband of his navy blue jogging pants, getting them down far enough to expose the growing bulge in his white briefs.

"I like this idea," Orlando said, laying his head back on his pillow.

"Shh," Allie told him. "Relax. Rest."

She put her hand on his thigh, feeling the strong beat of his pulse. He shivered at her gentle touch.

"A little higher," Orlando directed. She shushed him again.

Allie hesitated only a moment before finding the front opening of his briefs and tugging the head of his cock free of them. As their son's first birthday reminded her, she'd been with Orlando (in one way or another) through one year and nine months now. Still, she always felt a little amazed at the sight of his naked cock. So fat. So beautiful. She looked at his face, daring him to say something else. She stroked his cock affectionately. It grew longer and fatter in her hand. Allie smiled.

She leaned in, cupping his balls in one hand, feeling their weight. He exhaled heavily, but didn't open his eyes.

Allie closed hers, leaned in, and ran her tongue along the underside of his cock, from the head down to the base, then back up to the head again. She licked her fingers and tested the feel of her wet hand against the wet side of his dick. Hm. The feel was slippery, but not as slick as she wanted. She spit in her hand and tried again.

"Yeah," Orlando said. Allie opened her eyes, and watched him ball up a handful of the bed sheets in his fist.

Stroking him with her wet hand was only part of the plan. After a few more carefully placed licks, she got into a comfortable position between his legs, lowered her lips, and took the head of his cock into her mouth. She slid him back, further down her tongue, until her mouth got full, almost to the point of gagging. Further down his cock, her fingers never stopped moving. Now she let the action of her lips and tongue match the rhythm of her fingers.

She stopped, briefly, to gauge her effect on him. Orlando's hard breathing shook the bed. Both fists clenched sections of bedding. One knee was bent—and yes, inside his white athletic socks, his toes were curled. Allie had timed this pause perfectly; she'd brought him right to the brink of losing control, and then backed him off. This amused her. She decided to leave him hanging for a moment before taking him in her mouth once again. She paused again, long enough to spit on her fingers once more, and resumed working him over with her mouth and her fingers at the same time.

Soon, Allie had Orlando close to the edge again. She pulled away, intending to tease him some more. "Oh, come on," he said.

Allie relented, allowing him release. He came in great spurts on her tongue. She happily swallowed each drop of his precious seed.

"Tell Tony," Orlando muttered once he'd caught his breath, "his mommy is a very, very nice woman. God, I love you, Allie." Moments later, he fell asleep. Allie let him have his nap.

Chapter Five

Zen's feet, like the other women's, were bare. Four of them walked where the chilly, fifty-degree water of Lake Michigan met the warm sand on the first hot night of the year, early June, and a few minutes past the stroke of midnight. On the back of the wind, a troupe of monarch butterflies made its migration. Their vibrant lives, Zen thought, made an apt metaphor for Allie and Orlando. Though they had been married legally, and in the eyes of the Catholic church, for almost six months now, they were about to begin yet another new life, as a couple consecrated to the Goddess.

Zen felt Allie squeeze her right hand. She felt as nervous and excited as on her first wedding day, but Zen knew Allie had no reason to be. She was certain of the rightness of this marriage. With her left hand, Zen squeezed Gillian's hand. The moonlight wedding on the beach had originally been Gillian's dream, filtering down to Allie through Zen. Gillian's midnight ceremony would have been on the sunrise coast of Lake Michigan, the Wisconsin side, where Allie's took place on the sunset side. Allie's deep connection to Pagan Spirits farm meant she envisioned her wedding at Weko Beach, where Kameko had often taken the twins in the summer to get away for an afternoon. Given the perfection of this night, Zen was grateful to Gillian and Allie's collective romantic imagination.

She saw Orlando first, holding Antonio against his chest, and felt Allie's pulse race. Then she saw Ramesh, his skin positively golden under the light of the full moon. Allie's hand broke away from Zen's first, and Allie ran up the beach to her bridegroom. Touched by her eagerness, Zen dropped Gillian's hand and ran into Ramesh's arms, tearing past Paul Phillip and his boyfriend Chris.

Ramesh, casual but stylish in his favorite bright-pink button-down shirt and slightly rumpled khakis, had been talking to the overdressed Adam Schumann. Overdressed, because as he stood near the fire of driftwood illuminating the beach, he was visibly drenched in sweat. Allie's best friend's husband didn't seem to mind the break in conversation. He took Jane in his arms and smiled over at Allie and Orlando. They'd crushed Tony in between them, briefly, before handing him off to Bojana.

Melissa and Kameko got everyone into place, forming them into a loose circle. Ramesh and Zen held hands. She looked up at him, and his dark eyes sparkled in the moonlight.

"I want a traditional Indian wedding," he whispered into Zen's ear.

She was stunned, speechless. Ramesh had never mentioned marriage before. Zen wasn't sure she was ready, but as he said the words, something inside her liked the sound of them.

When Zen didn't answer, Ramesh took her in his arms again and kissed her. "We can talk about it later," he said. She squeezed his hand tightly, smiling.

Zen wanted to talk about it then, but there was too much going on around her. Armin arrived, along with his mother, Catherine. So, too, did Armin's biological father,

Vlad, Vlad's wife Annie, and their sons Sasha and Peter. Zen sensed a lot of tension. Fortunately, Allie and Orlando were too happy, too complete with each other to think about past wrongs and ruined relationships. They were diplomatic to their guests. Zen found it funny to finally see how much Armin looked like his half-brothers.

Moments later, Melissa prepared to begin the ceremony. "We'll begin with a prayer of thanks to the Goddess," she said, raising her hands solemnly over the little circle of guests on the dark beach. She faced due north. "Lady of the North, we call down your blessings upon us—"

"Wait!" a female voice called from off in the distance. "Don't start the wedding without me!"

Zen noted the mildly annoyed look on Melissa's usually serene face as Melissa turned around.

"Who's that?" Ramesh whispered to Zen.

"I don't know," Zen said, struggling to make out the face of the woman coming rapidly toward them. She wore an odd outfit, with long floral-patterned surfer shorts and a torn mesh jersey over a long-sleeved black t-shirt: Astrid. Her light-colored hair, still streaked with green, as far as Zen could tell in the weak light, was elaborately done up with chopsticks.

"What the fuck is that?" Vlad said in a low voice, though loudly enough for Zen and Ramesh to hear. Adam chuckled. Annie looked toward the lake, chagrined, as the others murmured and wondered aloud who she was, though in less vulgar terms.

Astrid scrabbled across the sand in her flip-flops, coming to stand beside Gillian. Gillian launched into full-on public display of affection mode, grabbing Astrid around the waist and smooching her. Their lips made a loud smacking sound as they separated.

Astrid then shrugged and said loudly, "You guys, I am *so* sorry I'm late." To Gillian she said, "I couldn't get off work early enough to make it on time." Then, to Melissa, she said, "Please, go on with the ceremony."

Zen wasn't quite sure, but she thought maybe, for the first time in the ten years she'd known Melissa Stargazer, Melissa rolled her eyes, however slightly. But her whole demeanor soon changed, as she took on the official aspect of Pagan priestess.

"Let us begin with a prayer of thanks to the Goddess for bringing all of us here together tonight to celebrate the union of Allegra Van Zandt and Orlando Parisi. Lady in heaven, Mother of us all, Giver of life, Taker of breath, Maker of war and of peace..."

* * * *

"The wedding was cool," Ramesh said as he crossed the floor, stepping around Kameko's rowing machine. Zen had slipped out of her red dress and stood beside the bed in her strapless bra and panties. She untucked the sheets and tossed the black bedspread off to the side.

"Yeah," Zen agreed. "I would say I liked it better than my sister's first wedding to Orlando, but frankly, I'm a little biased."

"What was up with Gillian's girlfriend?" He laughed.

Zen shuddered. "I've tried so hard to like Astrid, 'cause Gillian's so crazy about her, but that woman rubs me the wrong way. Not that I've had much face time with her. Every time she comes to pick Gillian up from the store, she's in such a hurry. I'd be surprised if she's said forty words to me the whole time I've known her."

"Maybe it freaks her out that you can read her feelings," he suggested.

"Maybe," Zen said, shrugging. "Maybe she has abysmal social skills. You saw what she wore."

"You mean *Gill and Astrid's Excellent Adventure*? I thought it was kind of cool, actually, in a post-punk California stripper kind of way." He took off his pink shirt. He hung it on the closet door knob and sat on the bed to take off the sandals he'd worn in the car.

She laughed loudly, then remembered Kameko and the baby were trying to sleep in the next room.

"You don't really have much room to talk," Ramesh continued. "I heard a rumor that when Allie married Paul Phillip, you finished out your sister's wedding reception in a plaid number held together with safety pins." He placed his sandals gently on the floor in front of the closet.

"Ugh, don't remind me," she said, struggling to re-bury the memories of her one forgettable night with Chris, Paul Phillip's wedding caterer/boyfriend.

"You've got to admit, though," he said. "Watching Astrid and Gillian make out is kinda sexy."

She got up and crossed the room, to her overnight bag. "I admit nothing. Gillian's my best non-twin-sister girl friend. I don't think of her like *that*."

He watched her dig through her bag. "What, did you forget to take your pill or something?"

Zen shook her head. She reached into the bag and pulled out what looked like an oversized wooden cigar box.

"No wonder that thing was so heavy," he said.

She ignored him, opening the box and taking out the familiar object inside: her sculpture of Kali.

"What did you bring that thing for?"

Zen placed Kali on top of the dresser, where her stereo used to sit. "To thank her," she said. "I don't know if I ever told you this before, Ramesh, but the second time I ever met Orlando, I was getting all of these sexual vibes off him. I wanted him, but I also knew he was married. I prayed to Kali to guide me toward the right decision."

Ramesh stared at her, but said nothing. Zen sensed jealousy.

"Look, I'm not saying hopping into bed with Orlando was the right thing to do. But if you step back and look at the grand scheme of things, if he hadn't met me, he never would have met Allie. Now you look at them, and they're so happy, married twice, and the parents of the cutest fourteen-month-old around."

"Lucky bastard slept with both sisters," Ramesh muttered.

Zen ignored him. She knelt in front of the dresser, then bent forward until her forehead touched the floor.

"What are you doing?" Ramesh asked her. He took off his pants and sat on the bed in his boxers.

She didn't look up. "This prayer pose is borrowed from ancient Greek tradition. The Greeks used to touch their faces to the ground to pray to Persephone and Hades. Because they ruled over death and held the only keys to a soul's chance at resurrection, Persephone and her husband were simultaneously feared, respected and loved."

He let her say her prayer, then added, "Don't ever let my mom see you do that."

She came to bed. "Why not?"

"She would say that you're not treating Kali properly. To you, that thing is a only a statue, but it represents the divine. To my mom it's a statue that represents the divine, and it's also a place where Kali's spirit or power resides, and so it *is* Kali. She would also tell you a goddess is to be treated like an important guest in one's home. You would bathe her, give her meals, dress her—never neglect her. Mom would say you haven't been doing your duty as a woman."

"I thought your mom was an ear, nose and throat doctor," Zen said, getting under the sheet beside him.

"No, she's an ophthalmologist, but her religious life is only one part of her professional life. Look, don't let her see that thing in your apartment, okay?"

She looked him in the eyes. "Why? Am I going to meet your family soon, Ramesh?"

"I'm considering it," he said. He lay back and reached for her hand. She let him take it. "If I asked you to marry me, Zen, what would you say?"

"I don't know," she said. "This marriage thing is kind of sudden. We haven't even moved in together yet."

"Maybe we should get married first. I mean, if you want to. You would let me know if you wanted to get married, wouldn't you?"

"Yeah, of course," she said. "I think I do, someday. I hadn't thought about it before today."

"Really?"

"Well, I thought about it, but not seriously. I sort of imagined we'd always be together, but I didn't know what you wanted."

"I want you," he said. "Listen, don't worry about it. You and I will come to a decision when we're ready. We don't need to rush things because your sister's wedding was so romantic."

She turned off the light. "It was, wasn't it?"

He leaned over and kissed her lips, running his hands gently across the smooth skin of her belly. Her skin shone with sweat, but this only strengthened his desire for her. "Ramesh?" Zen said in between kisses.

He kissed her neck, then paused. "Yes, my love?"

"Go to sleep," she said, giggling.

He didn't seem quite as amused by this request. "Don't you want to make love?"

"The walls are paper-thin," she whispered, "and Kameko's got amazingly good hearing for a woman in her seventies."

"I can be quiet," he whispered back. "I can't guarantee you'll be quiet when I make you come, but that's up to you." He slipped his fingers between her legs and rubbed her clit through her panties. "Please, Zen? How about if we go outside? We won't bother anyone out there."

She relented. "Okay, maybe a quick one," she said. She quickly threw on a t-shirt and a pair of shorts, and Ramesh also grabbed a pair of shorts. Neither bothered to put their sandals back on. Creeping down the back staircase, they snuck out through the kitchen and past Kameko's gated garden.

"Here," Ramesh said, pausing under the large tent at one of the picnic tables set up for the next day's wedding reception.

Zen wrinkled her nose, though she wasn't sure Ramesh could even see her face in the moonlight. "Are you kidding? People are going to eat off that thing tomorrow."

"Then their wedding feast will be seasoned with the flavor of love," he said. He stripped out of his shorts and sat on the tabletop, motioning for Zen to sit beside him.

She gave up, stripped out of her own shorts and t-shirt, and sat on the picnic table.

"Lay down," he said. She obeyed. She bit her lip to suppress a loud giggle as he kissed his way down her belly.

"This is what I love about the lake," he said, in between kisses laid gently on her hipbones. "You breathe the lake air, and it gets in you. Your skin tastes like it."

"That's sweat," she said.

He shook his head. "It's freshwater, sand, night air, full moon light, the flight of monarch butterflies." He kissed the inside of her thigh. "This part here? It tastes like the apple orchard, the wheat field, and the barley. All of these things get inside you and become part of you."

She relaxed, stretching out her arms, spreading her legs wide for him. Ramesh shifted from lying on his side beside her to lying on his belly between her legs. "What else do I taste like?" she taunted him.

He took some of her flesh between his lips and sucked her as if sucking an oyster from its shell. This pleased her, and she grunted her delight.

"Lake perch."

She grabbed her shirt and whacked the side of his head with it, laughing.

"Okay," he said. "I'll be serious." He slid back into position. She relaxed once again and closed her eyes. Ramesh took his time, sampling the tastes of her pussy lips and her clit. Zen got lost in the blissful sensation. He surprised her by trailing the tip of his tongue around the mouth of her pussy. All at once, his tongue slipped inside her, exploring her. He did this again and again. She liked this, a taste of bigger and better things to come. The delicious anticipation sent her to the edge. When the tension reached its crescendo, Ramesh seemed to know she reached the point of no return. Caressing her thighs, he kissed his way up her lips, then took her clit in his mouth and sucked.

Zen couldn't hold back any longer. Her orgasm came upon her all at once, the muscles of her pussy clenching hard, gushing with wetness. He penetrated her with one finger, and then two. His intrusion extended her pleasure. Zen arched her back and struggled to keep from crying out as Ramesh drew his fingers in and out of her.

She knew this would only make him want more. He sat beside her, kissing her face. She loved the taste of her own arousal on his lips. He knew exactly what Zen liked. He took her hands and helped her sit up. Taking care not to fall off the edge of the picnic table, he lay on his back. He moaned softly as she mounted him.

Zen took a moment to watch the blissful expression on his face before she closed her eyes. She felt what he was feeling: a heady mix of desire, love, comfort and dizzying pleasure. She loved this moment, the moment she could feel the sensation in Ramesh's body as well as her own while their bodies were connected. It felt as if their souls were connected. She breathed in the wind, which carried the scent of the apple trees. An owl called in the distance, and Zen couldn't imagine a feeling closer to paradise than this.

When she moved, it felt as if she moved in slow motion. Ramesh moaned a little louder. Zen leaned in and kissed him to silence him. Soon, though, she found she needed to sit up straight to work her hips the way she wanted. She loved the way his cock felt, how it worked so deep inside her when she rode him like this. He always seemed to find the secret place inside her that took her breath away. She could carry on in this breathless, ecstatic state only so long, though, before the pleasure drove her back over the edge.

This time, she reached the edge at the exact moment Ramesh did. As the force of her orgasm washed over her, Zen felt the spasms of his release inside her. She rocked her hips, wanting to keep up this blissful feeling forever. It wasn't only the friction or the orgasm feeling so good, she realized. It was the palpable sense of devotion and of peace between them.

At last she held her body still. She leaned in and rested her head on his chest, not separating from him. "I don't want to move," she said.

Ramesh ran his hand down her bare back. Though it was a hot night, she felt goosebumps rising. "I know what you mean, but we can't sleep on a picnic table."

"You're right," she said, though she was still in no hurry to pull her body away from his. Ramesh lay there, looking up at the stars, until Zen finally decided she could let him go long enough for them to put their clothes back on. They hurried back into the house and under the sheet. Comfortably back in bed, Zen snuggled up to Ramesh and fell asleep listening to his heart beat.

* * * *

The following evening's celebration at Kameko's farm was a simple affair compared to Allie and Orlando's wedding reception at his church's social hall. Kameko served salad and fresh fruit on one of her picnic tables for those who'd attended the previous night's festivities.

Bojana sat at the end of the long picnic table, feeding bits of pastry to Antonio. Orlando sat next to his mother, with the baby on his lap. As Antonio chewed the corner of a sweet roll, Bojana's neatly manicured hand reached out to Orlando's face.

"Here," she said. "Some for you."

He took the bit of pastry from his mother's fingers and laughed. "Mom, you don't need to feed me anymore. What's Allie going to say if she sees me eating out of your hand?"

"I'm going to say it's time for you and I to dance, Mr. Parisi Van Zandt," Allie said. She's walked up behind Orlando while he was distracted by the baby.

Bojana crooked her head and smiled, holding out her arms. "I'll take the baby. You two go dance." Orlando handed Antonio off to his mother, rose to his feet, and held out his hand for Allie in a grand gesture. She took it, and they slow-danced to a romantic ballad.

The long picnic table and the buffet occupied one end of the tent. At the opposite end, Ramesh and Zen had set up the bar on a third picnic table. Across from them, the DJ had set up stereo speakers and a laptop full of songs. In the gap between tables, Orlando and Allie danced.

Catherine Westmore danced with her date, Gary. Catherine hadn't formerly introduced herself to Zen, but Zen overheard Catherine reminding Orlando he knew Gary from Catherine's office. Gary wore gray slacks and a long-sleeved white button-down. He'd started out with a gold-and-silver striped tie, but had taken it off in the summer heat. Even under the shade of the tent, the heat felt stifling. It was too bad, because his tie had matched nicely with Catherine's form-fitting, short, silver evening dress.

Annie Davidovitch, after two glasses of cherry wine, danced by herself in the corner, seeming not to care who saw her. Her sons and Armin had gone off exploring the farm. Her husband staked out the table nearest the bar and helped himself to generous amounts of chilled vodka.

Paul Phillip, as Zen remembered from when he married Allie, had always loved to dance. Zen had to admit, he and Chris, dressed in matching khaki shorts and white button-down shirts, made an attractive couple. She tried not to watch them, though. She didn't want Chris to think she thought about him.

The only couples who didn't dance were Astrid and Gillian, who sat at the buffet table picking at their fruits and veggies, and Ramesh and Zen, who hung around the bar.

Kameko came over to where Zen was leaning against the bar table. "Zen, pour me a sparkling water over ice, please."

"Sure thing," Zen said, reaching for her ice scoop.

"Then get out there and dance!" Kameko said, smiling. She put her hand on Ramesh's sleeve. "You've got a gorgeous man here. Show him off. Ramesh, what's your favorite song?"

Ramesh's eyes lit up. "I like Pearl Jam, and Led Zeppelin—"

"That DJ's got a couple of Pearl Jam songs," Vlad said in his heavy Russian accent. Zen hadn't noticed him coming up behind Kameko until he spoke. Two hours into the reception, Vlad was clearly feeling the effects of his liquor. He took another chilled shot glass from the bowl of ice and staggered back to his table.

"Have fun," Kameko said, before sauntering off to talk to Melissa. Melissa stood behind Bojana, trying to get her to tell folk tales from Slovenia.

Ramesh finished off his bottle of cider and threw the empty into the recycling bin. He leaned in close to Zen. "I don't like the way he was looking at you."

"Who?" Zen said, watching Allie and Orlando dance. She was somewhat distracted.

"The big scary Russian guy," Ramesh said. He leaned against the table beside Zen, close enough to press his hip into hers. "Vlad. I don't trust him."

Zen was about to say something, but the U2 song that had been playing ended, and Ramesh's Pearl Jam tune came on. "Don't embarrass me out here," Zen told Ramesh as he took her hand and pulled her out to the dance floor.

Ramesh was a better dancer than Zen remembered. They finished out the first song, then a second, before Allie tapped Zen on the shoulder. Allie and Orlando had danced virtually non-stop for forty-five minutes before then.

"I'm ready for a cold drink," Allie told her sister. Allie's usual no-drinking rule was very, very relaxed that night. "How about you guys?"

"We were only getting started," Ramesh protested. "Then again, we've got all night."

Allie and Orlando sat at the long picnic table, opposite where Bojana held Antonio. Antonio looked as if he were ready for another nap, resting his head on his grandmother's shoulder. Allie pulled out chairs for Zen and Ramesh.

"What does everybody want?" Zen asked. "I'll get it."

"I'll help you," Ramesh said, stealing a glance at Vlad.

She put her hand on his shoulder. "No, you look tired. I'll get it. Cider for everybody?"

"Sounds great," Orlando said. "That is, unless you feel like grabbing me the bottle of Bertoluccio. I do have a family tradition to uphold here. Speaking of which, I think

I'll go grab another handful of Mom's cookies. Be right back, Allie." He kissed her cheek before he went.

"You two look really happy together," Ramesh told Allie.

"So do you and Zen," she said, smiling up at Zen.

Zen bent and kissed the top of Ramesh's head. "I'll be right back, too." She hurried over to the bar, keeping one eye on Vlad as she fished four ciders and the Bertoluccio bottle out of the ice bucket underneath the table. She pressed the cold bottles against her body to keep from dropping them. The sensation was refreshing, but she couldn't bear it much longer.

She placed the bottles on the picnic table in time to hear Catherine, seated across from Orlando, talking to Ramesh. "You look so familiar," she said. "I can't quite put my finger on it. What's your name?"

"Ramesh Sudhra," he said.

Catherine's eyes widened. "Sudhra? As in David Sadguna Sudhra?"

Ramesh gave her half a smile. "He's my dad."

Catherine gasped. "No way!" she said.

"Why is she doing that?" Zen whispered to Ramesh.

He turned to Zen. "Didn't I ever tell you what my dad did for a living?"

She shook her head. "Something in medicine or science, like you and your mom, I assumed."

Catherine laughed loudly. "David Sadguna Sudhra is *not* a doctor," she said. "But he played one on TV."

Zen cocked her head at Ramesh. "It's true," he said. "Dad played Dr. Ali Mirza for seven seasons on *Journey Toward the Sun*."

"The soap opera?" Zen said, giggling. "How come you never told me your dad's an actor?"

"He *was* an actor," Ramesh said. "He mostly does voice-over work now."

"I knew it!" Catherine said. "That was him in the long-distance commercial with all the spinning umbrellas, wasn't it?"

Ramesh nodded. "Some of Dad's finest work," he said. "I don't like to talk about it because I don't want to make it sound like a bigger deal than it is. Plus I used to get a lot of shit as a kid."

"Why?" Zen asked. "Was he a really bad actor?"

"Not *really* bad," Ramesh said with a smirk. "He played a Pakistani. That probably doesn't mean anything to you, but there aren't a whole lot of Indian-American actors on TV, and people used to give him grief for not playing an Indian character. If you knew my dad, you'd know: he'd have played an Italian guy if that's what the script called for. As long as he was in the spotlight, he was happy."

"He was handsome while he was on TV," Catherine said. "I bet he's gorgeous now."

Zen looked from Ramesh to Vlad to Orlando to Gary, a small, white-haired man with pale skin and glasses. He reminded Zen of no one so much as the white rabbit from *Alice in Wonderland*. She half-expected Gary to pull out a pocket watch and announce he was late for a very important date. She looked back at Catherine and said, "You have widely varying taste in men, don't you?"

Catherine ignored her. "Will you tell your father I'm still one of his biggest fans?"

"Dad will be glad to hear that," Ramesh said. He took a long sip from his cider bottle. "Zen, how would you feel about another dance?"

"Sounds great," she said. "Allie, I'll talk to you later." As they stepped out onto the dance floor, just in time for a slow dance, she asked him, "What's up?"

"I thought Orlando's ex-wife was being rude, ignoring you like that," he said. "You seemed a little uncomfortable around her, anyway."

She shrugged. He slipped his arm around her waist and held her to him. "I did help break up her marriage," she said. "I guess I really don't want to spend a lot of time with her."

The awkwardness of the moment was quickly forgotten, though. Zen and Ramesh danced, drank, and talked for hours. As Ramesh ran inside the farm house to use the bathroom, Zen kept dancing by herself. The DJ put on a fast Punjabi song, and Zen closed her eyes and danced. Lost in the music, she twisted and spun, working her muscles.

She got along fine, until she backed into someone. She opened her eyes. "Sorry," she said, turning to see the injured partyVlad. She should have known by his solid build.

"No problem," he said, smiling. He set his empty shot glass down on the nearest table. "Which one are you again?"

"I beg your pardon?"

Vlad thought for a moment. "Orlando's new wife has a twin," he said. "Are you the wife, or the twin?"

Zen laughed. "I'm the twin," she said. "The easy way to remember is this: the wife has brown hair, and the twin is blonde. My name is Zen, by the way."

He nodded solemnly. "Zen, dance with me."

She took a step back. "If you'll excuse me, I was about to have a word with my friend Gillian." She looked around quickly for Gillian. Gillian and Astrid, wearing the same clothes they'd worn to the wedding, were out on the dance floor, take turns spinning one another and laughing wildly. She made her way toward them.

"Wait!" Vlad said behind her. "You're friends with the hot lesbians? Introduce me to them!" She pretended not to hear him. Seconds later, Annie got up from where she sat talking to Catherine to guide Vlad back to his table.

"Gillian, can I talk to you for a minute?" Zen asked, tapping Gillian on the shoulder. "Privately?"

Gillian stopped spinning Astrid and nodded. "Babe, I'll be back in a moment." They walked a short distance outside the tent. "What's going on?" Gillian asked Zen.

"Nothing," Zen said. "I haven't had much chance to talk to you, in between going to school and how often you've been seeing Astrid lately. How are things going with her, anyway?"

"Fine," Gillian said, with stars in her eyes. "I'm totally into her, Zen. I mean, yeah, we do spend pretty much all of our time together, except when she's at the club, and some of my friends don't like her, but so what? We make each other happy. That's all that matters, right?"

"Your friends don't like her?" Zen said, looking across the dance floor at Astrid. She wasn't the only one. Vlad watched Astrid intently as Astrid danced by herself. "Why?"

Gillian shrugged. "Stupid stuff," she said. "They're jealous, especially Mike. He wants me to spend time with him. Why should I spend time with my friends, though, when I'm wasting precious time I could be spending with the woman I want to spend the rest of my life with?"

"Everybody needs friends, Gillian," Zen said quietly. "I need you. If I didn't have you to help me run the store, I wouldn't be able to keep it open while I'm working my way through nursing school."

"That's not a friend, Zen," Gillian said. "That's a co-worker. I do what I do because it's my job."

Zen couldn't believe what she heard. She hoped it was only the effect of the honey wine and cider Gillian and Astrid had been steadily consuming. "You only work at Light and Shadow because you have to?" Zen asked her. "I thought you liked it there. I thought you liked working with Corey and me. I thought you liked learning more about your Wiccan faith, being part of the Pagan community."

Gillian shook her head. "I'm sorry, Zen. I think I gave you the wrong impression. All of those things are important to me. Of course I like working with you and Corey. Being with Astrid is the most important thing in my life, though. Isn't being with Ramesh the most important thing in yours?"

Zen thought as she watched Ramesh come across the fallow field and back to the tent. "Zen, Gillian, can I get you something to drink?" he called as he crossed over to the bar.

"No, thanks!" Gillian yelled. She said to Zen, "I'm going back out on the dance floor. Astrid looks lonely without me."

Actually, Zen thought, Astrid looks fine without you. Astrid, spinning herself, slowly made her way over to where Adam Schumann stood, nodding his head to the beat of a Berlin remix while Jane had another piece of cake. When she thought about it a moment, Zen realized Jane had not only had three pieces of cake, but also avoided the fruits of Pagan Spirits' labor and drinking only the non-alcoholic apple punch. This led her to suspect there was a baby Schumann on the way. All the more reason to steer Astrid off her collision course with Adam.

As Gillian reached Astrid, Zen watched Ramesh stop to talk to Orlando. Orlando and Allie had been slow-dancing moments earlier. Allie stopped to talk to Annie after Annie wondered out loud where the boys were. Both Allie and Zen knew exactly where Armin, Sasha and Peter were: lying on their backs in Kameko's garden, eating handfuls of fresh strawberries off the plants. Zen watched Gillian snake her way between Astrid and Adam, smoothing making her intervention look like a dance move.

Engrossed in Astrid and Gillian's drama, Zen lost track of Orlando and Ramesh. Then she felt a hand on her shoulder. "Ramesh, I—"

As she turned toward the man behind her, she saw it was not Ramesh, but Vlad. "I asked you to dance with me," he said. "You said you were talking to that lesbian with the really nice ass. Now you're done talking to her, and you can dance with me."

Zen didn't like the feelings she read from Vlad. The amount of vodka he'd imbibed gave him an inflated sense of confidence, and he was now so bold he was almost aggressive. She didn't read any real maliciousness, but she knew she'd better watch her step. Vlad didn't seem to have too many boundaries at the moment.

She looked over at Ramesh, who still chatted with Orlando. Orlando seemed to notice Vlad and pointed him out to Ramesh as they spoke. Zen knew Ramesh would be there to rescue her soon. "Okay," she said.

The next song was a fast one, to Zen's relief. No touching required. She and Vlad stood face to face, moving in time to the music. She was surprised that he moved so well, at his size, and after all the vodka he'd consumed. She almost enjoyed herself, until he reached in, grabbed her by the elbows, and pulled her closer to him, close enough that he could grind against her.

Zen stepped back. "Thanks," she said. "It's been fun, but I should go find Ramesh now." She looked over. Ramesh and Orlando had moved closer, but still not close enough to see everything. Zen turned to go.

Vlad caught her arm. "Where are you going?"

"Let me go," she said, trying to pull away. His grip was strong. If he hadn't been feeling aggressive before, he was now. He saw her as a challenge, and one he thought he could overcome.

"Zen, you're a beautiful woman. I think you should give me some pussy."

"Get away from her," Ramesh said, suddenly standing at Zen's side.

Vlad let go of Zen's arm. Zen was relieved, but only momentarily. In the next moment, Vlad elbowed Zen out of the way. She lost her balance and fell on her rear end in the grass. Vlad cocked his fist and jacked Ramesh's jaw, sending Ramesh to the ground.

Jane screamed. Ramesh struggled to his feet, as Vlad got ready to hit him again. Orlando stepped in between the two of them. "That's enough," he said. "This is my wedding, Vlad."

His words had no effect on Vlad. A split second later, Orlando took a swing and hit Vlad square on the nose with a loud "crack." The punch sent the big Russian sprawling backwards, arms flailing as he lost his balance. As Vlad hit the ground, Zen knew he was out cold. Blood seeped from the nose, which was probably broken.

"Not at my wedding," Orlando said, looking down at Vlad.

Allie and Vlad's wife came running over. Allie helped her sister up. "Are you all right, Zen?"

Zen nodded. "Are you okay, Ramesh?" He didn't answer her, but Zen sensed he was more angry and embarrassed than physically hurt. Vlad was big, but Ramesh was stronger than she'd realized.

"I'm so sorry," Annie said to Orlando, as Allie came to his side. Now that she knew neither Zen nor Ramesh was badly hurt, Allie fixed her gaze on Orlando, beaming with pride. Zen sensed she'd gained a new respect for her husband.

Zen went to lay her hand on Ramesh's shoulder, but he pulled away from her, wiping his bleeding lip on the back of his hand. Instead he focused on Orlando. "Why didn't you let me finish it?" he asked. "Why can't you mind your own fucking business?"

"This is my wedding reception; I thought it was my business," Orlando said. "Besides, he's twice your size. I didn't want you, or anyone else, to get hurt."

"You didn't want Zen to get hurt," Ramesh said angrily. "Guess what? She doesn't need you to protect her. She isn't yours to protect anymore, Orlando. You had your chance with her, and you blew it. You made your choice."

Ramesh stormed off toward the farm house. Orlando stayed where he was, wrapping his arms tightly around Allie. Zen chased after Ramesh.

When she caught up to him, she said, "Orlando was only trying to help, Ramesh."

He glared at her. "Why do you seem more concerned about him than about me?"

"I'm not," she said. "I know you aren't hurt badly, because I can feel your feelings. You're very angry, though."

"Do you want to know why I'm angry?" He didn't give her time to answer. " I'm angry because I think you and Orlando never got over each other. I think somewhere in the back of his mind he still thinks he's got both you and Allie, and you're not doing anything to discourage him."

"You're wrong," she said. "What Orlando and I had was nice, but it wasn't long-term. The way he loves Allie, that's real. He fell in love with her the moment their bodies connected in the wheat field. By that time, he and I were only friends. I've never stopped caring about him, but I began to fall out of love the moment I realized he wanted me to be...well, what Allie is."

"The mother of his child," Ramesh said bitterly. "He told you that was what he wanted."

"Yeah," she said, as they paused on the back steps.

Ramesh nodded, as if he'd suddenly put the pieces of something together in his head. "You never told me that, Zen."

"I haven't told you everything about my relationship with Orlando," she said.

"You haven't told me anything. I knew you were lovers, and that's all. I knew he made you feel good. You didn't tell me that he seriously cared about you, Zen."

"I didn't tell you that he didn't."

"You didn't tell me anything, Zen." He turned away from her, reaching for the back door. "I'd like to go home now. Don't worry about packing your stuff; I'll call a taxi."

"Ramesh, no," she said. "You can't take a taxi to Chicago. That's more than a hundred miles."

"I'll go to town and rent a car," he said. "I need to be alone right now." He went to close the door, but Zen put a hand on the door and prevented him.

"Don't go," Zen said loudly, hoping he would hear her through the door. "Please don't leave me alone now, Ramesh. You can't leave me alone every time you get angry, especially about things in my past I'll never be able to change."

As Ramesh stared at her, Allie came up behind them. "Let me talk to him, Zen," Allie said, putting a hand on her sister's shoulder. The two women looked into each other's eyes for a moment. Zen nodded, and walked back over to where a crowd had gathered around Vlad and Orlando. She stood beside Kameko.

"What are we going to do with him?" Kameko asked Orlando.

Annie spoke up. "If a couple of guys can help me get him into the back of the minivan, I'll leave him in there for the night. He'll wake up and figure out where he is."

"You sound like you're speaking from experience," Orlando said.

"This happens all the time," Annie said. "Catherine, will you round up the boys for me?"

Catherine nodded. "I'll go get Sasha and Peter; Gary and I will take Armin. Is that all right with you, Orlando?"

"Fine," he said. "Annie, pull the minivan up behind the barn. Gary, are you any good at heavy lifting?"

* * * *

"May I talk to you for a moment?" Allie asked Ramesh. He stood halfway in, halfway out of the back doorway, one foot resting on the stairs, looking down at her.

"I guess so," he said. She followed him into the kitchen. He sat at the weathered butcher-block table, and Allie sat across from him. "Why did Orlando have to get in the way? It isn't his place to defend her. He didn't even give me a chance to get my revenge. How do you stand it, Allie? How can you look at Zen and Orlando together and not lose your mind?"

"Well, I'm not going to go to bed with you so you and Orlando can both say you've had twins, if that's what you're thinking."

He smiled half-heartedly.

"I understand why you're upset," she said. "Sometimes I look at my sister, then I look at Orlando, and it kills me to imagine the two of them together."

He suddenly looked very interested. "You mean you never got over it? You still get jealous?"

She shook her head. "In my case, I pretty much had to. Orlando and I had a baby on the way. Yeah, I fell in love with him, but only after many sleepless nights. Even now, my heart knows I can trust Zen and Orlando together, but some little part of my brain still tries to tell me otherwise. "

She still has feelings for him. I know she does."

"Of course she does. She wouldn't be human if she didn't. I still have feelings for Paul Phillip, and he's queer as a three-dollar bill." Ramesh smiled slightly. "Look, Ramesh, don't walk away from Zen tonight. You're upset, and that's understandable. Nobody expects to get punched in the face at a wedding reception. But if you walk away from Zen when she needs you, you might not be able to walk back into her life when it suits you. If you and Orlando hadn't come between her and Vlad tonight—"

"I know," he said. "It could've gotten really ugly. All the more reason why I wanted to be the one to protect her. I don't need his help to defend her."

She patted his hand. "That's the adrenaline rush from the fight talking," she said. "Your body wants to prove you're the alpha male. That's fine, as long as you don't hurt your alpha female in the process." She got up from the table. "I'm going to check on things outside. When you get your shit together inside your head, you may want to join us."

* * * *

Zen and Kameko sat across the picnic table from a very downbeat-looking Sasha and Peter when Allie returned. Zen stood and rushed to meet her sister halfway between the farmhouse and the tent.

"What did he say to you?" Zen asked desperately.

"He's angry, and he's jealous of Orlando. He thinks he should have been the one to protect you from Vlad."

Zen took in a deep breath and took in the information, along with some of the calm Allie radiated. There was jealousy in the mix, too, though. Zen sensed it from her sister from time to time. It stung her, but she'd gotten used to the sting.

"Is he really going to leave?" Zen asked as they walked back to where Kameko sat.

"I don't know."

Zen took a look back at the farmhouse. A hand touched her, and she wheeled around to see Armin. He put out his arms, and she hugged him to her. "Goodnight, Auntie Zen," he said. Annie was loaded Sasha and Peter into the minivan, two rows of seats in front of their passed-out father.

"Goodnight, kid," she said, planting a kiss on the top of Armin's head. "I hope I get to see you again soon."

"Maybe you'll invite us to *your* wedding soon," Catherine said. She looked beyond Zen at the farmhouse.

Zen turned around and saw Ramesh coming toward them. She smiled.

Chapter Six

Zen looked at the clock: eleven minutes past eleven at night. She doubted Light and Shadow would have any more customers. On this glorious summer night, anyone with any sense went out partying with friends, enjoying a quiet glass of wine on the balcony, or lying on the rooftop gazing up at the cloudless sky. She wished she had the leisure time. She wished she didn't have to study for yet another organic chemistry exam.

More than anything, she wished Ramesh was there. She'd stopped counting the number of days since she'd seen him. Whatever the number, it was too many. The text messages, e-mails, and phone calls helped, but her heart and her body keenly felt each moment that he was in India while she was stuck here in Milwaukee. She missed his breath on the back of her neck as she fell asleep.

She tightened her grip on the chemistry book, as if that might make her concentrate better on its contents. She willed herself to think about electrolytes: calcium, sodium...Ramesh. It was no use. She couldn't stop thinking about him. Her heart ached.

She sensed the man at the door before she saw him or heard his footsteps. Zen didn't look up from her book. He wasn't giving off any vibes that signaled trouble. He wasn't drunk or high, though he was a little lonely.

The door opened and closed, triggering chimes. He stood in front of the counter, waiting.

"Hi, Mike," Zen said without looking up from her electrolytes.

"Hey, Zen. Have you seen Gillian?"

She put her book down on the counter. "She was here until about nine, but Astrid came and got her."

He was disappointed, and frustrated. Zen knew that frustration well. "Did they tell you where they were going?"

"Do they ever?"

He shook his head sadly. "I miss her, Zen. She used to be one of the guys. God, you're going to think I'm the biggest asshole for saying this, but I don't care how happy she and Astrid are together. I just want her back, you know?"

"I do know," Zen said. "I don't think you're an asshole at all. She's my friend, too, don't forget. She's in love with Astrid. Love is selfish. Love wants to shut out the world and be completely wrapped up in itself."

He rested his hand on the gargoyle's head. "She's not in love with Astrid. She's in *lust*. Right now, Astrid is Gillian's shiny new toy."

"I don't know—"

"I do," he said firmly. "Real love would never be this selfish. Real love would open up and let Gillian's friends in. When two people are truly in love, they make everyone around them feel that love, and it makes us all better people. Astrid—I don't know. There's something about her I don't like, Zen."

Zen stood and stretched her legs. "Is it the green hair?"

He smiled slightly. "No. I kinda like the green hair. She's a sexy girl. It's more to do with her chosen career. I find it hard to trust a woman who takes money from horny men each night in the name of feminist art."

She shrugged. "I haven't seen her act, so I'm not the ideal judge. It may well be very artistic." She went around the counter to the light switches and turned off the lights in the back of the store.

"I've seen her act. Whether you're dancing to Ludacris or Holly Near doesn't matter too much while you're shaking your tits in someone's face. Excuse my language."

"I've heard worse," she said. "Usually from Gillian." The door chimed again, and three women walked in, dressed for a night of bar-hopping in short, black dresses. They giggled as Zen raised her hand dramatically. "Ladies, I sense you're hear for a reading. Unfortunately, I was about to close the shop for the evening. The Goddess tells me she wants you to learn to deal with disappointment. And you!" She pointed to the tallest of the three. "Stay away from the guy with the tongue ring."

"I don't know anyone with a tongue ring," the woman protested.

"You'll meet him later tonight," Zen said. "No charge for the quickie reading, but come back tomorrow and we'll do the whole shebang."

She allowed them some time to look around the shop. One of them bought a good-luck charm shaped like a vulva. As the women left, she turned back to Mike, "Want to come with me to O'Connor's?"

"Yeah, I'd like that."

She shut off the second set of lights, collected her books, and grabbed her purse. Once Mike went out the door, Zen set the alarm.

Recently, Zen had been working on her spell craft, and the closing of the shop each night was one of her favorite opportunities to use magic. After setting the alarm, she placed a protective spell—her own invention—on the shop.

She didn't mind the two-block walk to the pub, although the night was hot and she began to perspire through her thin t-shirt. It felt good to be out of the shop and away from organic chemistry. It felt good to talk to a human being again.

"How's Ramesh?" Mike asked her.

"I haven't seen him since my sister's wedding reception, actually. He went to India on some family business, something about his dad's mom. We keep in touch, but it's not the same as actually being together."

She sensed his embarrassment at asking a loaded question. "You probably didn't want to talk about," he said.

"Are you kidding? Between Ramesh being in India and Gillian being off in Astrid-land, I haven't had anyone to share with. It's actually kind of a nice change. That is, if you don't mind listening."

"Not at all," he said. "So, how was the wedding reception?"

"Unexpectedly complicated. Orlando's former best friend, the guy who slept with Orlando's ex-wife and was secretly the father of Orlando's kid, got completely wasted at the wedding reception and came on to me."

"No way."

"Yeah, and it gets even worse. When Ramesh came to defend me, this guy hit him in the eye. Orlando decked the guy, and Ramesh got pissed off that Orlando didn't let him finish it."

"Whoa, there," Mike said. "I think I'm going to need a score card to keep up with this one."

On the way, they talked about Mike's job managing the pizza place and his band. As Zen took her seat on her favorite bar stool, Brittany O'Connor poured her the usual Michelob Light.

Brittany O'Connor was a beautiful woman, and she wore her beauty confidently. With her short, chocolate-brown hair and small, elfish ears, she looked as if she could have been a cousin to Zen and Allie. She was even the same height as the Van Zandt sisters. Zen and Allie were minimalists when it came to make-up, though, while Brittany liked layers of color. Tonight, her eye shadow was the same shades of green and gold as the striped polo shirt under her black apron.

"What are you having, Mike?" Brittany asked. Mike was only a semi-regular at O'Connor's. He'd usually show up only if Gillian and some of their mutual friends were with him, but he lived in the Third Ward, and preferred to drink at Trinity.

"Vodka martini, very dry," he said.

As she turned to get it for him, Brittany said over her shoulder, "You guys just missed Ramesh."

Zen did a spit take, spraying the bar. "What? Ramesh was here? That doesn't make any sense, Gillian. If he were back in town, he would have told me. I didn't even know he'd flown home yet. What did he say to you?"

Brittany shrugged. "Not much of anything. He had a couple of drafts, kept to himself, and left. Did you guys have a fight or something?"

"I guess you could say so," Zen said. "He got decked at my sister's reception when he tried to defend me from a jerk who tried to get a little too friendly."

"Yikes," Brittany said. "But that wasn't your fault, was it?"

"No," Zen said. "That wasn't all, though. Ramesh thinks Orlando and I still have feelings for each other. Don't leave me hanging here, Brit. Ramesh must have said something to you about me. Spill it!"

Brittany shook her head. "Remember the first time Orlando came in here, Zen?"

"Of course," she said distractedly. "I'll never forget it. He looked beautiful, wearing his best blue suit with the Gucci shoes. He was *so* sad. But that's beside the point, isn't it? You have to tell me what Ramesh said—"

Brittany stuck a cocktail napkin under Zen's beer mug and went on as if Zen hadn't said anything. "I told you he looked like trouble, and stay away from him."

"You said no such thing," Zen said. "In fact, after *I* told *you* I was going to stay away from him and mind my own business, you told him I'm a witch and sent him to me for a reading."

She shrugged off Zen's comments. "Either way, he was trouble, wasn't he? Married to your sister, and still making trouble for you and Ramesh."

"It wasn't Orlando's fault," Zen said. "It was my fault. I wasn't completely honest with Ramesh. I never told him how deeply I was involved with Orlando."

Mike took a slug of his martini, finished it, and set the empty down on the bar hard. He seemed a little disappointed the conversation had steered away from him, and made up for it with a rousing soliloquy. "Why can't we be honest with our feelings?" he said. "Why didn't I ever tell Gillian how I really feel about her? Now she's off with Astrid, they'll probably have a lesbian wedding, and I'll never have another chance."

"Another one?" Brittany asked him.

"Another lesbian wedding?" Mike asked her in return, somewhat addled.

Zen put her hand on his shoulder gently. "No, hon. I think she's asking you if you want another martini."

"Oh."

"Hey, that reminds me of a joke," Britney said brightly. "A Latin professor walks into a bar and orders a *martinus*. The bartender looks at him funny and says, 'Don't you mean a *martini*? And the Latin professor goes, 'Look, buddy, if I want more than one I'll let you know.'" She laughed at her own joke.

Zen rolled her eyes; she definitely wasn't laughing. "Britney, if someone in this bar doesn't tell me *right now* what Ramesh said to you while he was sitting here, I'll jump behind the bar and—"

The door opened, and Zen turned her head. She caught a glimpse of the man who walked in, recognizing his body instantly without seeing his face, and smiled. She spun around on her stool, happy to see Ramesh. She took a deep breath and tried to sense his feelings.

He ran to her, threw his arms around her, and held her against him. As he ran his fingers through her loose hair, Zen pressed her cheek to his chest and felt his heart beating.

"Ramesh—"

"Let me go first, Zen," he said. "I sat hear for a half hour rehearsing what I would say when I got to Light and Shadow. Only, I got there, and you'd already closed for the night. I'm glad you're here. Are you ready?"

"I'm not sure," she said.

"That's okay." He pulled away from her to look her in the eyes. "I don't think anyone's ever really ready for this; here it goes anyway. Zenobia Van Zandt, I love you. I've needed some time to get my head straight about what was going on in our lives; thank you for allowing me that. I have to apologize for what I said to you at the farm, because I don't care about the past. All I want is you, and I know I want to be with you for the rest of my life. I've missed falling asleep with you beside me, waking up with you, holding your hand. Zen, will you marry me?"

As he said this, he dropped to one knee on the floor in front of her bar stool. Then he pulled the ring from his pocket, holding it up for her to see. Breathless, Zen took the ring from his fingers. It was beautiful. The sparkling blue stone was large enough to be impressive, but not so large it was gaudy. A sapphire so deeply blue it was almost black, it was set inside the petals of a flower fashioned from white gold. She'd never seen anything like it before.

She turned it around and around in her fingers, watching the way the light played off the facets.

"The flower is a lotus," Ramesh said. "The lotus is a symbol for Kali, and the jewel is a symbol for Shiva. The ring represents their union, wholeness, completeness."

She stared at the ring, but her mind was elsewhere. Zen was thinking, not of her future with Ramesh, but of their past. She hadn't even known his name then, the night Kameko and the other women had placed the crown of oak leaves on her head and told her she was the May Queen. She was only twenty-one, barely old enough to drink the Beltane wine legally. By then she had been familiar with the customs experienced by all the guests at Pagan Spirits Farms on Beltane night: the feast, the maypole dances, the brave ones who leap over the bonfire. She would learn that night of the other sacred custom, whispered about in conversations but never fully explained while she listened: how she, as Queen, was to run far out into the wheat, where the May King would be waiting for her, to consummate their ritual marriage. It seemed like a dream, or a scene from a movie. He looked to her like a Hindu god, like Shiva, and when she looked down at herself she realized she was his goddess.

Zen couldn't explain her memories of that night, why the dream seemed so real, why she truly believed she, and the man she now knew as Ramesh, had truly become goddess and god on that warm late-spring night. As she held the ring in her hand, staring at the lotus and jewel that symbolized the most sacred part of her life, Zen felt the magic of that night.

He took her hand and slipped the ring onto her finger.

"Zen," Ramesh said, "please say something."

"Yes," she said. "Yes, I'll marry you."

Ramesh leapt to his feet and embraced Zen and kissed her with such hunger, it reminded her not so much of Beltane as of the night she'd been released from her vow of celibacy. He kissed her mouth, then the bridge of her nose, then the middle of her forehead.

"Thank you," he said at last. "I thought you were going to say no."

"Never," she said. "I never could."

There weren't many people in O'Connor's that night, but the few who were there broke into applause. Brittany and Mike clapped the loudest.

Ramesh reached into his pocket again, this time slapping his American Express card onto the bar. "Brittany, a round for everyone, please."

"Sure thing." Brittany poured another Michelob and set it down in front of Zen.

Ramesh pushed the frosted glass back toward Brittany. "I mean, everyone except me and Zen. We have our own celebrating to do, in private."

Zen blushed, holding Ramesh's hand tightly. Ramesh slapped Mike's shoulder. "We'll see you around, Mike. I don't mean to leave you hanging, but Zen's just made me the happiest guy on the planet. There's only one possible way I can imagine this evening ending."

Nothing more needed to be said. Ramesh led Zen outside.

"Aren't we going to take your car?" she asked him as he started off toward her apartment.

"Are you kidding? I've got it parked for the night, and there's no way I'm going to find a parking spot closer to your place."

Her apartment on Farwell wasn't at all far, but the trip home had never seemed so long. It felt nice to be walking hand in hand again, though. Though the night was warm, the heat from Ramesh's body comforted Zen, as if she'd been reunited with a lost part of her soul.

They barely managed to get inside the apartment and get their shoes off before Ramesh took Zen's face in both hands, touching her cheeks gently with his fingertips as he seemed to drink in the sight of her. He leaned in for the first butterfly kiss, brushing her lips lightly with his. She strained against him, her mouth searching for a deeper kiss, but he pulled away.

"No hurry, Zen. I'm here now. We've got all night."

They stood at the doorway, Zen leaning against the wall as Ramesh kissed her softly on the lips, barely allowing the tip of his tongue to penetrate her mouth. She ran her fingers down the side of his body, feeling the curve of his hips. Wonderful as it felt to have him here, kissing her again, she also felt a twinge of frustration. She wanted more, and she wanted it now. Ramesh's insistence on this slowly pacing was both exhilarating and maddening.

He seemed to know, however, exactly how long he could keep her desire at bay. Moments later they sprawled on the couch, kissing madly and tossing throw pillows out of the way in their quest to get as close to one another as is humanly possible.

Ramesh, who'd ended up on top, let Zen up enough to allow him to take off her clothes. He started with her socks and worked his way up. He took off her panties, then paused to move her thigh out of the way, lower his head and kiss her pussy. "You're wet," he said.

"Mm," she responded.

"Let's see what we can do about that." She thought he would take off her shirt next, but instead he unzipped his shorts. He started to get naked, but stopped himself. "Let's go to bed first."

"Why?"

"Because," he said, raising his eyebrows suggestively, "it's easier to sixty-nine when you're on top."

Zen ran to the bedroom; Ramesh chased her. She let him finish undressing and find a comfortable spot in the middle of the bed, taking off her own shirt and bra as she went into the bathroom. She took a short shower, washing her pussy. She emerged from the bathroom wrapped in a towel, but let it fall to the floor.

Ramesh smiled. "Do you want me to wash up?" he asked her.

"I'll have to smell you," she said. She didn't often ask him to wash before sex. She liked the raw, sweaty, male scent of him. In the back of her mind she knew he probably enjoyed the raw scent of her, too, but Zen was insecure.

She knelt on the bed, brought her lips to Ramesh's stiff, waiting cock, and tasted him with her tongue. She inhaled. His skin smelled clean. Instantly, she wanted another taste.

"Hey!" he said as she took most of his cock inside her mouth. "You've got to let me have some, too."

"Sorry," she said, straddling him, giving him a nice view of her ass. "You're just too yummy for your own good."

"I guess I shouldn't complain," he said. "I've got a beautiful woman willing to suck my dick. The thing is, I want to eat her pussy."

He put both hands on her hips and pulled her lovely ass closer. His hot tongue between her lips felt so good, Zen almost lost her rhythm. With some concentration, she ran her tongue down the length of his shaft, then up again. She sucked the head of his cock for a few seconds before pulling back and starting her pattern all over again. This created enough sensation to keep Ramesh interested, but not enough to make him come. The last thing she wanted was for this session to end too soon.

Ramesh seemed to have a different idea. He did his best to keep Zen on the razor's edge between pleasure and a sensation so intense it was almost pain. He sucked and nibbled at her clit with abandon that put her tame tongue-lashing to shame.

Zen stepped up her game. She cupped his balls with one hand, and with the other, she stroked his shaft. She licked her palm to make it slick. At the same time, she rolled the head of his cock around her tongue. Every few seconds, she would barely scrape him with her teeth. Each time she did, he shivered.

"Oh, stop. Stop!" he exclaimed, after his last shiver.

"What's the matter?" she said. "Did I bite too hard?"

"No," he said. "It feels too good."

"Hey, I'm only trying to do to you what you're doing to me. If you want gentle, then you have to be gentle."

"Okay," he said. To demonstrate, he barely touched his lips to the inside of her thigh. The feather-light touch was tantalizing, making her want more. "How's that?"

"Mmm," she said. She took a deep breath. Two could play at this game, she decided, touching her lips to his cock as lightly as a butterfly lands. She used her breath, her lips, and only the very tip of her tongue to tease him the way he teased her. She could have kept at this all night.

After many minutes of soft touches, though, Ramesh got bolder. His long tongue made unbelievably deep passes between her lips, stroking her clit along the way. Zen had never known a man with such a long and skillful tongue before, almost as if he were born for this. His sudden audacity took her by surprise, and before she could regain control of herself, Zen realized she was about to come.

Ramesh then pulled out his dirtiest trick yet: he made a growling sound deep in his throat, like a cat's purr. The vibrations against Zen's cunt were more than she could bear. Ramesh must have known this. He licked and sucked her aggressively, steering her over the edge. She came hard and fast. Ramesh didn't relent, drawing out her orgasm until she was forced to pull her ass out of his hands and away from his persistent mouth. As she did, he groaned as if disappointed.

Now she took her turn to make him groan with pleasure instead of frustration. She returned to her familiar pattern: cupping his balls, running her tongue up and down his shaft, stopping at regular intervals to suck his head, scraping its sensitive underside with her teeth. This time, though, she went at it with the same determination he'd extended to her. She licked him harder, sucked him more forcefully, squeezed his balls until she wasn't sure if she hurt him. She got the result she wanted, though. Ramesh's moans grew to a violent crescendo as Zen drained him.

She couldn't suppress a laugh as she lay beside him, proud of the way she'd reduced him to a moaning, spent heap. As she lay her head on his pillow, Ramesh put his arm around Zen. She leaned in and kissed his lips, savoring the taste of her cunt on his mouth.

"Good night, my love," he whispered.

"Good night," she said, thinking those were the very words she wanted to hear every night for the rest of her life.

* * * *

"She's coming," Ramesh said. Zen looked up from the bouquet in her hands. She'd been thinking the baby's breath looked at little wilted, but it was too late to do anything about that now. "Big smiles."

She smiled. She felt nervous, and it didn't help that she could feel the tension coming from Ramesh, too. Meeting the Sudhras was nerve-wracking enough, but now that she'd seen David Sadguna and Nalini's front yard, Zen felt more anxious than ever. Everything about the two-story, suburban house was perfect, from the weedless lawn to the spotlessly clean, freshly painted cedar siding—the color of ginger, with dark green trim— to the brand-new welcome mat. Even the irises in the flower bed seemed to be symmetrical. In the late afternoon sun, everything about the Sudhra home sparkled.

The door opened. Nalini Sudhra stood there, unsmiling, examining Zen and Ramesh like cultures she viewed through her microscope. "Yes?" she said.

Nalini Sudhra was in her early fifties, and her brown-black hair had started to turn gray. Clearly, Ramesh had inherited his narrow nose and full lips from his mother's side of the family, though not his curly hair. Nalini's hair was stick-straight and pulled into a tight bun. She wore a lavender blouse, neatly pressed black slacks, and a string of pearls.

Ramesh didn't seem at all pleased with her chilly reception. "Mom, you haven't seen your only son in six months." He stepped around her, into the foyer. Zen remained on the top porch step, unsure if she should follow. "Don't you have something more to say?"

"Who's the blonde?" Nalini said.

Zen felt mixed emotions from Ramesh's mom. She had so many of them, she was a little hard to read. She seemed to be happy to see Ramesh, though chagrined at his taste in women, and resentful of the way he'd been treating her. Zen decided to try to be as pleasant as possible. She couldn't force Ramesh's parents to like her.

She remembered the flowers, and held them out. "These are for you, Mrs. Sudhra," she said.

For half a second, Nalini almost smiled. She took the flowers. "Sadguna, bring me some water!" she called up the stairs. "Ramesh is here."

"Zen, get in here," Ramesh said. "Don't let her intimidate you. Have a seat on the couch around the corner. Mom, you know perfectly well who she is. She's the woman I'm going to marry."

Zen nodded. She stepped inside the foyer. It was even more perfect than the front yard, without a speck of dust in sight. The house smelled of a mouth-watering blend of spices Zen couldn't identify and roasted chicken.

A family portrait, blown up to almost life size, hung on the wall beneath the stairway's banister. Ramesh and his younger sister Priya were teenagers in it. David Sadguna was looking off into the distance above his family, with one arm crooked and his hand on his hip. It reminded Zen of Superman in the old TV series. Now that she looked at the portrait, she thought she did recognize David Sadguna from TV after all. His soap had been enormous popular twelve years before, before Zen and Allie came to live with Auntie Kameko. One of their previous, elderly foster mothers had been a soap opera fan.

"Hey, your dad does look familiar," Zen said, pointing at the portrait. "So that's where you got your curly hair from."

"Sadguna!" Nalini called up the stairs again.

After a moment of tense silence, David Sadguna came down the stairs, carrying a bottle of water.

"That is *not* what I meant when I asked you for water," Nalini said testily to him. Nonetheless, she took the bottle from his hands.

"How was I supposed to know? You didn't say you had flowers. Hi, you must be—what is it? Zen?"

As he spoke, Nalini shook her head and went off, Zen presumed, to get a proper vase to put the flowers in.

"Yes," she said, offering her hand for him to shake. "It's nice to meet you."

Catherine had been right about one thing: as handsome as he'd been on TV, David Sadguna was even more so in real life. Zen glanced at Ramesh. If genetics were any indication, her fiancé would only get more handsome with age.

"David is a stage name," he said, still holding onto her hand. "As Ramesh may have told you, for many years I starred on *Journey to the Sun*. The producers gave me a name everybody can pronounce. You can call me Sadguna." He kissed her hand, then let it go. "Those are lovely flowers you've brought us."

"Thank you," she said.

"Can we sit down now?" Ramesh said impatiently.

"Of course." Ramesh went around the corner into the living room and sat on the couch. Zen sat beside him. Sadguna settled onto the arm of the couch.

Nalini returned with the flowers, now inside a crystal vase. She stood over them, her arms crossed and her brow furrowed.

"So," she said to Zen, "my son thinks he's going to marry you."

Zen's mouth popped open.

"Nalini, please," Sadguna said. "This is exactly why Ramesh only visits once every six months."

"He's right, Mom," Ramesh said, taking Zen's hand.

"I'm sorry, Ramesh, but as the matriarch of this household, it's my obligation to make sure my children uphold the family traditions. It's bad enough you've turned your back on Hinduism."

"No, I didn't," Ramesh protested. "I totally believe in the gods."

"How can you believe in something you don't even understand?" Nalini said, raising her mild voice slightly. "When was the last time you visited a temple?"

"I went to the temple every day when I was visiting Grandma, actually. Listen, just because the way I pray is different from the way you pray—"

"The way you pray," she interrupted, "is what you've learned from dabbling with these Neo-Pagans. That isn't a real religion, Ramesh. These people don't have any connection with the places their ancestors came from the way your father and I do. Zen, where is your family from?"

The question caught her off guard, and it took her a moment to answer. "My mom was Dutch, I think," she said. "I could be anything on my father's side."

Nalini nodded, as if Zen had just proved her point. "Neo-Pagans have no real roots, no real connection to their ancient traditions. Zen is Dutch. She comes from Vikings who worshiped Odin and Thor. Do you worship Odin and Thor, Zen?"

She smiled. Thor had been the name of the last guy she'd dated before Orlando. He'd been a vain, spray-tanned, body-waxed workout fanatic. The first words that came to mind were, "Thor worshiped himself." She didn't say them, though. Instead she said, "I believe there is only one divine being, a Goddess with many names and many, many female and male forms."

Nalini studied Zen for a moment. "Ramesh told us about some of the Pagan holidays you celebrate. I couldn't believe my ears. Do you want to know what I think?"

"It doesn't matter what you think," Ramesh said, squeezing Zen's hand tightly. "You're not the religious police, and you can't tell us what to do."

Nalini looked hurt. "European Paganism is vulgar," she said. "Earth-bound. Materialistic. Neo-Pagans celebrate the seasons, food and drink, sex, the human body, but miss the higher spiritual truths of all these material things, these symbols."

Zen didn't know what to say. She was tempted to thank Nalini and Sadguna for a lovely afternoon and dart out the door, whether Ramesh followed her or not.

"How would you know?" Ramesh spoke up angrily. "This is exactly why I've all but cut you out of my life. You think you know me, but you don't, and you certainly don't know Zen. Not that it matters. I'm marrying her no matter what you say."

Nalini looked suddenly triumphant. "How well do you two really know each other?" she asked them. "I'll bet he's never even told you his real name, Zen."

"His full name is Ramesha," Zen said. "It's one of the many names of Vishnu. Ramesh is a family nickname he got after his sister Priya started calling him by that name when she was very little. It stuck, and it's what he's gone by ever since."

"Zen and I are practically living together, Mom," Ramesh said. "Most nights I stay with her. I take the train from Milwaukee to Kenosha, and then another train to get from Kenosha into the city, to get to school in the morning. I'll ride the train four hours a day to be with this woman. That's how much I love her, Mom."

"I'm glad to hear you're taking your studies so seriously," Nalini said sarcastically. "I thought you really wanted to be a medical researcher."

"I don't need to defend my life to you, Mom. You raised me, fed me and clothed me for eighteen years. Thank you very much. But I'm a grown man now. I make my own decisions, and if you don't like them, that's too damn bad." He crossed his arms defiantly.

The words must have stung her, but she hid the hurt. "I'll bet you didn't know Ramesh was engaged to be married to another woman," Nalini said sharply.

"That's not what happened," Ramesh said. "You tried to arrange a marriage for me, but you know perfectly well Remma and I had no intention of marrying one another. And Zen already knows all about it."

"That's right," Zen said. "Remma eloped with another guy. What was his name again?"

"Arun Gupta," Sadguna said. "Nice guy. I think he's a manager at the big downtown IKEA now."

"Something like that," Ramesh said. "He and Remma have a daughter now. Zen and I don't keep secrets from one another."

"Any good parent would try to arrange a decent marriage for her son," Nalini said. "I only want you to be happy, instead of chasing after some whim. Priya intends to marry the man your father and I chose for her."

"Of course," Ramesh said. "Priya does everything you say. She's the good child."

"You're a good child, Ramesh," Nalini said. "I never said you weren't. I do think you'll be sorry if you neglect the traditions of our culture."

"Our culture?" he said. "You mean people from South Milwaukee?"

"You know what I mean," Nalini continued. "Please don't be offended, Zen. I'm sure you're a perfectly nice person. It's only that, if you'd come from a family with very strong religious and social customs, and you were strongly tied to those traditions even though you were living in the United States, you would understand the way I feel. I want my family traditions to continue the way they have for the past thousand years or more. What do you know about *puja*? Where's your respect for the sacredness of marriage?"

"You don't understand," Ramesh said. "You never will."

No one said anything for a long time. Finally Ramesh rose to his feet and announced, "I'm going outside; I need a cigarette before dinner. Zen, come with me."

Nalini looke scandalized. "Ramesh, you're smoking cigarettes now?"

He helped Zen up from the couch, then glared at his mother. "Yeah, Mom. I smoke, I drink whiskey, I have sex without condoms, and I drive without my seatbelt on. And guess what? There's not one damn thing you can do about it."

Hurriedly, he escorted Zen out the front door and around to the side of the house. Zen stepped carefully, avoiding standing in the iris bed.

"Ramesh, you don't smoke," Zen said.

"I know, but there's something I want you to know, Zen." He grabbed her hand.

She looked into his eyes. "You don't have to say it. I already know."

"I'm going to say it anyway. I don't care what they say. I don't care if they don't like you, or don't think you're right for me. I don't care if they disown me. I'm never going to give you up."

"Ramesh, I know," she said quietly. "She *is* your mother, though. I don't want you to have a strained relationship with her for the rest of your life. We're going to have to figure out a way to reconcile the part of your life with your parents in it with the part of your life with me in it."

"Know this, Zenobia Van Zandt: the part of my life with you in it will always come first. Do you know when my spiritual life began?"

She cocked her head and looked at him funny. It was an odd question. "When?"

"At Beltane," he said. "That was the first moment I knew for sure I had a soul, and there was a power greater than myself in this world. You did that for me, not Nalini Sudhra."

"She's your mother, Ramesh," Zen said. "You have to respect her. The way you talk, you make it sound as if it wouldn't bother you if you never saw your parents or Priya again."

"Sometimes respecting your parents means respecting them from a healthy distance," he said. "You come first. Now, are you ready to go back into the storm?"

Zen looked up at the nearest window. She would have sworn the curtain moved; perhaps Nalini was looking to make sure Ramesh wasn't really smoking a cigarette.

"I guess so," she said. "The reception might be chilly, but as least the food smells good."

"Oh, my mom can cook," Ramesh said with a certain amount of pride.

As they stepping back into the house, Sadguna stood in the foyer. "I think I know how to defuse this," he said. "Ramesh, you ask her how Priya is doing in school. She'll be too distracted to give you any more shit."

"Dad, I'm not afraid of her," Ramesh said. As soon as Nalini announced the chicken was ready, though, Sadguna sidled up beside her.

"Nalini, sweetheart, tell Ramesh and Zen about that fellowship Priya won," Sadguna said.

Zen and Ramesh sat down to the most delicious meal she'd tasted in years, while Nalini hardly ate a bite. She was too busy rattling off Priya's accomplishments. She almost seemed to have forgotten Zen was there as Zen enjoyed chicken tandoori and its flavorful side dishes.

When they left the Sudhra house that night, Zen said to Ramesh, "They hate me."

He shook his head. "Mom hates the fact that you're not a Hindu girl from an Indian family. You can't do anything about that, Zen. Dad likes you, though."

She thought for a moment. "Do you really think your dad likes me?"

"I know so," he said. "As we were leaving, he whispered in my ear, 'She's a very beautiful woman.' Trust me, that's a high compliment coming from him. Beauty is something he thinks about twenty-four hours a day. If he's not studying himself in the mirror, he's studying beautiful women."

She smiled. "We are going to have beautiful babies some day. I mean, if that's what you want."

"I'll be really disappointed if we don't have at least one."

"Really?"

"Absolutely. You've seen how happy Orlando is when Armin and Antonio are around."

"I've done more than see it," she said. "I can feel it, remember? He does get very peaceful and content when his kids are happy."

"He loves Allie, obviously, but his kids are his world. I want to be that happy some day, Zen. And I can only be that happy with you."

"I feel guilty," she said. "I feel as if I'm ruining your relationship with your mom."

"Don't talk like that," he said. "It's nothing to do with you. Priya's always been the good child, and I've always been the black sheep of that family—and not just because I'm darker than Priya."

"That doesn't *really* matter, does it?" she asked him.

"It does to some people. I know a lot of women who are jealous of Mom because she's so fair-skinned. Of course, Priya's got her coloring. I wish I had a dollar for every time I've heard women whispering, 'He's so good-looking; it's too bad he's not light-skinned like his mother.'"

"People really say those things?" Zen asked.

"Sad, but true," he said. "It's not just Indian-Americans, either. It's something about human nature. If you were in the Netherlands, you'd probably be taking shit from the natural blondes."

She laughed out loud.

"Don't let my mom worry you for one more second, Zen," he continued. "She'll like you once she gets to know you. In the meantime, my dad likes you. He likes to let my mom think she gets her way all the time, but the truth is, if he's patient, he can talk her into just about anything."

"You mean he can talk her into liking me?"

"Maybe," Ramesh said. "He talked her into letting him move to Los Angeles while he was filming *Journey To the Sun*. There were years when I was a kid when Priya and I wouldn't see him for months at a time."

"You stayed here in Wisconsin?"

"Yeah. Mom had her ophthalmology practice, and Priya and I were enrolled in a private school. It wasn't very easy for us to pick up and move to pursue his acting dream. We did stay with him during the summers, and Mom would take a couple weeks off so we could all be together for a while. I think Mom always thought it wouldn't last very long, anyway."

"She was wrong," Zen said. "He was on TV for almost a decade."

"She's wrong about you and me, too," he said. "Some day she'll change her mind about our marriage, the way she changed her mind about Dad's acting career."

"I don't know," Zen said. "I don't want to take you away from your family, Ramesh. Don't forget, I've been through this with Orlando. I permanently ruined his chances of having a happy life with Catherine. Even though I know he's happy with Allie, it's still hard to forgive myself for destroying their relationship."

"You're not destroying anything, Zen. That was completely different." She didn't answer him, and they sat in silence for a few moments. Then he said, "You're not getting cold feet about marrying me, are you?"

"No," she said, "not at all. I don't think you realize how much you'll miss your parents until they're gone, though. It'll always be too late for me, but it's not too late for you."

"Oh," he said thoughtfully. "So that's what this is about. Zen, I'm sorry for what happened to your mom, and I bet it sucks not having a clue who your dad is. At least I can always point to the TV and find mine." She laughed a little, so he went on. "They'll come around." He reached for her hand.

She took her hand off the steering wheel and held his. "I want to believe that," she said.

"That's good enough for now, Zen."

Chapter Seven

Gillian had fallen asleep watching the late, late show. She realized this as soon as she heard Astrid's key in the door. She sat up, wiped the drool from her chin, and smiled. At last, the light of her life was home.

Astrid came in, locked the door behind her, and backed up against the door. "It's freezing out there," she announced. She wore only a short skirt, a thin t-shirt, and a green military-style jacket.

"I guess summer is finally over," Gillian said, stretching. "How was work? No, wait, before you tell me, come here and kiss me."

Astrid's face lit up at the suggestion. She came toward Gillian, pausing in front of the TV to pull a tube of her favorite frosted pink, vanilla icing-flavored lip gloss from the pocket of her jacket. She applied the lip gloss slowly, letting Gillian stare at her shiny, infinitely kissable lips. She sat on the couch beside Gillian, close enough that Gillian could feel the chill of night air on Astrid's skin. Reflexively, she rubbed Astrid's arms, trying to warm her.

As she did, Astrid leaned in for a kiss. Astrid sucked Gillian's top lip while Gillian sucked Astrid's bottom lip. Gillian felt the rush of blood to her nipples and her clit as Astrid kissed her. Astrid smelled good, like female flesh mixed with cotton candy, with a whiff of the fruity shampoo she liked so much. When Astrid slipped her tongue between Gillian's lips, Gillian's hands shot out to feel the gentle weight of Astrid's breasts beneath her t-shirt.

Astrid took off her jacket and let it drop to the floor. Gillian ran her hands along Astrid's bare arms and up her sleeves. She moved her hands up to Astrid's shoulders as they kissed. The gentle pressure welling up in Gillian's nipples and clit became more urgent. She slid her hands down the front of Astrid's t-shirt, found Astrid's nipples through her bra, and squeezed them gently.

"Oh yeah, nice," Astrid moaned.

"You like that?" Gillian asked, laughing. "It'd feel better if you'd take off your shirt."

Astrid shivered. "Let's go to bed and get under the blankets first." She stood up and held out her hand for Gillian.

Gillian took it. "Is my baby cold? I can make my baby hot."

They walked, hand in hand, into the bedroom. There, Gillian stripped out of her jeans and sweater. She got under the blankets in her bra and panties, lying back to watch Astrid get naked. As soon as her short skirt, t-shirt and bra hit the floor, Astrid dove under the blankets.

"No panties today?" Gillian asked as she dived onto Astrid, eagerly feeling her breasts with both hands. "Naughty girl."

"Squeeze my nipples again," Astrid said. Gillian didn't hesitate to comply, leaning in to kiss Astrid's lips as she did. She felt Astrid's hand snake down between her own legs. As Gillian kissed her and played with her nipples, Astrid manipulated her clit.

Knowing Astrid was pleasuring herself made Gillian's clit ache, and her pussy surge with wetness. But she would suffer, gladly, as long as she got to watch Astrid.

"Vibrator," Astrid whispered. Gillian reached into her bedside drawer and pulled out Astrid's favorite toy. Made from a textured, jelly-like material, Astrid's vibrator was red and shaped like a long, thick penis. Gillian checked to make sure the battery was working, then turned it on high. Astrid didn't stopping rhythmically rubbing her clit while Gillian worked the head of the vibrator between the slick lips of Astrid's cunt. Astrid's toes curled. Despite her obvious delight, though, Astrid was tenacious, holding onto control for the many, many minutes Gillian worked the toy in and out of her slick walls.

At last, Gillian heard the tell-tale signs that Astrid couldn't hold on any longer. Her breathing grew quick and shallow. When she uttered a short, sharp "Yes!" Gillian knew it was time. She drove the vibrator in deeper and held it there, as deep as it would go. Astrid shouted, her body twisting and turning, simultaneously trying to escape and prolong the all-encompassing pleasure. Gillian didn't let up on the pressure, though, prolonging Astrid's writhing, almost unbearable ecstasy.

As Gillian finally, reluctantly, turned off the toy and pulled it free from Astrid's pussy, Astrid lay on her back, panting, recovering. When she finally caught her breath, she said, "Your turn." She took the vibrator from Gillian's hand and turned it on low. Gillian got on her hands and knees on the bed, presenting her ripe pussy for Astrid's inspection.

Astrid explored Gillian's pussy with her fingers first, running her fingertips over Gillian's lips and around the opening lightly. Gillian moaned, straining to get some pleasure from these light touches. "I'm ready," she said. "I've been waiting so long."

"Waiting for this?" Astrid said, laughing. She introduced the tip of the vibrator into Gillian's pussy. Gillian shivered all over.

"Yes," she said.

Astrid drove the vibrator in slightly, reaching under Gillian to massage her clit with her fingers at the same time. The dual sensations left Gillian temporarily breathless. Astrid took Gillian's silence as encouragement, and turned the vibrator up to medium speed.

"Faster," Gillian squeaked.

"Not yet." Astrid brushed her blonde and green hair out of her eyes, not caring that her fingers were sticky with fluids from Gillian's cunt and her own. The sweet, perfumed, sweaty smell of their bodies hung heavy in the air. Gillian breathed it in, intoxicated. She pumped her hips as Astrid slowly rotated the head of the vibrator inside her.

"More," Gillian begged.

Astrid laughed. "Okay, you asked for it," she said. She pushed the vibrator as far as she could into Gillian's cunt, spinning it passionately as she did. Gillian was caught off guard by her sudden, intense orgasm. Despite the wild contractions of Gillian's pussy, Astrid didn't stop turning the vibrator around and around, touching every part of Gillian from the inside.

Astrid then twisted the base of the vibrator and turned the speed down to low. "We're not finished yet," she said. "I think you've got one more of those in you."

Carefully, Gillian lowered herself to the mattress, lying on her belly. "Please," she said. "Faster. More."

"You had the nerve to call *me* a naughty girl?" Astrid snickered.

"I've been waiting all night for you," Gillian said.

"I'm here now, Gillian, and I'm all yours. Still working the vibrator in and out of Gillian's slippery walls, she lay beside Gillian, nearly on top of her. Gillian's heart raced. Lying on her belly with her lover on top of her had always been one of her favorite positions with a male lover. It felt even better with Astrid, who understood her anatomy and knew exactly how rough, and how gentle, to be.

Astrid laughed and turned the speed up to high. With a little shifting, she brought her lips to Gillian's breast and suckled at her nipple. She rolled her tongue, allowing the nipple to get wet with her spit. The gentle roll of Astrid's tongue sent Gillian's head spinning. Gillian felt an incredible tension build up in her belly, traveling through her pussy and to the tip of her clit. Then her orgasm flooded over her. It was so good, Gillian actually cried. She felt the hot tears falling down her cheeks.

Astrid's mouth moved up Gillian's neck and to her lips. They kissed as Astrid switched the vibrator off and withdrew it from Gillian. They kissed until they got exhausted and started to drift off to sleep.

"Thank you," Astrid whispered as Gillian was drifting in and out of awareness. "You warmed me up."

Gillian wanted to say, "You've warmed me, too, not just in my body, but also in my heart." She was too sleepy for words, though.

Early in the afternoon, Gillian woke up in the fetal position. The night had been so cold, she'd curled up under the thin sheet. Astrid always had been a blanket hog. Gillian reached for Astrid, but found only blankets. Astrid's perfume hung in the air, but she was gone.

"Astrid?" Gillian called. There was no answer.

What seemed like moments later, Gillian's phone went off, vibrating quietly and flashing with red and blue lights. Gillian got out of bed groggily and hunted around on the floor until she found the dirty jeans she'd been wearing the night before. Her cell phone was still strapped to her belt. As soon as she picked it up, the phone stopped vibrating.

She waited a moment, then listened to the voice mail message from Zen. Zen's message was simple: "Gillian, call me right now."

Gillian sank into the couch and dialed Light and Shadow. "Zen? What's wrong?"

"Astrid called me," Zen said calmly. "She called the shop because she couldn't reach you on your cell phone. She says you've got the damned thing on vibrate."

"What are you talking about?" Gillian asked. She was still so groggy. "What's going on?"

"Astrid called me from jail, Gillian," Zen said.

"What? Did she tell you what happened?"

"She didn't tell me anything. All she said was, she needed to talk to you." She gave Gillian a phone number.

"Zen, I'm sorry," Gillian said. "I mean, I'm sorry you had to get involved in this. There has to be some kind of mistake. I've been with Astrid for nine months, and I've never seen her do anything illegal. She doesn't use drugs...I can't imagine how this could have happened."

"Don't freak out about it," Zen said calmly. "Call her, find out what's going on. As you said, it's probably some kind of misunderstanding. You two'll have it straightened out in an hour or two."

"Thanks, Zen."

"No problem, kid."

Gillian hung up and checked her cell phone. There were seven missed calls from a number she didn't recognize. She dialed the number Zen gave her. A woman answered, letting Gillian know she had called the county women's holding facility and asking if she was calling for a prisoner. *Prisoner.* The word sent chills down Gillian's spine as she imagined Astrid sitting in a cold, dark cell wearing only her short skirt and thin t-shirt. She could only imagine the loneliness, confusion and anxiety Astrid must be feeling.

"Yes," Gillian said. She cleared her throat. "Astrid Dejonghe."

"Hold, please." Before Gillian had time to respond, the woman put her on hold. Gillian listened to a static-y Chicago song for three or four minutes as she waited impatiently. She swung her legs wildly, kicking the couch, to burn off some of her nervous energy.

The woman at the jail came back on the line. "I'm sorry," she said. "We don't have anyone by that name here."

"Well, you had her there a while ago!" Gillian shouted into the phone. She'd completely lost her cool. She wanted to know where Astrid was, and she wanted to know immediately. "She called my friend from there. She's pretty hard to miss: tall, petite blonde with green streaks in her hair."

"Hold, please," the woman said again. When the on-hold music started again, Gillian screamed into her cell phone. It was more than fifteen minutes before the static-riddled music ceased, and a human voice returned. This time, it was Astrid.

"Gillian?" she said. "Gillian, can you come down to the county holding facility right now? They won't let me go until I post bond. It's five thousand dollars, which I don't exactly have, but I thought if you'd let me borrow five hundred of it, I could at least pay a bail bondsman—"

"Slow down, Astrid," Gillian said. "You're talking a mile a minute, and I just got out of bed. I woke up, and you were gone. Where did you go?"

"Home," Astrid said. "I wanted to go home for a few minutes to grab some clean clothes. You were sound asleep, and I didn't want to wake you. I was going to be right back."

"How did you end up in jail, then?" Gillian said. She couldn't believe she had to say those words to the woman she loved and trusted.

"It was so unbelievable, it was like a scene from a movie. I couldn't believe it was actually happening to me. The police were waiting for me when I got to my apartment. They had a warrant."

"Explain this to me so it makes sense," Gillian said. Her heart was sinking by the minute. She still hadn't heard Astrid protest her innocence. "Why did they have a warrant? What are they saying you did?"

"I was charged with theft and fraud," Astrid said. "They think I stole credit card numbers from the club and tried to pass myself off as someone else. They keep accusing me of things I didn't do. I can't believe this is happening to me, Gillian. It's all a big mistake, and I can explain the whole thing as soon as you get me out of here."

"When I asked for Astrid Dejonghe, the woman who answered the phone told me there was no one there by that name," Gillian said with a sigh. "Is that your real name, Astrid?"

"Is it my real name?" Astrid echoed. Gillian sensed she was trying to buy herself a few more seconds. "Yes, but it's not the name I gave them when they arrested me. I had a credit card on me with a different name, so I gave them that name."

Cold fear gripped Gillian's heart. She didn't want to listen to any more, but she had to know the truth, no matter how painful. "Why did you have a credit card with someone else's name?"

Astrid's voice dropped to a whisper, making her sound like a little girl. "Why did I have a credit card with someone else's name on it? Well, it's my great-aunt's, my grandma's sister's. She's like a third grandma to me. She gave me permission to use one of her credit cards. I have a letter from her stating so in my apartment, but the cops wouldn't let me look for it before they arrested me. Look,

Gilly, I've done a couple of things I probably should've had better sense than to do, but it's not like they're making it sound. I don't deserve any of this. Now, are you going to give me the third degree, too, or are you going to come here and help me sort this all out? You know I don't have anyone else in town."

Gillian sighed again. It felt to her as if her soul would come out of her body along with her breath, and it was a struggle just to keep breathing. "You want me to come bond you out of jail," Gillian said dryly. "You want me to bring five hundred dollars with me. Where do you think I'm going to get five hundred dollars?"

"You can pay with cash or a credit card," Astrid said. Her voice sounded suddenly bright. "I'll pay you back out of my tips from the club. You know I can make three to five hundred on a good night."

Gillian closed her eyes, and memories of watching Astrid work came flooding back to her. Astrid was a beautiful woman. She had a beautiful body, and the way she moved it—a truly artistic blend of stripper, belly dancer and ballerina moves—entranced men and women alike. Astrid was right about one thing. She could easily earn five hundred dollars in a night. And since that was true, why would she bother to steal credit card numbers? Then again, if Astrid was doing so well at the club, why didn't she have the money lying around where Gillian could get to it for her? Gillian would have liked to sit with her eyes closed, remembering Astrid for her graceful stage act and beautiful body, but too many questions swirled through her mind.

"What will happen if you don't bond out?"

Astrid sounded shocked. "Don't you have five hundred dollars, Gilly?"

"Whether I do or don't, I asked you a question first. What happens if I don't show up?"

"I have a hearing at ten o'clock Monday morning," Astrid said. "I'll have to wait here until then. That's two whole days, Gilly. I know you wouldn't want to leave me here for two whole days!" She began to cry.

"I've got to go," Gillian said. Astrid's tears sounded false to her. She couldn't believe all her trust in Astrid had been misplaced. It hurt almost as much as the moment her parents had asked Gillian to leave their house. "I need some time to think. Don't worry, I've got the number to call to reach you. What name should I ask for again?"

"Lilith Hurley," Astrid said, adding in her girlish whisper, "that's my great-aunt's name."

Gillian hung up the phone. She wanted to scream, cry, and throw all of Astrid's things out the window. Or were they Lilith's things? How could she ever know? She'd never be able to trust Astrid/Lilith/whoever to tell her the truth again. She felt like such a fool.

She was tired. She lay in bed, trying to fall asleep again, but it was no use. Excuses and rationales for what happened with Astrid played over and over in her head, along with doubts, disappointment, loneliness, and hope. When she could no longer stand the loop, Gillian got up. She took a long shower, as if she could rinse this awful stain out of her hitherto-perfect relationship with Astrid. It didn't help.

After a few hours of this agony, she remembered Astrid kept a small bottle of pills hidden behind the medicine cabinet. One of the many red flags that should have warned her about Astrid, she told herself. But that didn't matter now. She'd never asked how Astrid had acquired the painkillers—which, sure enough, said "Lilith Hurley" on the label. She simply filled a glass with diet cola and her favorite spiced rum, took two of the pills, and lay on the couch. At first she felt no different. Then the numbing pulsations that clouded her mind began to make less and less sense. Soon she slept deeply.

* * * *

The next day, Zen returned home from visiting Gillian at her apartment.

"What's going on?" Ramesh asked her, looking up from the stack of undergraduate exams he was grading. "Is Gillian all right?"

"She's fine. She's going to need a few days to get her shit together, though, so Corey's going to come in and work a few of her shifts. She promised she'd get back to me on Tuesday." It was Saturday.

"Did she tell you what Astrid did?"

"She didn't know."

"She needs some space," Ramesh said. He sat on a stool at the kitchen counter. "Gillian's a sensible girl. If she really needed you, she'd reach out."

"I always thought Gillian was a sensible girl, too, before Astrid came along," Zen said, taking a seat on the couch. She looked up at the painting hanging over the TV, Bouguereau's *Nymphs and Satyr*. She'd looked at it every day without paying much attention. This time, however, she focused on the satyr, so distracted by the beauty of the nymphs he didn't recognize their plans to drown him until it was too late.

"Ramesh?" she said.

He put down his red pen. "Yes?"

"Have you ever noticed the nymph with the green ribbon in her hair and the bright red lips looks like Astrid?"

He stared at the painting. "I suppose she does look a bit like her."

Zen seemed unable to take her eyes off the painting. There was nothing she could do for Gillian except wait, and she felt frustrated and anxious.

Ramesh seemed to understand how she was feeling. "Come here, Zen. I'll ask you the questions from these first-year Biology exams, and let's see if you can do better than my students."

"Thank you," she said. "You create a good distraction."

"I thought about taking off my pants," he said. "But this way we get some studying in."

She sat across from him at the counter. "We'll take off your pants later," she said.

On Tuesday afternoon, Zen had finished classes for the day and was home alone, having a late lunch, when Corey called her. "Gillian's coming in this afternoon," he said as soon as she answered the phone.

"Corey, calm down before you give yourself a heart attack. The last thing the paramedics need to see is the leather bustier you're wearing under your shirt."

"How did you know?"

She laughed. "You know, I always tell people I'm not psychic, but maybe I am, a little bit. My point was, we're not doing Gillian any good by acting as if Astrid's arrest is some big deal. When she comes to work, treat her the way you'd treat her any other day."

"Gotcha. Make fun of her Goth clothes and black eyeliner, ignore her for a few hours, then make out with Riley in the back room."

"Is that what you really do when I'm not there?"

"Only on days when Riley's working." Riley was employed by Cousin's, the sub sandwich shop next to Light and Shadow, though he rarely did much actual work.

"Well, I'm glad to hear you and Riley are together again, but I don't want you making fun of what she's wearing or how she does her makeup. Leave her alone about what Astrid allegedly did."

"Can I tell her horror stories about women's prisons I've seen in campy old movies?"

"Corey, be serious."

"Okay," he said. "But admit it, Zen: you're dying to know what happened with Astrid, too."

"I'll be anxious to hear whatever Gillian wants to tell me, but I'm not going to press her for details." She let him off the phone and went back to her lunch. Zen did a few hours of studying, but soon decided she'd go to the shop and see how Gillian and Corey were doing. After all, it was getting close to Halloween, the second-busiest time of year for Light and Shadow.

When she got there, though, Corey was alone, except for a handful of customers. "Where's Gillian?" she asked him.

"I don't know," Corey said. "She never called, and she never showed."

She set the books she'd brought on the counter. "Did you try calling her cell?"

"I left her two different messages," he said. "She never called me back."

"That's not a good sign," Zen said. She got out of the way so Corey could ring up some herbs for a customer.

"Anise seed and bloodroot," Corey said, smiling at the customer. "You must be making a love potion."

"I'm going to try," the woman said with a sly smile.

"Use pure water, and remember to let the bloodroot steep for a good, long time," Corey advised. "The stronger the potion, the better."

"The smell of the potion is a key element," Zen interjected. "I've made a few of them in my day, and anise seed alone doesn't do it for me. It's a lovely smell, but it simply doesn't remind me of that first blush of new love the way the smell of roses does, and cinnamon...when you meet someone who smells like cinnamon, it's so warm and comforting, it makes you want to come nearer."

"I don't want to drink rose petals," the woman said, the smile falling off her face.

"You don't have to," Zen said. "When you're taking your ritual bath to purify yourself for the potion-making, put a few drops of rose oil in your bath water, or spray yourself with a rose-scented body spray. I'd steep a cinnamon stick with the anise seed, though."

"Thanks, I'll try that," the customer said. She winked at Corey as he handed her the paper bag with her magical items inside, then left.

Zen turned to Corey. "It's not like Gillian to leave us hanging like this. She always either calls or shows up."

"What do you suggest we do?" he asked her. "Call the police? What would we tell them, that our co-worker's late for the first time, and she didn't call first? That's nothing, Zen."

"I know," she said. "I hate this feeling of not knowing, and not being able to do anything about it. I'll stay here and help you out, Corey. Maybe we'll get lucky, and she'll show up."

Gillian came in around six thirty. She looked as if she hadn't showered, eaten or slept in days. Instead of her usual shiny black Gothic style, she wore a gray hoodie and faded red sweatpants. Zen ran to put her arms around her.

"Sweetheart, are you okay?" Corey asked. "You look awful." Zen stomped on his oversized foot for that one.

"You don't have to tell us anything that's none of our business," Zen said. "We just want to know you're all right."

"She took off," Gillian said. She sounded more stunned than anything, but Zen sensed she was deeply sad. It reminded her of the sad, crushed vibes she'd picked up from Orlando when he suspected Catherine had cheated on him.

"What do you mean, took off?" Corey asked, leaning against the counter. Zen helped Gillian into one of the plush blue chairs near the books.

"I shouldn't have bailed her out," Gillian said sadly. "I told her no at first, but after I went to visit her, I changed my mind. I pulled the money out of my savings. I gave her the five hundred for the bail bondsman, and then I gave Astrid another two thousand to get a lawyer. She told me she wanted to go home to her own apartment, and I let her go. What was I thinking? By the time I got there, she was already gone. Gone for good, too. Her door was open, most of her stuff was gone, and her landlady said Astrid told her to throw out everything else and keep her deposit. She disappeared without a trace. I keep thinking she'll call me, or knock on my door, or I'll turn around and she'll be there." Tears fell down her cheeks. Zen didn't have tissues, so she grabbed the stack of sub shop napkins from behind the counter and handed them to Gillian.

Gillian wiped her face. "My heart aches for her, but my mind knows better. All this time, she's been nothing but a con artist. I can't believe I fell for her. I can't believe I'm that naive! What could I have done to bring this kind of bad energy on myself?"

Zen hugged Gillian tightly. "You didn't do this to yourself," she said. "Astrid did this to you. She's the one who put out the bad energy, and she's the one who'll reap the consequences of it."

"I can loan you back the money if you need it," Corey offered. "You can pay me back a little at a time. I won't even charge interest."

Gillian shook her head and wiped away another tear. "I don't need it now," she said. "I'll have to start saving again from nothing."

"Is there anything else we can do for you?" Zen asked.

Gillian nodded. "Coffee," she said. "A tall mocha with whipped cream and chocolate sprinkles, and a shot of creme de menthe syrup, from Brewed."

"I'll get it," Corey said. "Zen, anything for you?"

"My usual," she said. "Espresso macchiato. Two sugars."

He stopped to ring up a celestial-patterned scarf and a pumpkin-shaped candy dish for two women, then went to the coffee shop up Brady Street.

When she and Zen were alone in the shop, Gillian said, "I thought she loved me, Zen."

"I'm sure she was in love with you in her own way, sweetie," Zen said. "Some people don't know how to act decently. You couldn't have known she had another face hidden behind the one she presented to you."

Gillian smiled through her tears. "You should have seen it," she said, "when you did my tarot reading."

Zen laughed. "You're a better tarot reader than I am," she said. "I tend to cheat and read people's feelings instead of looking at the cards. Speaking of which..."

She didn't say so, but Zen sensed an entirely different set of feelings coming toward the door. The person coming toward them was content, secure, and infectiously happy. Zen had the odd sensation of being caught between one very happy person and one miserable person. It made her feel hot and cold at the same time.

The happy person, she could now see through the glass front door, was Ramesh. As he came in, he saw Gillian, and some of his excitement fell away. He leaned in close to Zen and gave her a subtle kiss on the back of the neck.

"Gillian," he said, "how are you?"

"I've been better," she said. "Have Zen tell you about it later; I don't think I feel up to rehashing everything again right now. Zen, if it's okay with you, I'm going to take a look around the stock room and see if anything needs put away."

"Are you sure?" Zen said. "If you need another night off, Corey and I've got it covered."

"I'd rather keep myself busy," she said. "It helps ward off the bad thoughts."

Zen gave Gillian another hug. "It wasn't your fault," she said. "Keep telling yourself that."

"I will." She went in the back.

Zen looked at Ramesh. "Astrid ran off with a wad of Gillian's cash," she said. "Apparently she's a fugitive from the law now."

"It doesn't surprise me that Astrid would do something like this," Ramesh said. "She was sexy as hell, but there was something you couldn't trust about her. I have a hard time trusting any girl who's that sexy."

"What are you saying? That I'm not sexy, and that's why you can trust me?"

"No, not at all." He abruptly changed the subject. "Is Gillian really going to be all right?"

"What other choice does she have? We all get our hearts broken sooner or later. This was just Gillian's time, I guess."

He put his arms around her. "My time was the year after I was king of Beltane," he said. "When I came back to see you again and couldn't find you, I got a little obsessed. For months afterward, I felt as if I was infatuated with a ghost."

"Well, it all worked out for you and me. How was your day? Did your lab rats do anything cute today?"

"Maybe," he said. "I wouldn't know, because I didn't go to campus today."

"What?"

"I was talking to a wedding planner," he said. Instantly, his concern for Gillian dissipated and his happiness returned. "Her name is Sumati, and she's from Pune, like my mom and dad. You'll like her, Zen. She reminds me a lot of Melissa, but with henna instead of ink tattoos. Well, you'll get to meet her soon enough. I told her we could meet her on Saturday."

"Whatever you want," Zen said.

Ramesh nodded. "We can go over the details then, but I thought I'd run some ideas past you now. Do you mind?"

She looked at him. "Now is not a really good time, Ramesh."

"That's okay," he said "The store *is* kind of busy tonight." A customer brought a pair of earrings and a spell book to the counter for Zen to ring up.

"It's not only that," she said as the customer left. "We've both got a lot on our minds with school. Look, we've got a semester break in December. How would you feel about putting off the wedding stuff until then?"

He looked deflated, but though some of his excitement had waned, he felt no less content or secure. "I have plans for our semester break," he said.

"What plans?"

"It's a surprise. It's my Winter Solstice gift to you. Ride the train to Chicago with me on Saturday and meet Sumati. Please."

"I said I would go," she said. "I still think we should wait before we make too many plans. We don't even know if your family is going to participate in this wedding."

"They are," he said. "Have a little faith in me, Zen. I have a secret weapon here."

"I thought we weren't keeping secrets from each other anymore," she said.

"This is different. This isn't something that could possibly hurt you," he said.

"Let me be the judge of that," she snapped. "I know what happened to Gillian and Astrid isn't going to happen to us, Ramesh. I trust you. I want to feel like an active participant in our wedding plans, though. Right now I feel as if you're making all the decisions, and I'm along for the ride."

"I didn't know you felt that way," he said. "You never mentioned any of this before."

"You never hired a wedding planner, without telling me, before," she said. "We'll talk about this another time. Corey's back with Gillian's coffee."

Ramesh opened the door for Corey, who used both neatly-manicured hands to hold a cardboard tray with four coffees. "I'm a little bit psychic, too," Corey said. "I knew Ramesh would be here, and I knew he'd want chai with lots of milk."

"Thanks, Corey," Ramesh said, taking his tea from the tray. "You're not really psychic, are you?"

Corey frowned at him. "Thanks for spoiling it," he said. "Actually, Zen, Ramesh parked his stank old Dodge in front of the coffee shop, and I saw him get out while I was in line."

"Hey, my car may be old, but at least it's clean. When's the last time you hosed down the back seat of your car? I bet it looks like a Jackson Pollock painting back there."

"Wouldn't you like to know?" Corey asked, arching his eyebrow.

"You wish. You totally nailed the chai with extra milk, though," Ramesh said. He handed Zen her coffee.

Corey only smirked. "Where's Gillian?" he asked.

"Stock room," Zen said. Corey went back to find her.

"Now that Corey's back, why don't I get us all some take-out? Gillian likes that Vietnamese place around the corner, doesn't she?"

"Yeah. Now you're talking," Zen said. She set her coffee on the counter, and Ramesh caught her up in his arms and gave her a long, deep kiss. When they separated, he went to get orders from Corey and Gillian.

Zen sat on the stool behind the counter. She turned around to face a shelf of beautifully rendered statues of the Goddess with many names and many faces. Here she'd found the smoke-gray jade statue of Kali she kept in her bedroom and the statue of the Virgin Mary she'd given to Orlando, the one he and Allie now kept in their bedroom. The sculptures all came from the same artist, a local woman named Mercedes Vallejo. Mercedes either made them from new materials or refashioned and repainted existing sculptures, often ceramic lawn ornaments. When Mercedes showed up with her sky-blue pickup truck packed with art treasures, Zen never knew whether she was going to get an Aphrodite, an Isis, a Kuan Yin, or a Xochiquetzel. On this particular day, the shelf held a sculpture of Hecate, depicted as a robed and partially veiled old woman with long, wavy hair peeking out from her veil.

Mama, Zen said, silently addressing the divinity represented by the statue, I need your guidance again. I want to marry Ramesh, but I'm scared. I don't want him to lose his relationship with his parents and his sister because of me. I know he loves me, but I don't think he understands what it means to lose your parents. He hasn't been through it the way I have. Please help me do the right thing. If he and I are meant to be together, then let me marry him. But if he's meant to be with another woman, one who gets his family's approval, please don't let me stand in his way. I ask you to give me a sign that this marriage is the right thing to do. So let it be.

"Spring rolls?" Ramesh said. Corey stood right behind him.

Zen jumped. She'd been so lost in prayer she'd forgotten about Ramesh, Corey and Gillian and about ordering take-out. "What?" she said.

"Do you think we should get spring rolls along with our entrees?" Ramesh clarified.

"Definitely," she said. She watched him pick up the phone and dial. Goddess above, he was beautiful. And kind, and thoughtful. And he wanted to marry her so badly. Zen would wait impatiently for the answer to her prayers, hoping that what she wanted was what was meant to be.

"What are you having, Zen?"

"Spicy noodle salad," she said.

He smiled. "That's what I want, too."

"Scary," Corey said. "Your gift of empathy even extends to feeling what he wants from Le Colonial Noodle."

Zen couldn't help but smile.

Chapter Eight

Zen looked at her reflection in the mirror. After weeks of late-night study sessions, preparing for her end-of-semester exams and the term papers that went along with them, she finally looked rested. The dark circles under her eyes were gone.

Carefully, she peeled at the tape holding the gauze pad to her upper left arm. She was afraid of what would be underneath. The last time she'd peeked, it had been a bloody mess, and she'd had to ask Ramesh to help her clean it. It stung like hell. She swore she'd never get another tattoo, and could hardly believe she'd been able to endure the ones she'd gotten so far. In the back of her mind, though, she knew she would do it again and again.

She peeled the gauze back and smiled. The result looked beautiful. On Zen's arm, Kali stood with two of her arms raised in a gesture of protection. In another hand, she held a lotus blossom, filled in with delicate rose-colored ink. In the opposite hand, she held a sparkling diamond. Melissa had inked Zen's second tattoo with the same artistic touch as her first, with exquisite attention to tiny details. Zen marveled at both the eyesight and hand coordination that Melissa, well into her 70s, still possessed.

Zen threw the used gauze in the trash can and cleaned the tattoo. Ramesh stood in the doorway. "How does it look today?"

"You tell me," she said. She threw away the cotton ball and let him look at her arm.

"It's really cool," he said.

"I thought you were going to say, 'Don't let my mom see it.'" They laughed.

The phone rang. "I've got it," he said. He went into the bedroom, emerging a moment later holding the phone out to her. "It's Kameko."

Zen took the phone. "Hello?"

Kameko wasted no time getting to the point. "Melissa says you're not coming home to the farm for Winter Solstice," she said.

"She's right," Zen said. "Ramesh wants me to go somewhere with him."

"Where?"

"I don't know. He won't tell me. He made me get a passport, though."

"Sounds exciting," Kameko said. "Your sister and the kids and I are going to miss you here, but I'm happy for you and Ramesh. We'll make some extra pine cone bird feeders and hang them on the evergreen for you."

"Thanks," Zen said. "I'll come see you and Melissa when we get back. Whenever that is."

"Happy Solstice, Zenobia. May the goddess bless you with light."

"And you, too, Auntie Kameko. I love you."

"I love you, too, Zen. Have fun on your trip." She hung up the phone.

Zen looked up at the doorway, where Ramesh stood. He held out a little box, carefully wrapped in shining red and pearlescent white striped wrapping paper, with a little sprig of holly on top.

"What is it?" Zen asked, leaning against the bathroom sink.

"Our destination," he said.

Zen couldn't imagine where Ramesh wanted to take her. She couldn't imagine where he'd gotten the money for an international vacation, really. He earned a small salary as a professor's assistant at school, and a bit more money from research projects he was working on, but that was all. She was nervous and excited. Ramesh, she sensed, was just plain excited.

She unwrapped the thin box and looked inside: two sets of boarding passes and tickets. She scanned them to find out where they were going.

"Read 'em out loud," Ramesh said.

Zen nodded. "There's a flight out of O'Hare to Atlanta. Then one on Lufthansa. We're going to Germany?"

"Yeah," he said, "but that's not the final destination."

"Mumbai," she said, turning over the last ticket. She could hardly believe what it said. "You're taking me to India."

He put his arms around her, pulling her close to him. Zen could feel Ramesh's heart beating. "You'll love it," he said. "Nothing you've ever seen, heard, or read about India will prepare you for the actual experience of Mumbai."

"I've never been outside the country, other than the one summer Kameko took Allie and me to see her daughter in Seattle and we went to Canada for a few hours."

"India is hot," he said. "If you go in the summer, it's hot and humid, but while you and I are there, it'll be hot and dry. It's huge, sprawling, noisy, and more crowded than Marshall Field at Christmas. It's weird, though, because even though you're in the midst of this enormous modern city, it's like you stepped back in time. It's very spiritual. You feel Kali's presence wherever you go. You see her in the women's faces. Going to India is like going to Kameko's for a Pagan festival, only the festival never ends."

Zen smiled. "Is that why you're taking me there?"

"No," he said. "We'll stay in Mumbai for a couple of days, see Bollywood and some of the other tourist stuff there, but then we get on a train and go to Pune. My grandma wants to meet you."

"Really?" Zen said. She pulled away from him to see the expression on his face.

"Well, yeah," he said. "Marriage is a really big deal to Hindus, and as the matriarch of the Sudhra clan, she pretty much has to meet you. In fact, she helped me pay for the trip so she could. You'll see; she's like our Kameko."

"I hope she'll love me," Zen said. "What happens if I meet her, and she feels the same way about me your mother does?"

"Zen, do you ever listen to me?" Ramesh said with a sigh. "I've told you: I don't care if my family hates you. I don't care if they disown me or tell all their friends I'm dead. There is no future for me without you. Have some faith in us, Zen."

"I know, Ramesh. I only hope our future together doesn't mean you have to lose your past."

He pulled her in close again and kissed her neck. "Grandma's the ace up my sleeve," he said. "Once you've won her over, she'll win my mom over to you."

"I hope so," she said. "Your grandma speaks English, right?"

"Yeah," he said. "She's a native English speaker. Hindi and Marathi are her other native languages."

"Do you speak any Hindi or Marathi?"

He smirked. "Mom made Priya and I take lessons in Marathi over the summers when we were kids. I know a few words, but I never got anywhere near fluency. Priya, on the other hand, speaks like a native. She and Mom have these whole conversations in rapid-fire Marathi in front of me, and I don't understand a word."

"Good," Zen said. "Then you'll be in the same boat as me."

"Tons of people in India speak English, especially in the really huge cities like Mumbai and Pune," Ramesh said. "It's Indian English, but it's pretty much the same. You hear it on the phone all the time when your business calls get routed to an Indian call center. You and I will get along fine."

She let him hold her, pressing her ear to his chest to hear his heart beat again, and took in his emotions. He was so happy and excited. Zen felt excited, too. She hoped this adventure had a happy ending.

* * * *

Zen stirred her screwdriver with her red plastic stirrer and took a short sip. "How long is this flight, anyway?"

"Long," Ramesh said. "And we'll lose so many hours due to the time difference, it will be as if we've been flying an entire day. And that's just to get across the Atlantic. I highly recommend you try to get some sleep."

"In a little while," she said. "I'm too excited to sleep. I've never been to Europe before."

"I haven't either, really," he said. "I've flown to and from India four times in my life, always through Germany, but I've never really seen Germany. I wonder what it's like?"

"Good beer, I'm guessing. Fatty foods. Blonde, blue-eyed people, really fast-moving Volkswagens, and highly efficient trains."

"Doesn't sound like my kind of place," he said. "Except maybe the Autobahn part. I could get into that."

"Yeah, right. I can totally see your Dart on the Autobahn." She laughed. "Allie's been to Europe twice now. She loves it."

"Twice?" he said. "I remember when she and Orlando took the baby to be baptized in Slovenia, in the little village Orlando's mom came from. She has all those great photos of the mountains and the Adriatic coastline."

Zen nodded and took another sip of her drink. "She said the same thing about Lake Bled that you said about India: that you can feel the goddess everywhere. She had the same experience when she and Paul Phillip went to Greece. They had this deal, though. For every Pagan temple they visited in Greece, they also had to visit an early Christian site. That way, he wouldn't feel like he was worshiping idols."

Ramesh laughed. "He's a good little Baptist, right?"

"Right," Zen said, catching his point. "Paul Phillip's funny like that. His Baptist upbringing comes out at the oddest times."

"Except when it comes to living with another guy, right?"

"Yeah, that's the funny part," she said.

Zen finished her drink, sat back, and closed her eyes. She'd never been a nervous flyer, and the gentle drone of the Punjabi music she could barely hear through Ramesh's headphones soothed her. Soon she was asleep.

When Zen awoke, Ramesh sat beside her, sleeping soundly, with the melted ice of two whiskey and sodas still on his tray in front of him. She wondered what time it was in Milwaukee, but realized it was a moot point. She was far from Milwaukee, far from anything she'd ever known. If she reached over Ramesh and opened the window shade, she would see one of two things: the Atlantic Ocean, or the continent of Europe. She felt a little thrill of excitement at the thought.

The perceptible change in her own emotions made Zen suddenly aware of the myriad feelings around her. Ramesh, sound asleep, was inaccessible to her. She'd never been able to get a good reading on a sleeping person's feelings, even if it seemed obvious that he or she was in the middle of a horrible nightmare. Dreams were off-limits to her gift of empathy. The other passengers' feelings, however, were wide open books. She got especially strong vibes off the people who were panicky flyers.

Momentarily distracted from looking out the window, she looked around the cabin instead, scanning the faces of her fellow passengers. Some of them, clearly, were Germans. The middle-aged couple directly behind her and Ramesh, for example, was having a soft conversation in German. Zen had the disconcerting experience of knowing their states of mind without being able to understand their words. In Milwaukee, this happened to her rarely, mostly in the Vietnamese restaurant near the shop, and in the taqueria over by Gillian's apartment, or when a certain elderly Polish couple came in to O'Connor's and argued in Polish.

The Germans weren't arguing. If she had to guess, Zen would have said they were talking about all the things they missed about home while they were on an extended business trip to the United States. They felt homesick. She surmised they missed the food most of all; they also felt hungry. The in-flight meal hadn't yet been served.

As Zen continued scanning the cabin, the brief thoughts she'd had of Milwaukee alerted her to something she may otherwise have missed. Six or seven rows ahead of her and Ramesh, there was a woman with short, dishwater-blonde hair, streaked with flamingo-pink highlights. She could only see the back of the woman's head, but that back of the head looked unnervingly familiar.

Zen felt her anger rising. "Astrid," she said out loud.

Beside her, Ramesh stirred. "Did you say something, babe?" he asked her.

"Yes," she said, shaking his knee until he opened his eyes. "Over there, the blonde. Does she look familiar to you?"

Ramesh sat up to get a better look. "Not really," he said. "Should the back of her head remind me of the back of the head of someone I should know?"

"She looks like Astrid," Zen said quietly, "except Astrid's hair had mint green stripes, and that woman has pink stripes. But stripes are easy enough to change, and if you're the kind of person who'd walk around with green stripes in your hair, you're the kind of person who'd wear pink stripes, too."

Ramesh yawned widely. "Yes, I see your logic." She didn't need empathy to know he couldn't have cared less. "Have you ever dyed your hair an off color, Zen?"

Zen blinked twice. "Ramesh, I'm not trying to discuss hair fashions with you. This could be Astrid, the fugitive! Don't you care that this woman not only broke Gillian's heart, but also stole a good chunk of Gillian's savings? And she may be on the plane with us. This could be our chance to bring her to justice!"

She realized her voice had gotten a bit loud, and that the other passengers were starting to stare. The middle-aged German woman gave her a slight snort.

"That would be highly improbable," Ramesh whispered. "It's too much of a coincidence. Of all the flights toward all of the destinations in the world, what are the chances she'd be on the same one as us?"

Zen thought for a moment, then said, "Is it a coincidence, Ramesh? Or is it fate? Divine intervention, perhaps? I can imagine the same Goddess who decided you and I would be together and compelled you to take me to

India also wants to resolve this thing with Astrid and Gillian. I know you believe in Her unseen hand, Ramesh."

"I do," he said, "but before you get carried away with divine intervention, why don't you go up there and check to see if it's really her?"

"Okay," Zen said. "I have to use the bathroom anyway."

She got out of her seat, made her way up the aisle, and went into the unoccupied bathroom. Having finished her business, she made her way back. Zen stopped in front of the dishwater blonde, almost toe-to-toe with her. Slowly, she looked into the woman's face, thinking of all the things she wanted to say to Astrid.

The dishwater blonde woman, Zen now saw, was at least fifteen to twenty years older than Astrid, with lined features and kind gray eyes. Her pink locks of hair were the only thing about her that suggested youth. Her sophisticated, pink business-casual suit and general demeanor suggested a suburban, working grandmother rather than a twenty-something stripper.

"Yes, young lady?" the woman said with a thick German accent.

"I'm sorry to bother you," Zen said. "I thought you were someone else."

Zen sat down beside Ramesh, who'd had the flight attendants bring him two blankets, one for each of them. He was wrapped securely in his, with his eyes closed. As she settled under her blanket, he asked her, "So, was it her?"

"Not even remotely," she said. "Just some middle-aged German woman with pink streaks in her hair."

"That's too bad," he said. "Astrid would have made the flight to Munich more interesting, that's for sure."

"Is that all you can say?" Zen said, slightly offended. "What about Gillian? Astrid is still out there somewhere!"

"The police will find her one of these days. She probably hasn't even left Milwaukee." He yawned again. "You never did answer my question, Zen. Have you ever done anything radical with your hair color?"

"Yeah," she said, calming down. "During my punk phase, I wore my hair spiky and blood-red. It matched all the ripped-up plaids."

"Nice," he said.

"How about you, Ramesh? Ever experiment with any colors?"

"Of course. What American teenager hasn't had at least one terrible home dye job?" he said. "Remember the summer when all the major league baseball players were getting their hair bleached?"

She giggled. "Yeah. They still do that sometimes."

"Well, there was one summer when I was in high school when it was really popular. A bunch of guys on the baseball team and I all bleached our hair together."

She laughed quietly, trying not to draw stares from the other passengers. "How'd that turn out?"

"Kind of orange," he said. "I'll show you the pictures sometime. Don't be offended, Zen, but do you mind if I get back to my nap? I was having the most beautiful dream. You were in it. As a matter of fact, so was Astrid."

"I don't want to hear it," she said, leaning back and closing her eyes tightly. Before long, Ramesh was napping again. Zen wished she could get back to sleep, but the thought of being somewhere over Europe—possibly—was too exciting. She could feel the mounting excitement in the other passengers, too.

She reached across Ramesh and opened the window shade. She saw nothing but darkness.

* * * *

When the long flight finally ended, Zen and Ramesh waited their way through German customs. As soon as they got into the airport itself, they found the terminal for their next flight.

Zen looked up at the enormous digital clock on the wall. "Two hours to go," she said, looking over at Ramesh.

"I'm not sitting still for two hours," he said. "Not after that flight. Let's go explore."

They went into the duty-free shop, where they debated buying a bottle of Scotch. In the end, they decided against it.

"There must be a place to get a beer here," Ramesh said. "When in Germany, drink Heineken, right?"

"Heineken is Dutch," she said. "If you really want to do something German, let's go *there*."

She pointed out a food stand underneath a brown-and-white striped awning, attended by a very fat, bearded man in a grease-smeared butcher's apron. In front of him, behind a glass case, was a huge selection of sausages, assorted meats, and cheeses.

"Are you kidding me?" he said.

"Okay, I admit the sausages look a little—shall we say, exotic? But what's the point of going on an international adventure if you're not going to experiment a little?"

"You make a good point, my little adventurer," Ramesh said. "Look, when we get to India, you definitely can't be buying just anything off the street vendors and eating it. You've seen the rough parts of Chicago and Milwaukee, and you think you know what poverty is, but believe me, Zen, you're going to have a whole different idea about it when we get to Mumbai. Our standards of food preparation are very different from theirs."

As he spoke, Zen made her way over to the food stand. The vendor spoke to her in friendly German. Zen understood few of his words beyond "Guten tag." She scanned the selection of foodstuffs and finally pointed at a bright yellow wheel of Jarlsburg, loosely wrapped in clear plastic.

"Some cheese should be safe, right?" she asked Ramesh.

"Sure," he said.

She laughed as she handed over some euros in exchange for a chunk of cheese wrapped in brown paper. "Danke," she told the man. She then broke off a piece of the cheese between her thumb and forefinger, and popped it in her mouth.

"How is it?" Ramesh asked.

"Wonderful," she said. "Sharp, milky and creamy at the same time, and spicy in a way I've never tasted before. And I eat Jarlsburg all the time in Wisconsin. The Jarlsburg in Milwaukee isn't this smooth, and doesn't have the same aftertaste. I wonder if Germans make it a different way than Americans do."

"You *are* my little cheesehead."

"Try some."

She handed him the entire chunk, paper wrapper and all. They moved out of the way as a large group of nuns, carrying coin purses and talking excitedly in German, lined up at the food stand.

Ramesh broke off a piece of cheese, then handed the greasy paper back to Zen. She raised her eyebrows, awaiting his verdict.

"Okay, it's good," he said. "It's really good. This is what I'll always remember when I think of Germany."

"See?" she said. "Don't be afraid to try new things."

"I'm not afraid," he said. "I'm warning you to be cautious about what you put in your mouth." She laughed. "I'm serious, Zen! When we get to India, we'll have some really good *rassogolla*. You'll love it, I promise."

After the cheese-tasting experience, they found a bar and sipped Beck's until it was almost time for their next flight. They boarded the plane to Mumbai with a few other Americans, some Europeans, and a broad mix of Asian people, mostly dressed in business suits.

Zen's first experience of Mumbai, once she and Ramesh got out of the international airport, was of an overwhelming crush of humanity. She soon learned the city was actually a series of islands, renowned for the fisherman who worked from its shores. She was amazed; she'd never imagined an Eastern version of Venice.

Their first day went by in a blur: taxis, navigating their way through streets that ranged from glamorous to decrepit, with every variation in between. She saw a bewildering array of signs, some in English, some she could read but not understand, and some in scripts Zen had never even seen before. She witnessed dazzling lights, desperate poverty, sounds ranging from the sacred bells of Hindu worship to calls to prayer from the Muslim minarets to the hip-hop beat of Bollywood soundtracks. The skyscrapers awed her, more vast and intricate in their architecture than anything she's ever seen in Chicago and Milwaukee, and the smells—Zen had never experienced such a dizzying blend of mouth-watering cuisine (foods, of which Ramesh's gajar barfi had been a single flake in a blizzard), spices, and nauseating city smells of unwashed human bodies and urine, all permeating the atmosphere in a cacophony of scent.

Ramesh took her to the Gateway to India, then to Chowpatty Beach. They bought handfuls of flowers from little girls with baskets and even saw a snake-charmer, something Zen could hardly believe still existed. Then there was the Gandhi memorial, followed by the Hanging Gardens.

At the end of the day, Ramesh took Zen to a four-star restaurant. Their server spoke English and was kind enough to explain the menu items to Zen. Even Ramesh wasn't familiar with some of the things on the menu. He knew he wanted *Bhel poori*, a savory dish made with puffed rice, and ordered it for himself and for Zen as an appetizer. The server brought it, along with a glass of white wine for Zen and bottle of Kingfisher for Ramesh. Ramesh had a certain fondness for Indian beers, and sometimes drank Kingfisher even while Zen had her Michelob at O'Connor's.

Ramesh, not bound by ritual obligation to refrain from eating other creatures, had a dish of *jhinge batana*, a spicy shrimp served with shredded coconut and coriander leaves as garnish. Zen tasted the sauce; its blend of chilies, cumin, coriander and tamarind was overpowering to her taste buds. She was much happier with her own, vegetarian entree, the *bharaleli wangi*, stuffed eggplant. The spicy stuffing also had tamarind, coriander and cumin, but in much more reasonable quantities. Plus, the fried coconut and brown sugar gave it a sweetness that balanced out the spiciness.

Despite the sensory overload of being in a place as gilded as Las Vegas, yet on a grander scale and without the sense that it had been laid out purposefully, Zen was aware of one thing: there was a peace here she'd rarely felt in the United States. She understood then what Ramesh had meant when he'd said India was like one of the Pagan festivals they'd celebrated together. It had the same feeling of timelessness, the same sense of the uselessness of concern for everyday problems. Mumbai lacked the certain anxiety Zen always felt in large groups in the U.S. In its place, there was a calm. She knew this wonderful absence was the presence of the Goddess. This ease, this contentment *was* the Goddess. Peace was one of Her many faces.

As she and Ramesh took a taxi from a temple dedicated to Ganesh, she leaned against Ramesh's shoulder. "Where are we going?" she asked him, for the first time since she'd taken the tickets out of the box. It appeared Ramesh spoke enough Marathi to tell the taxi driver where they wanted to go.

"We'll stay in a hotel tonight," he said. "Tomorrow there will be some more time for sight-seeing before we get on the train."

"Train?"

He nodded. "To Pune, to see my grandma," he said. "We'll stop at one of the bazaars and buy you something to wear tomorrow."

"Something to wear?" she asked, more interested than offended. "You don't like any of the things I brought to wear?"

"Of course I do," he said. "I like 'em fine. I love the black knit dress with the leggings, even though it might be too hot for you to wear tomorrow. Hell, you could go naked, for all I care. I just like to buy you things. I wanted you to have something authentic. You know, like a souvenir of your trip to Mumbai."

"Do you think I need to change the way I dress to make a good impression on your grandma, Ramesh? I thought you were so sure she and I are going to love one another."

"You are."

"But only if I'm—what? Not too Western for her? Is there anything else about me you'd like to change, Ramesh? How about my accent, or the color of my eyes?"

"Whoa, crazy woman, slow down," Ramesh said. "I don't want to change anything about you. I love your blue eyes. Hey, you were the woman who wanted to eat German cheese. Whatever happened to 'when in Germany, do as the Germans do?'"

"I'm sorry if I'm overreacting," she said. "I'm nervous. I want your family to like me, and so far, I've been failing miserably."

"Stop saying that," he said. "My grandma is easy to impress. You'll make a great impression on her no matter what you're wearing." He put his hand on her cheek and kissed her.

The taxi headed south and took them to the Marine Plaza Hotel with its gorgeous view of the sea from Zen and Ramesh's room. They had another drink in the lounge, then went to bed. Too tired from crisscrossing the city in search of tourist attractions, neither of them made an attempt to initiate sex. This was rare for Zen and Ramesh, who usually liked it at night and often fell asleep naked together. This time, they fell asleep in one another's arms, fully clothed.

The next morning, Ramesh woke Zen up early. They went for a dip in the hotel's glorious glass-bottomed swimming pool. If they'd been alone, this would have been the perfect place for a canoodle. However, as they were sharing the facilities with a troupe of businessmen from Saudi Arabia, sex would have to wait.

They dried off, threw on a pair of jeans apiece, and went to the hotel's café for a caffeine boost. After a quick breakfast and a couple of espresso macchiatos, Zen and Ramesh headed off to Colaba Causeway.

At the bazaar, though, Zen changed her mind completely. She saw so many beautiful things, so inexpensive: jewelry, incense, brass candlesticks and other antiques in both European and Asian styles, all kinds of crafts, shoes, leather belts and handbags, and every style of clothes Zen could imagine. She ended up with a traditional-style pants suit in a rose color. Ramesh wanted to buy her things, and she wanted to let him. She also got a pair of gold shoes and handful of rings with semi-precious stones. She was especially fond of the toe ring with the smoothly polished chip of rose quartz.

Zen and Ramesh had lunch at Leopold's Café, then hopped back into a taxi and visited the Victoria Terminus railroad station. From there, they would take a train to Pune.

The train to Pune was horribly cramped. Fortunately, the woman who sat on the other side of Zen from Ramesh spoke English.

"My name is Lakshmi," the woman said, extending her hand for Zen to shake. "What's yours?"

"Zenobia."

"What do you do, Zenobia?"

"I'm a student. I'm studying to become a nurse-midwife."

"I've never been a midwife, though I've had about every other kind of job you can imagine. I did once work as an office manager at a women's clinic, though. Of course, I came about it in a roundabout way. I started off as a chemist, and then a pharmaceuticals representative, and then the office manager at the clinic. I've been near a lot of pregnant women and new babies, but thank the gods, I've never had to attend an actual birth."

"So far, I've only attended one birth," Zen had to admit. "And that was when my sister gave birth to my nephew."

It seemed strange to her then that she was spending the holidays so far away from Allie and Antonio, and the rest of the family, and her own familiar corner of the world. She turned her head and looked at Ramesh, though, and didn't regret a moment of it.

"You'll be a fine midwife," Lakshmi said. "You have the gift. I can tell, though I've only just met you."

I do have a gift, Zen thought, and not only the gift of empathy. She looked at Ramesh again and thought, my whole life has been a gift from the Goddess. She said a silent prayer of thanks.

During the three-hour trip, Zen and Lakshmi talked about labor and delivery. Zen began to feel euphoric, as if she truly belonged here, belonged to this land. Was this the spiritual promised land she'd dreamed it was?

At the train station, Zen slipped into the ladies' restroom, which was as crowded as the train, and far from ideal. Still, she took off her Western clothes and stowed them in her travel bag, putting on the pink outfit Ramesh had bought for her at the bazaar.

She and Ramesh walked out of the train station hand in hand. Pune, it seemed, was as sprawling and multicultural as Mumbai, though the architecture of the large buildings was less modern and, somehow, less British. The sun rose high in the sky, and the mid-day heat reflecting off the buildings and cars felt stifling.

"It's hot," Ramesh remarked. "Hot and dusty."

"We should get something to drink," Zen said, looking around.

"I could go for a beer," Ramesh said.

"There," Zen said, pointing out a street vendor. "He has tea."

Ramesh bought two mugs of chai tea from a street vendor. The mugs weren't entirely clean, but the hot, milky tea refreshed them. Zen finally understood why Ramesh liked so much milk in his tea. As he and Zen walked around drinking them, she noticed street signs pointing out the way to the airport.

"If there's an airport here, why didn't we fly to Pune?" she asked him.

He smirked. "You can't really experience India without seeing the Victoria Terminus. Or without being crammed onto a passenger train."

She had the feeling she could see almost as many things to see in Pune as in southern Mumbai, and she and Ramesh hadn't even been able to take in half of them. This time, he seemed insistent on getting to his grandmother's house, so sightseeing would have to wait. They got into a taxi, which took them through downtown and out toward the suburbs.

As they neared Mrs. Sudhra's house, Zen noticed the colorful designs on the ground. They looked like colored chalk.

"What is it?" she asked him, whirling around to study the intricate patterns. "This must have taken your grandma hours to do."

"She's surprisingly quick at it," Ramesh said. "She's been doing it for years. Her whole life, really. They're called *yantras*."

"I've seen it in front of other houses, too," she said. "It can't just be art."

"You're right," he said. "It's a form of *puja*, an action-prayer."

"Can I learn how to do it?"

"You can, but if you're going to take it on, don't take it lightly. My grandma gets up an hour early every morning as part of a vow she made to Lakshmi."

"The woman from the train?"

He looked at her as if she were insane, but she felt his amusement. "The goddess of prosperity."

"I feel it," Zen said. "I feel the presence of the Goddess. I feel *shakti*."

The front door opened. "I thought I heard someone speaking English," the white-haired woman in the doorway said. Zen guessed she stood a little under five feet tall. She was slightly plump, but well-dressed in a white blouse with a ruffled collar, a colorful scarf, a navy blue skirt that reached her knees, and black satin ballet flats. She wore no makeup, but her fingernails glittered with scarlet.

Ramesh smiled broadly as he went to embrace her. She said more, but in Marathi. The only word Zen could make out was "Ramesha."

Zen felt suddenly self-conscious; she wished she were wearing her Western clothes again. "Mrs. Sudhra?" she said shyly. "Hi, my name is Zenobia Van Zandt—"

"I like the sound of that," Ramesh's grandmother said. "Zen-o-bya Van Zandt. Very musical." Her English was slightly tinged with a British accent.

Her remark caught Zen off guard, so Ramesh stepped in. "Grandma, I'd like you to meet Zen, the one I told you so much about."

Grandma blinked in the bright afternoon sun. "Do you mind if I call you Zenobia? Zen is nice—it reminds one of the Japanese school of Buddhism—but I really like the sound of Zenobia Van Zandt. Or, Zenobia Sudhra, as I'll have to say shortly. Ramesha, didn't you say you're going to get married on Midsummer Night?" She laughed and extended both of her hands to Zen, who took them. The women laced their fingers together as Ramesh's grandma studied Zen. "You needn't call me Mrs. Sudhra, dear. You may call me Hetal. You're going to be part of the family."

Ramesh and Zen both nodded. "Ah, Midsummer Night. It's not popularly celebrated in your culture anymore, other than in Shakespeare's play. Once, Europeans believed it was the one night of the year when the veil between the fairy world and ours was at its thinnest, when a mortal could most easily slip and fall into the fairy realm. And who are the fairies, after all, but faint reflections of the ancient gods? This is why, when the Christians came to the British Isles, they had to replace Midsummer Night—Litha—with Lammas." She laughed, a musical, bell-like sound. "But listen to me, droning on as if I'm giving a lecture in introductory folklore. Zenobia, you must let me braid your hair for the wedding. Come inside now and I'll make you some tea and biscuits."

The first thing Zen noticed as she stepped inside Hetal's house was the family portrait. It took her a few seconds to pick out Ramesh, who must have been seven or eight years old at the time. He was smiling, and one front tooth was missing. He sat next to Priya, who wore an elaborate, ruffled, sunflower-yellow party dress. Behind them to the left stood Ramesh's parents, and on the right were his paternal grandparents. They all looked very happy.

As she glanced at the portrait, Zen noticed the scents of coriander and cardamom in the air.

"I took a few days off from work to be with you," Hetal told Ramesh. "I expect the bank will get along without me until Friday. I baked ginger biscuits this morning. Excuse me for a moment while I get them, yes?"

"Thanks, Grandma," Ramesh said, sinking into a large chair. Zen sensed he felt perfectly at home in this house. Based on Hetal's warm reception, Zen was beginning to feel at home, too.

Zen wandered around the small, cozy parlor, looking at the pictures on the walls, then the bookshelf. The books were in various scripts: some titles in English, some in the Roman alphabet but in another language, and others completely indecipherable to her. It was like reading the street signs in Mumbai.

At the end of the bookshelf there was a door. Ramesh opened it; inside there was a squared-off wooden table, nearly black from great age. Zen could see it over Ramesh's shoulder. In the center of the table was a statue of a goddess, lovingly surrounded by a garland of fresh flowers and other offerings.

"Lakshmi," Ramesh said.

Zen stood, staring at the goddess's statue in awed silence. Hetal entered the room, carrying a plate stacked high with homemade ginger cookies. Zen breathed deeply. The scent reminded her of something, a memory buried deep in her subconscious. It wasn't a visual memory. She closed her eyes, but could conjure no images. It was more of an emotion, a sensation. The only name she could put to it was the one word that escaped her lips: "Mama."

She didn't know whether she was remembering her own mother, or responding to the presence of Lakshmi in the room. Suddenly she felt warm and loved.

Zen opened her eyes. She saw Ramesh staring at Hetal, unsure of himself. Was Hetal disappointed that Ramesh didn't seem to know how to make puja, how to pay his traditional respects to the Goddess? Zen couldn't tell. Hetal was harder to read than most people. It was as if she kept her feelings sealed in a vault inside her head. This didn't bother Zen, though. She was more concerned about showing her own respect for the force she felt in this house, the universal mother, the Creator, the place she came from.

"Have a biscuit," Hetal said, smiling as she held out the plate.

Ramesh made the first move, taking a cookie off the plate and placing it at the feet of the Goddess. As he did, he made a slight bow. Zen sensed the sincerity of his intentions. She imitated Ramesh's gesture. To her surprise,

Hetal did the same. The three of them sat down in the parlor and made themselves comfortable.

"Your mother worries about you," Hetal said to Ramesh. "She has her heart in the right place. She wants what is best for you, and in her understanding, what is best for you is to keep the traditions our family has observed for these many thousands of years. She is not wrong, Ramesha."

Ramesh sighed and took another cookie off the plate. "I don't mean to disrespect my mother or the family, Grandma. I never meant to turn my back on Hindu tradition, but there was no way I was going to marry Remma Gupta." He took a bite of his cookie.

Hetal smiled approvingly. "Have a biscuit," she said again, holding the tray out for Zen.

Zen took a biscuit and brought it to her lips. Its smell was divine. She tasted it, and the flavor was as sublime as its smell indicated. Tears filled her eyes, as she could not shake the impression she was eating more than gingerbread. It seemed to Zen she was tasting maternal love itself.

Hetal set the tray of cookies aside and took a book from the shelf. The title of the book was in a script Zen couldn't read. Hetal sat beside Zen on the sofa and opened the book. It was lavishly illustrated with pastoral scenes and love scenes. Zen recognized the basic storyline. She knew the handsome god with blue skin was Krishna, and the beautiful women who surrounded him were *gopis*, the cowgirls of India.

"Ramesha, do you remember the story of Radha?" Hetal asked.

Ramesh finished his cookie. "Of course," he said. "She was married, but she was unhappy with her husband's family. Although her mother-in-law warned her never to wander off the trail as she drove the family's herds through the forest, Radha disobeyed, and Krishna seduced her."

"Do you remember the point of the story?" Hetal prompted, sounding very much like a schoolteacher.

Ramesh shrugged. "She probably got punished somehow, for not listening to her mother-in-law."

Grandma shook her head. "Not at all."

Ramesh looked chagrined, but Hetal gave him a comforting smile. "It is one of the greatest love stories of all times," Hetal said. "Their love was true, and pure, because it had no purpose. Their coupling was an act of pure joy, not a marriage undertaken for social reasons, or to produce children. So it is with you." She touched Zen's leg. "And you." She nodded to Ramesh. "Your love is not correct. It is not rational. Therefore it is pure."

"We *will* have children," Ramesh said, catching Zen's eye. "At least two. Maybe three."

Zen raised her eyebrows; she and Ramesh had never actually settled on a number, although both agreed they wanted to be parents one day. She was going to say something to that effect, but Hetal interrupted her.

"Of course you will," Hetal said. "The point is not that you shouldn't want to marry and raise a family. It only matters that your love begins as a spark of fire that begins to burn, and soon is blazing out of control."

"Our love began with fire," Ramesh said. "Quite literally. I looked across the bonfire at you, Zen, and there you were, my strong and beautiful Kali." She looked down at the ring on her finger, the jewel nestled in the lotus.

"I have several things to show you," Hetal said. "This afternoon, we'll go to the Empress Botanical Gardens and have tea at a nice restaurant. Tomorrow we'll see Pataleshvara Cave Temple and spend some time in the gardens. After that, you'll make the journey to Khajuraho."

"Khajuraho?" Zen asked. "Is that nearby?"

Hetal shook her head. "I've booked you a flight. I regret I won't be able to spend any more time with you, but I'll see you again before your wedding. You must visit the temple of Shiva at Khajuraho before your marriage."

Zen looked at Ramesh. "Did you know she'd booked another flight for us?"

"Of course," Ramesh said. "We've been planning this ever since I came here to get the engagement ring from her. When we go home, Grandma reports to my mom all about how you and I have had this great spiritual awakening in India, and resolved to be good Hindus as well as Pagans."

"We're going to lie to your mother?" Zen asked Ramesh.

Hetal answered for him. "No," she said flatly. She followed this definitive remark with a smile. "I'll go make some tea, yes?"

* * * *

When Zen woke, alone in the guest bedroom, it was still dark. She felt a hand on her shoulder, nudging her awake gently. She smiled. This must be Ramesh coming to say good morning, she thought, sensing a hint of wonderful joyous emotions.

"Get dressed, Zenobia," a voice said. Instead of Ramesh, it was Hetal. Zen opened her eyes. "If you are a willing student, I would like to teach you a *yantra*."

"Really? Of course I'd love to learn," Zen said.

"Just listen and observe," Hetal said, "I'll give you a moment to get ready."

She got out of bed, put on her slippers, and went for her suitcase. She was somewhat perplexed by what to wear. The morning still felt chilly, but somehow putting on her favorite pair of jeans and a comfy sweatshirt seemed disrespectful. She didn't have any more Indian clothes to wear. She settled on a pair of flat-front khaki slacks and a soft pumpkin-orange sweater. She left her slippers on and made her way out to the front of Hetal's house.

Hetal walked back and forth with a broom, sweeping the sidewalk in front of her home until it was free of dust, leaves, and the dropped blossoms of the hyacinths that grew on either side of the front door. Zen thought of Allie, who used the traditional birch broom to ritually purify her meditation space. The sun had barely come up.

"This is part of the *puja*," Hetal said. "It's the first thing I do every morning, before my first cup of tea. When it rains, I make the *yantra* on a wall inside the house. I prefer to be outdoors, in nature, though."

Zen noticed, sitting on the steps, hammered brass bowls filled with different colors of fine powder: a bright yellow, like turmeric, a chalky white, a red like chili powder, and a vibrant pink. They may have been the spices they reminded her of; the smell of spices hung in the air, as Zen had noticed when she'd first seen the *yantras*. Hetal knelt, chanted a short prayer, and stuck her hand in the white powder. Sprinkling it on the ground, little by little, she made the shape of a triangle. The triangle pointed upwards, away from her body. Zen crouched beside her.

"This is always the beginning," Hetal said. "It represents Shiva." She brushed the powder from her hands and took some of the yellow powder from the bowl. Overlapping the white triangle, she carefully drew a yellow triangle pointing in the opposite direction. Together, the two triangles made the familiar image of a six-pointed star. "*Shakti*," Hetal said as she wiped the yellow powder from her hands. "The female principle. We begin our sacred diagram with the union of these opposite forces, male and female, for this is the source of all life."

Zen watched as Hetal made the *yantra* larger and more complex, a colorful masterpiece of overlapping geometric figures.

"Don't worry about learning all of the details yet," Hetal told Zen. "As long as you get the basics."

"Can you teach me? I want to learn everything I can from you."

"Yes," Hetal said, smiling. "Follow me inside, and I'll show you how the *puja* continues. The *puja* you are learning is thousands of years old." She plucked a handful of fresh blossoms from the hyacinth to the left of the door.

Zen followed Hetal into the family room, where they stood before the image of the goddess. She respectfully laid the hyacinth blooms at the goddess's feet. Then she touched the goddess's feet with her right hand and said a prayer aloud in Sanskrit. She repeated the same prayer, touching the goddess's knees. The ritual continued with Hetal touching the goddess's lower belly (the womb, Zen thought), navel, heart, and forehead, all while repeating the same words. She then touched the feet again, and started the ritual over. Hetal did this three times in all.

As she finished reciting the final mantra, Hetal looked at Zen. "This is *nyasa*, the ritual of caressing. You don't have to learn the mantras in Sanskrit, unless you would like to as a special act of devotion. You can repeat them in English, in your own words. It's the intention of your heart that matters, not your vocabulary."

"I want to learn all I can," Zen insisted. "Can you teach me the Sanskrit words?"

"I'll write the words down, spelled phonetically, for you to practice. And I'll tell you something else." She dropped her voice to a very low whisper. "The ritual of *nyasa* need not be performed on the image that represents a god or goddess. It may also be performed on a living person who embodies some aspect of the divine to you."

Zen smiled, picturing herself reverentially touching Ramesh while reciting an impromptu prayer to Shiva, or to Cernunnos, or to one of her many images of the male aspect of the mysterious creator of the universe. She watched as Hetal anointed the goddess with oil and gave her offerings of fruit, perfume, and scented water. Zen pictured herself performing these rituals at home. She wondered if they would become a natural part of her everyday life, as they seemed to be with Hetal.

When she completed the *puja*, Hetal went to the kitchen and made coffee. The scents and sounds of brewing coffee seemed to awaken Ramesh, because he was there moments later. Wearing green pajama bottoms, he sat across the table from Zen as Hetal cooked them a breakfast of Irish oatmeal.

When the oatmeal was on the table, Hetal stirred hers and said, "You know, when Nalini first joined our family, I wasn't sure she and Sadguna were going to make it as a couple. She was so down-to-earth, and my Sadguna always had his head off in the clouds. She was insistent upon going to medical school in the U.S., and he wanted to stay here. He dreamed of acting in movies, you know."

"I didn't know that," Zen said. Ramesh sipped his coffee with an amused smirk.

"It's true. That boy of mine would have traded the family cow for a handful of magic beans if Nalini hadn't kept her eyes on him. I know she might seem a little stiff at times, Zenobia. I thought so at first, too. Especially the time she reorganized my pantry while I was out at the market. She said my shelves weren't organized logically."

Zen laughed. "That wasn't even the worst of it," Ramesh added. "She went into the closet and grouped grandma's saris by color to make it easier for her to find her clothes in the morning."

"And she does the same things to Sadguna, Ramesha and Priya, of course," Hetal said. "Remember how she used to look in your backpack to make sure it was organized?"

Ramesh snorted. "I'll never forget that, Grandma. She did it until my freshman year in high school. After she threw away my Walkman, though, I put my foot down."

Hetal laughed, and so did Zen.

That afternoon, the three of them said goodbye in a whirlwind of tearful hugs and kisses. "We'll meet again in half a year," Hetal said, looking into Ramesh's watery eyes. "When it's time to prepare for the wedding."

"We're not coming back to see you after we visit Khajuraho?" Zen asked Hetal. "There's so much more we need to discuss."

Hetal shook her head. "We've discussed all we need to. The rest can be said without words." She kissed Zen's cheek, then said to Ramesh, "You have my blessing."

Ramesh wiped away his tears of joy on his sleeve as the taxi driver honked the horn impatiently.

Ramesh and Zen passed the first part of the flight to Khajuraho by playing "speed" with a deck of cards. After a while, though, they got tired, and sat back in their seats, holding hands. She looked over at him and noticed for the first time he hadn't been shaving since Mumbai. Ramesh was starting to grow a fine black beard, and Zen found it incredibly sexy.

"You look really good with a beard, Ramesh."

He raised his eyebrows suggestively. "Is it turning you on?"

"A little bit," she said, smiling.

"Good," he said. "Then you're in the perfect mood to visit the temples. Want to join the Mile High Club?"

Ramesh asked the flight attendant for a blanket. Zen wondered for a moment what exactly he intended to do with it as he spread the blanket over his lap. She heard him unzip his khakis, and seconds later he pulled her hand under the blanket with him, placing her palm on the head of his cock, so there could be no doubt about his intentions.

"Really?" she said, arching her eyebrows.

He nodded, giving her a smile so appealing she couldn't resist. Trying to be subtle, she moved her hand up and down his cock. Ramesh didn't make a sound, but his wide-open mouth and glazed eyes told her she was doing something he liked. To her pleasant surprise, the head of his cock was soon wet with a few drops of pre-come, giving her enough lube to keep her from having to spit on her hand. She wasn't sure how she was going to do that gracefully with a plane full of wide-eyed passengers watching. Fortunately, Ramesh had the window seat. As she leaned over him, Zen could pretend she was looking out the window.

Ramesh leaned back into his seat; his relaxed pose let her know she was doing well. He closed his eyes, but never turned his face away from her. She breathed in his scent, more musky than usual from the heat and the fact that he hadn't used his usual aftershave lately.

"Am I doing this right?" she whispered close to his ear.

"Yes," he hissed through clenched teeth. "You're almost there. One quarter of a mile to go."

She smiled. It normally would have taken her much longer to get Ramesh this close to coming. He hadn't been so ready to go since the night they'd ended her year of celibacy. Maybe the thought of all those people watching, probably knowing exactly what the two of them were doing, turned him on. She leaned in and kissed him as her fingers drove his cock the last quarter of a mile toward ecstasy.

Zen flicked her thumb over the head of Ramesh's cock, making sure to tease the tiny opening with a butterfly-light touch. Ramesh shuddered. Seconds later, his hips rocked involuntarily as he shot his hot seed into her hand. Her lips never pulled away from his as waves of pleasure washed over him. Her gift of empathy came as a blessing at moments like these.

When he recovered his senses, Ramesh whispered, "Let me do you now."

Zen was about to say something, but a flight attendant a few seats ahead of them interrupted her train of thought. "We'll be landing soon," the flight attendant said.

"I guess I'll have to wait," Zen said.

Ramesh smirked as he readjusted himself in his seat. "Good things come to those who have to wait."

The plane touched down, and an airport shuttle service took them from the airport to the India Airways office at Khajuraho. From there, they found a couple of bikes and rented them for the day. It was about a mile from the office, in the southern part of the temple complex, to the southernmost of the three groupings of temples. They visited Duladeo temple.

"This is the youngest of the temples at Khajuraho," Ramesh explained to Zen, flipping through the guide book he picked up from a street vendor along the dirt road that led to the isolated, ruined temple. "It's supposed to be the least impressive temple built by the Chandela dynasty. I guess we're working our way up to the more impressive ones."

Zen stared up at the elaborate carvings as she and Ramesh walked in the traditional clockwise circle around the temple to show their respects. They paused to consider the carved figure of a temple dancer. The dancer's back was toward them, though she looked at them over her shoulder, patting herself on the butt with one hand. Her clothes were scanty, her figure graceful and shapely. She wore a seductive look on her face.

"This is the least impressive?" Zen said. "These women are gorgeous, heavenly creatures. The sculptor was so respectful. He really loved women, don't you think?"

"He was probably a celibate monk," Ramesh said, laughing. "The women are attendants of Shiva and Parvati. They're in a playful, sensual mood because they're celebrating the sacred marriage of the divine couple."

"Beautiful," Zen said, never taking her eyes off the sculpture. Amazingly, she saw an endless variety of temple dancers and shapely musicians around the temple.

When they had soaked in the erotically charged, sacred carvings of the temple for a few hours, Zen and Ramesh rode their bicycles north. They had a small meal of curry and a Kingfisher Premium apiece at a restaurant called Agrasen. They rode past the vegetable market and the bazaar, heading slightly north and east to reach the temples of Nandi and Vishvanath.

Zen and Ramesh learned that Nandi, at which they arrived first, was a shrine to the bull said to be the vehicle of Shiva. They bought flowers from local children and left them as an offering.

As they left, Zen noticed a long line of women. All of them wore their long hair loose. "What's this?" she asked Ramesh.

He smiled. "Have you ever wondered where the human hair in hair extensions comes from?"

She was surprised. "They're lining up to sell their hair?"

He shook his head. "They're lining up to sacrifice their hair. It's another form of *puja*. It's considered an honor."

Zen took the ponytail holder out of her long, blonde hair, letting it fall loose. "I want to give my hair, too."

"Are you serious?"

"Will you still love me when I'm bald?"

"Of course. You do realize we're getting married in six months, right? It won't grow back before the wedding."

"Good," she said. "Let your family see the sacrifice I was willing to make. Let them see my prayer to Kali."

"They might think you're nuts," Ramesh muttered.

"Oh, shut up. I want to experience this ritual, if it's not going to be a problem with you."

"Go right ahead," he said.

Zen parked and chained up her bicycle. Ramesh kissed her goodbye and went back to Agrasen to wait out her *puja* at the bar. He promised to meet her again in an hour, approximately the time it would take her to get to the front of the long line of women.

His timing was exquisite; Ramesh returned right as Zen's hair was being prepared. "Are you sure you really want to do this?" he asked her as the scissors were lowered to her scalp.

"Yes," she said. "I need to do this." In a moment, she was shorn of her blonde locks. Zen was left with very short, very brown hair.

"What do you think?" she asked him as they hopped back onto their bicycles.

"I can't promise you I'm not going to think about Allie while we're having sex. I've never seen your natural hair color before."

She would have smacked him if she hadn't needed both hands to steer on the rocky road. "You've seen my natural color," she said. "Not on my head, though."

Ramesh took another look at the guide book as they approached Vishvanath. "This temple is about a thousand years old," he told Zen.

He may have given her a more extensive history lesson via the guidebook, but Zen wasn't listening. She was studying the elegant artistry of the temple's *sikhara*, its "mountain" or central pillar. The carvings depicted all aspects of human life. Zen and Ramesh paused to ponder the image of two men, one naked and the other wearing only a loincloth. The clothed man handled the naked man's cock.

Zen looked from the carving to Ramesh's face. He looked slightly embarrassed at the homoerotic image. "It has some esoteric spiritual meaning," he said. Zen didn't comment.

Ramesh seemed less embarrassed and more fascinated by the carving of a woman tenderly caressing a man's face. With one of her hands, the woman played with the man's balls. On either side of them stood two more figures, one female and one male. The woman seemed to be pleasuring herself, while the man had an erection and appeared ready to penetrate the first woman from behind.

Ramesh also seemed to like the image of a man running his fingers through a woman's hair with one hand and tenderly fingering her thin garment with the other while she reached out to fondle his cock. His leg wrapped partially around the woman's shapely ass.

"It's gorgeous," Zen said, as Ramesh stared at the carving perhaps a little longer than was necessary.

Taken all together, the temple of Visvanath was a wonder of architecture and fine art. Zen was entranced by the spiritual nature of this place, which was earthy and sensuous and palpable. She couldn't imagine how the temple's Hindu worshipers had let it fall back into the hands of the jungle before it was rediscovered in the Victorian era. In fact, she was amazed the Victorians didn't destroy these images. She could feel the spiritual energy of the place, and it made her feel peaceful inside.

Zen and Ramesh were so caught up in the wonder of the temples, they were late getting to the airport. By the time they found a taxi, and the taxi driver found the airport entrance nearest their terminal, they'd nearly missed their flight. The entire time, they felt rushed and half-frantic.

The first sign the peace they'd known in India was being restored came as they relaxed in their seats. Ramesh reached into the side pocket of his cargo pants, pulling out a deck of cards. "Want to play?"

She yawned. "I don't have the mental energy for a game of speed right now," she said. "Please don't be offended if I take a nap."

"It has been a long day," Ramesh agreed. "I might take a nap myself."

Zen was soon fast asleep, and dreaming. She dreamt, not of the fabulous temples she had just left, but of a misty forest. Zen was there. The air felt almost oppressively humid. Her thin clothes clung to her body. She didn't know where she was. She might have been in India, or back at Kameko's farm on a summer night, or somewhere else entirely. She looked around in all directions, trying to see what she could make out in the very low moonlight filtering through the trees. She could barely see at all. The hot, steaming forest loomed around her, full of strange sounds. She felt frightened.

Suddenly she was aware of a bright light—fire, it seemed. Yes, she could see it now: a torch. Someone was coming toward her. A new thrill of fear ran down Zen's spine, but she couldn't run. She couldn't see where she was going. Rooted to the spot where she stood, Zen watched, holding her breath, as the light came nearer.

Soon she could make out the shape of the man holding the torch, and she was no longer afraid. But no, he wasn't a man at all. Surely no man she'd ever seen before had such a well-proportioned and attractive body. No man had such a perfect face. Surely this was the being Auntie Kameko described when she told Zen and Allie about Cernunnos, the wild Green Man of the forest, consort of the Great Goddess. He looked more beautiful than she'd imagined when she lay in bed as a young woman, listening to the distant drum circle of the Beltane rites before she was old enough to attend. In her imagination, the Goddess's consort was pale-skinned, had striking eyes, and wore a crown of antlers tangled in his long, cocoa-brown hair. He looked, in short, the way Orlando must have appeared to her twin on the night Allie and Orlando consummated their sacred marriage.

As this figure drew nearer, Zen could see her earlier imaginings had been vastly wrong. His eyes were the deepest of deep browns, like the bark of an ancient tree, or the night sky right at the edge of twilight. His two eyes, like the eyes of a mortal man, fixed on Zen's face. He seemed to study her appearance. His third eye, in the middle of his forehead, seemed to see far beyond the physical world and look directly into her soul. She didn't find this being's scrutiny uncomfortable, though. Instead, it was like being bathed in a warm, inviting light. The longer he stared, the more pleasant his gaze became.

That the godly being before her had three eyes and stared into her soul did not disturb Zen. It only filled her with an electrical kind of wonder that made the hairs on the back of her neck stand up. Nor did it disturb her that this being who had at first seemed so human seemed now to have six arms. One held the torch, another a kind of wooden flute. Its music had been one the many strange sounds of the forest that night. A third hand stroked Zen's hair. She didn't object. His touch was as soft as a butterfly's wing.

It occurred to Zen then that perhaps the six arms and the third eye were a kind of illusion. It seemed to her he had powers she never would, and never could, understand—not, at least, in this lifetime. He moved in a way human beings couldn't, and she almost couldn't comprehend. The "extra" arms, then, were a kind of symbol, a kind of device created in her own mind.

It occurred to her, also, that the gentle being stroking her hair aroused all of her senses. He smelled like jasmine blossoms, a pinch of sharp cumin, and his natural, invigorating male scent. She inhaled, and his scent seemed to travel directly from her lungs to her pelvis. She felt the moisture between her legs. She wanted him. She wouldn't have minded at all to press her lips against his full, moist lips.

Those lips alone were worthy of the grandest temple at Khajuraho. His upper lip was cinnamon brown, and his lower lip was as soft pink as the cherry blossoms of Kameko's orchard. Both glistened with the honeyed dew from his mouth.

Zen sensed, too, that this godly being was open to receiving her devotion. If she gave him any sign she would allow it, he would have stripped her of her thin, clinging dress. He would have laid her among the bright plants of the forest floor, giving himself to her as much as her poor human body could handle it as she gave her body and soul to him.

As she had these thoughts, an achingly pure pleasure took root at the base of her spine. Spreading like fire, it filled her womb. The burning pleasure made her clit swell and her pussy salivate with moisture. It traveled down her legs and made her knees feel weak. It traveled up her spine and came out at her breasts as an amazing sensitivity to the fabric that covered them. The touch of the transparent material hummed at the surface of her skin like electricity. Drops of sweat glistened from every pore on her body. The pleasure rose to her face and became a smile, and a countenance beaming with welcome.

The light of the torch faded as the young god before her smothered the flame. Zen saw he hadn't needed the fire all along. Her god's body glowed with a light as eerily silver as the moon, but brighter. The forest leaves could do nothing to dim its radiance.

All at once, the thoughts that had seemed forbidden—sacrilegious, even—a moment before seemed inevitable. The god brought his lips to hers. In one fluid motion, their bodies entwined, her trembling flesh pressed against his. Mouth to mouth, belly to belly, legs to legs, beating heart to beating heart. She felt a great peace, knowing she and the god were, for the moment, inseparably one. Her mind was an open book to him, and she could glimpse the infinity inside his. Their coupling brought a sense of perfect wholeness. She felt as one, not only with the irresistibly beautiful god, but also with the forest. All beings, she sensed, were enveloped in this oneness.

Yet, this profound sense of wonder did nothing to diminish the physical pleasure of taking this being as her lover. She felt his kisses and caresses as keenly as if he were a mortal man. She responded as she did to her mortal lovers: she wanted to please him, as thanks for the pleasure he brought to her. She trailed kisses down his chest, then down his belly. Each kiss was planted with the deliberation of a prayer. He sighed like a mortal lover as her kisses reached the soft black plume of his pubic hair, then jumped to the broad head of his fat, straining cock.

With all the devotion to her lord of a medieval nun, Zen covered his cock in kisses from the tip to the base, then back up again. His taste was as pure and beautiful as his appearance. She was eager to repeat the pilgrimage, but he stopped her, gently laying a hand on her head. She stood, and he removed the thin fabric that wrapped around her hips.

Looking deeply into Zen's eyes, her divine lover placed his hand between her thighs. The mere presence of his fingers was enough to flood her pussy with juices. Yet he did more than rest his hand, stroking her clit with his thumb with all the skill and patience of a practiced lover, out to please his partner. He brought his other hand down the curve of her back, then between the cheeks of her ass. With two fingers, he playfully explored the entrance.

Zen worried, briefly, that the god would find her unclean. Another brief glimpse into his limitless mind convinced her there was no uncleanness here, only two beings in divine union, as if one.

She would have let him probe and explore her body for eternity. She sensed, however, that even this divine experience of oneness must have its fulfillment.

His fingers slid away from her clit, and he pressed her to him with a new urgency. She felt his thick cock press against her thigh. She parted her legs and let it slide between them. The god sighed, a noise that could only have been approval. Zen took a deep breath. As she breathed in, the extraordinary cock slipped inside her wet pussy. Unlike some of her previous experiences, there was no pain, despite the size of the organ. There was only a heightened sense of pleasure combined with this wonderful oneness.

Heightened pleasure, and a new sensation that burned like fire, though it was not in the least painful or unpleasant. She felt like the fabled burning bush, ablaze with divine light and heat, yet not consumed. She was acutely aware of her body and the body of her godly lover. She tasted him, smelled the perspiration that gleamed from his flesh , brushing her lips against his neck. She was present in the forest, her bare feet in the dirt and the hot, moist night air in her lungs. She couldn't say she was having an out-of-body experience. She was very much in her body, as was her young god. At the same time, her imagination began to soar. All at once the impossible seemed ordinary, and worlds she couldn't have dared dream of opened to her. She couldn't describe all the things that came to her mind; there were no words for them.

At last a word came to Zen's mind. She grasped at it as if it were her salvation, holding its sound and its silver, spherical shape in her mind, concentrating on it. Truth emanated from the center of it, and all things were possible around truth.

Her concentration on this single word was so intense, it drove the heavenly sensations in her body to the edge of her consciousness. In letting go of her physical pleasure, she somehow brought herself release. Her body was wracked with an orgasm that strained her muscles and made her blood pound through her veins. She might have doubled over from its strength if her lover hadn't held onto her so tightly. He held her against him, forcing her to ride out wave after wave of burning intensity.

When she became aware of his powerful arm around her waist, his solid grasp, Zen could no longer fight the urge to call out the word that obsessed her. Her shout seemed to come, not from her mouth only, but from the depths of her soul, and from her entire body.

"Shiva!" she roared, throwing her head back and squeezing her eyes closed so tightly it almost hurt. The rolling thunder of her voice, along with the fierce roar of pleasure in her bones, seemed to last an eternity.

When she finally opened her eyes, Zen saw Ramesh. He sat back in his seat, staring at her with wide eyes while trying to open a small packet of peanuts.

She flushed with embarrassment, looking around at all the faces of her fellow airline passengers. They stared at her with the same quizzical looks on their faces as Ramesh.

"Did I scream out loud?" Zen whispered to Ramesh. He nodded slightly.

Two flight attendants came running down the aisle, stopping in front of Zen. "Is everything all right, miss?" one of them asked in a thick German accent.

Zen swallowed, then nodded her head. "I'm fine," she said. "I had a dream. I'm sorry I bothered you."

The flight attendants exchanged looks. The one closest to Zen smiled.

"Please let us know if there is anything we can do for you," the second one said. She, clearly, was from India.

"Some water, please," Zen said, straightening up in her chair. The flight attendant nodded and went off in the direction of the beverage cart.

"Do you want to tell me what that was all about?" Ramesh asked her.

Zen shrugged. "It was more than a dream," she said.

Ramesh nodded knowingly. "Yeah. It was a wet dream." He laughed softly. "I have the feeling I wasn't your co-star this time."

"It was more than a wet dream, too," she said, though she couldn't help but laugh along with him. "We won't have to lie to your mother now."

"About what?" He opened his pack of peanuts, slipping some of them onto his tray.

"About the great spiritual revelation I had while we were in India," Zen said. "Hetal knew it would be true."

Chapter Nine

Zen carefully wrapped the delicate crystal glass in black tissue paper. After she wrapped its mate, she placed the pair upright in a paper bag. Light and Shadow's shopping bags were nearly the same cheerful cantaloupe color as the shop's walls, with a black handle. They said "Light and Shadow" in black Gothic letters, with the round part of the "g" filled in with yellow "light" and the word "shadow" shadowed with gray. Underneath, in a much more legible script, the bags read, "Where Magic Begins." Below that was a large black pentagram.

"Thank you," the young blonde woman said as Zen handed her the package.

"You're welcome. I hope your fiancé likes them, and that your wedding goes better than your wildest dreams."

The beaming blonde customer left the store. Zen came out from behind the counter and went down the aisle farthest from her cash register. She'd seen another shopper come in as she was helping the woman with the wedding goblets. She found the woman examining the goddess sculptures, paying special attention to a beautiful image of Nagina. The light-skinned Indian-American woman with her auburn hair done up in tight curls ran her fingers over the face of the serpent goddess.

"May I help you find something?" Zen asked the woman.

The woman straightened herself up, smoothing the wrinkles from the front of her red dress. As she looked into Zen's face, Zen noticed the resemblance between this potential customer and Ramesh. She looked so much like Zen's fiancé, in fact, the two of them could have been brother and sister.

"Are you Zenobia Van Zandt?" the woman asked.

"Yes," Zen said cautiously. "Do I know you?"

The woman shook her head. "You and I haven't met. I'm Priya Sudhra; Ramesh is my brother."

Knew it, Zen thought. She sensed a certain confidence from her soon-to-be sister-in-law.

"I'm here to tell you, you can't marry my brother."

Zen cocked her head, too stunned to say anything. She wasn't sure whether to be outraged or merely offended.

"Please, hear me out," Priya continued. "You know I don't mean anything personal by it, because I don't know anything about you as a person. You may be perfectly nice, and I'm sure my brother loves you very much. You simply can't marry him because, well—I don't mean to put you down, Zenobia, but you're not Indian."

Zen laughed. "I think Ramesh has already figured that out, Priya. For some crazy reason he wants to marry me anyway."

Priya frowned. "This isn't about what he wants. If you let a child choose what she wants for dinner, she's going to choose candy over vegetables most of the time. But a child can't live on candy alone, and the Sudhra family can't survive, as it has for thousands of years, if the oldest son is allowed to marry a non-Hindu, non-Indian woman."

Zen shook her head. "Ramesh is an adult, Priya. He's allowed to make these decisions for himself. Besides, the woman your parents chose for Ramesh rejected him and married someone else. That wasn't his fault."

Priya looked as if she were studying Zen's face carefully. "There are plenty of single Indian women my parents could fix Ramesh up with, but he won't let them. He won't even give these women a chance. And why is that? Because he thinks like a typical American, that everything on TV is the way things are supposed to be, and if another culture does things differently, well, the other culture must be wrong. And why is *that*? All because when he was an impressionable 21-year-old, he got himself mixed up in this Pagan nonsense and turned his back on the family's past."

"I beg your pardon," Zen said defensively. "Pagan nonsense? You're talking about my faith in the Goddess, one of the oldest faiths on earth."

"Oh, please," Priya said. "I don't doubt your faith in this mysterious, nameless Goddess, Zenobia. I do know your so-called religion bears little more than a passing resemblance to what ancient people believed. You know as well as I do the ancient pagans followed hundreds, maybe thousands of local religions. What was meaningful to them is, no doubt, far different from what is meaningful to you. What is meaningful to the Sudhra family, however, has never changed since ancient times. That is, until you came along."

"It's not true," Zen said. "What's meaningful to Ramesh is what's meaningful to me. We don't care about nationality, or about putting the right label on our beliefs.

We just live our lives. I would never try to keep him away from you or your parents—"

"But don't you see? That's exactly what you're doing," Priya interrupted. Her foot tapped on the floor, and Zen felt her impatience. "He has to choose, Zenobia. Your world, or ours."

"He has chosen, Priya. You have to accept his decision."

"I must do no such thing."

"There must be another way, some kind of compromise."

Priya's eyes focused on Zen's engagement ring. "That ring belongs to my grandmother."

"Ramesh went to Pune and got it from Hetal. He took me back there to meet her, and I received her blessing. What else do you want to hear, Priya? If the blessing of the matriarch of your family isn't good enough for you, what is?"

Zen was confused. Priya didn't seem the slightest bit angry at her; instead, she was supremely confident in what she was saying. She was honestly saddened by the thought of losing Ramesh to a non-Indian woman. Zen imagined Nalini, and perhaps Sadguna too, being disappointed in their son. Would they feel as if they'd lost him as a son? It didn't seem likely, but then what did Zen know? Priya did have a point when she implied Zen didn't know enough about Hinduism, or about the traditions Sadguna and Nalini were raised in.

Priya took Zen's hand in hers, studying the lotus-and-jewel engagement ring on Zen's finger. "This is more than the ring my grandfather gave to my grandmother when he married her, Zenobia. It's the ring the first-born son in the Sudhra family has always given to the woman who will become the family matriarch. It dates back to the seventeenth century."

She stared deep into Zen's eyes, and suddenly Zen saw four centuries of history staring back at her. The ring felt heavy on her finger. She loved Ramesh more than anything and couldn't imagine life without him. Still, maybe Priya had been right when she'd said this was about more than simply what she and Ramesh wanted for themselves.

When Priya held out her hand, Zen understood. She reluctantly took the ring from her finger and placed it on Priya's palm.

Priya smiled. "Thank you. I'm sorry for the disappointment, Zenobia, but I'm glad you understand what I'm saying." She took one last look at the statue of Nagina before she brushed past Zen and walked out the door.

Zen looked down at her now-naked finger and wondered what she'd done. For the first time in many Monday afternoons, Zen turned off the shop's neon "Open" sign. She gathered her school books and locked the front door. She could think of nothing else but getting to Ramesh. She didn't even bother to perform her usual spell before she left.

Traffic was bad, and it was more than two hours before she made it into Chicago. Even taking the expressway, it still took Zen forty-five more minutes to get to Ramesh's campus. It was getting late in the afternoon, but she didn't bother with checking for him at his apartment. This late in the school year—it was April—he was almost certainly in the lab.

She reached the decade-old, ivy-covered brick building and climbed the steps. The door was locked to anyone who didn't have a student i.d., so Zen waited for a student to enter and walked in behind her. She'd been there before, and knew where Ramesh's lab and office were. She checked the lab first, but there was no one she recognized there. She went upstairs to the faculty offices. Nearly all the offices were occupied, and the doors were closed, but the door to Ramesh's office was open.

As Zen walked nearer, she heard Ramesh's voice and realized he was talking to a student. For one brief, horrible moment, she imagined Ramesh alone in his office with that bitch, Kara Sarves-whatever. She breathed a sigh of relief when she heard a second male voice. She took a seat in a chair outside the office door and waited patiently for the student to leave.

The boy walked out, and Zen stood. She caught Ramesh's eye as he peered around the doorway. "Zen!" he said. "This is a nice surprise."

He tried to put his arms around her, but she pulled away.

"What's wrong?"

She shook her head, struggling to keep her voice steady as she held back the tears. "I'm so sorry," she said. "Ramesh, I love you, but I talked to your sister today."

He was suddenly bubbling with anger. "What did she tell you?" he thundered. "What did that rotten, lying little bitch say about me?"

Zen was taken aback at the force of his anger, but she understood. He really did love her more than he loved his sister. Realizing this only made things harder for Zen. Still, she had to get this over with as quickly as possible, even though there was no chance this was going to be painless.

"She didn't say anything bad about you, Ramesh. She told me the truth. She said there are some things more meaningful than the way a man and woman feel about one another."

He shook his head. "You're wrong. There's nothing more meaningful. Zen, you mean the world to me." He paused, staring at her hand. "What happened to your engagement ring?"

She took a step back, literally and symbolically stepping back from the temptation to fall into his arms and forget about Priya. "I gave it back to your family, where it belongs."

"What the hell are you talking about, crazy woman?" He half-laughed at his own attempt at humor. "You *are* my family. This doesn't make one damned bit of sense, Zen."

"I gave the ring back to your sister because it belongs to the Sudhra family matriarch," she said. "The matriarch should be a Hindu woman, an Indian woman. Your children should be Indian children. How arrogant of me to think I could get in the middle of centuries of family tradition." The tears wouldn't stay back any longer. She let them flow down her cheeks.

"How stupid of you to think your skin color, or where your family comes from, has anything to do with you being the matriarch of the Sudhra clan," he said bitterly. Tears flowed as freely down his cheeks as they did down hers. "I can't believe you even listened to her. Why didn't you throw Priya's stupid ass out on the street?"

"Ramesh, she was right. You haven't given your parents a chance to arrange a marriage for you."

"So what?" he said. "I want to marry you, Zen."

"I'm sorry," she said. "I can't do this to your family, Ramesh. I'll always love you, but I have to walk away."

He shook his head again, lost. "You're going to walk out on me? Do you know what your sister said to me the night I almost walked out on you, at Allie and Orlando's wedding reception? She said if I walked away, I should never expect to come back. I understand if you have pre-wedding jitters, but you cannot walk away from me now, Zenobia Van Zandt."

They stared into one another's eyes for a moment. Her heart ached from his acute pain, on top of her own. She looked away, then turned her back to him. "I love you, Ramesh, but I have to do this. It's for your own good."

"Fuck that," he said. "Fuck you." He turned on his heel and walked back into the office, slamming the door behind him.

Weeping, Zen left the science building and got back in her car.

* * * *

The phone, located inches from Ramesh's head, had been ringing non-stop for almost a minute. Ramesh didn't seem to notice. Since Zen had broken off their engagement, there wasn't much he did seem to notice. Nalini wished she had the same problem, but the telephone was driving her crazy.

"Ramesh, are you going to get that?"

He made no response.

Nalini walked into the living room and picked up the cordless phone. She glared down at her son angrily. Her anger soon broke, however, as she observed him. He was no more than a shadow of the Ramesh she knew. His face was pale and unshaven, his hair unwashed. He hadn't changed his clothes in a couple of days now. She recognized the classic signs of depression and knew her son needed help. She sighed, realizing what form that help would have to take.

She pushed the "talk" button, but walked into the kitchen as she spoke. "Hello? Yes, he's here, but he's...well, he can't take a phone call right now. I'll let him know you called. Yes, I did let him know about the other times. As I've said, he's unable...as soon as he can. Yes, goodbye."

Nalini left the phone lying on the kitchen counter. She sighed again, collecting her thoughts before she walked back into the living room. She didn't like any of this, and this was going to be the hardest part of it all.

She sat down beside her son on the couch. Ramesh didn't look at her. He didn't even blink. She picked up his hand and sandwiched it between her hands. "Son, I know you're disappointed because Zen called off the wedding. I know your heart is broken."

He answered her with a weak sort of grunt.

"Listen, you can't spend the rest of your life moping around on your parents' couch. It's not healthy."

His head turned toward her. The movement was slight, but Nalini perceived it.

"I'll admit Zen isn't exactly what your father and I had hoped for in a daughter-in-law," she said. "I really wanted you to marry a girl from Maharashtra. I was hoping for Indian grandchildren, with a traditional Hindu upbringing." She smiled slightly at the words, remembering how strongly Sadguna had wanted a traditional American upbringing for his son and daughter. It was a miracle she and Sadguna managed to stay together for almost thirty years now. "The gods simply had another destiny in store for you. Who am I to deny it?"

He snorted slightly. "What did you just say, Ma?"

"I said I think Priya was wrong. I hate to say it about my own daughter, but it's the truth. She shouldn't have interfered in your wedding plans, especially after you and Zenobia got Hetal's blessing."

Ramesh wiped at his eye. Nalini could see he was crying. "It's too late," he said.

"Nonsense," Nalini said firmly. "It's never too late."

* * * *

Zen stood on a stepladder in the back of the shop, peering into a box of herbs to take inventory. She kept count on her Blackberry. The light from the little device was the brightest thing in the dark, dusty store room. As she got ready to look into the next box, Zen wondered if there was a spell that would make the back room seem more cheerful. Not much had seemed cheerful to her lately, even when she was in Light and Shadow.

Gillian stood in the front of the shop, keeping an eye on the door while she worked on the front display case's Midsummer Night theme. There were the gold-painted plastic balls representing the sun, the healing herbs (also plastic, in this case), the crystals and trinkets representing the fairies, and even a loaf of bread in recognition of Lammas. Gillian had a flare for display cases Zen only wished she could possess.

Still, Gillian couldn't always help the customers and create the display at the same time. The front door chimed, and Gillian immediately called out, "Zen!"

Zen left her Blackberry on the highest shelf and climbed down from the stepstool. She came up front, expecting to wait on the customer who'd just walked in. Instead, she found herself face-to-face with Nalini Sudhra.

"Mrs. Sudhra," Zen said, more stunned than anything else. "What—what are you doing here?"

Nalini looked around, almost admiringly, at Zen's shop. Her eyes rested in the same place Priya's had, on the statue of the Hindu serpent goddess. Then she looked back at Zen. "I wanted to give you something."

Zen shook her head, certain whatever Ramesh's mother had to give her was something she didn't want. It was already hard enough to get through the day without thinking about Ramesh. She couldn't believe her eyes when Nalini held out her arm, opened her hand, and presented Zen with the lotus-and-jewel engagement ring.

"Gillian," Zen said, her voice cracking, "will you go in the back and count the bloodroot for me?"

Gillian looked up from arranging fake herbs and winked at Zen. "Sure," she said.

"Take it," Nalini said, pressing the ring into Zen's hand as Gillian left them in privacy. "Zenobia, I don't care what my daughter told you. She doesn't speak on behalf of the Sudhra family. The only person who has the right to do so is Hetal, and she already granted you her blessing. Zen, you have to marry Ramesh."

Zen continued to shake her head, unable to believe what she was hearing. "I thought you wanted him to marry a Hindu woman." She took the ring from Nalini, but didn't put it on. She stared at it as if it might disappear into thin air if she looked away for a moment.

"If Hetal thinks you're a good match for my son, then you must be a Hindu woman," Nalini said, shrugging her shoulders. "Now, come on, Zen. Sunday is my only day off; are you going to let me waste it waiting on you? Or are you going to get in my car and let me take you to Ramesh?"

Zen was still stunned. "Are you serious? Because if this is some kind of joke, it really isn't funny."

"Do I look like the kind of woman who tells a lot of jokes?" Nalini said. Zen had to admit she didn't. Nalini told Zen, "Tell your employee you're going to be gone for a while."

"Gillian, can you handle inventory?" Zen called to the back of the store. "I might be gone for a while, so call Corey if you need any help."

"Sure thing," Gillian called back. "Where are you going?"

"To answer the call of true love," Nalini said.

"Have fun," Gillian responded. Zen wasn't sure if she'd really heard Nalini's dramatic pronouncement or not.

She *was* sure, when they arrived at the Sudhra home, that being back in Ramesh's arms was the only thing in the world that felt right. When he slipped the ring back onto Zen's finger, she whispered, "I'm sorry."

"Me, too," he said. "I never should have let you walk out that door."

Ramesh pulled her in for the longest, deepest kiss they'd shared since she completed her vow of celibacy. Nothing, as far as Zen could tell, would ever separate her from Ramesh again.

* * * *

Zen clutched her beer bottle nervously as the house lights dimmed. Beside her, Gillian was refilling margarita glasses for Melissa and Kameko. This was a special occasion, a feast day, so even the Pagan priestesses allowed themselves to partake in alcohol. Brittany, like Zen, had opted for bottled beer. Allie gracefully swirled her martini glass, never spilling a drop of her blood-red cosmo.

Zen leaned over to her sister. "I take it you're not pregnant again."

Allie took a sip of her drink. "Not yet," she said. "Which of us do you think will have the next baby?"

"You," Zen said. "Definitely you. I'm not quite ready to give up my pills yet."

If she had more to say, it wouldn't have mattered. The speakers rumbled, and a male voice announced, "Ladies, gentlemen, and everyone in between, get ready! You are about to be dazzled by seven of the sexiest showgirls Drop Dead Legs has to offer!"

The music swelled, bass pumping, and the show "girls" appeared in a melange of pink marabou, fishnet, and spandex. Zen studied the blonde wigs closely, wondering if any of those hairs came from her own head.

"Which one is Corey?" Melissa asked, barely audible above the drone of the music.

"Third from left," Gillian said, licking the spoon she'd been using to dole out orange cream margaritas. "In the blue halter top."

Kameko nodded approvingly. "He makes a good woman," she said. She took a large slurp from her margarita glass, then ate some of the sugar from the rim.

A showgirl with fire-engine-red hair lip-synched her way through a techno remix of a Christina Aguilera song, and then the music quieted down to a reasonable decibel level. "Uh-oh!" the announcer shouted into the mike, "did someone say we have a bachelorette party in the house?"

Corey (known inside Drop Dead Legs as Blonde, James Blonde) appeared from backstage, nodding vigorously and pointing to the table where the women sat. Zen attempted to duck under the tablecloth, but Brittany snagged her. Corey took the mike away from the redhead.

"Don't be shy, honey," he said, using his most feminine voice. Zen seldom heard this voice; she was much more accustomed to the gray-suited, insurance salesman version of Corey Werwinski. "Come on up here and party with us! That is, if you're not too tired from all the pre-wedding humping you and your man have been doing." The audience roared with laughter. "Oops, did I let the cat out of the bag? This is one bride who won't be wearing white. I hope he got down on his knees when he proposed. Did he?" Zen nodded. "Good, because I know he's going to want you to get down on your knees for him!"

As the audience howled, Brittany and Gillian escorted Zen to edge of the stage, and two drag queens helped her up. "Ladies and gentlemen, let's hear it for Blonde, James Blonde!" the announcer said.

There was a wild whoop of applause, followed by the opening notes of "A View to a Kill." Corey struck a dramatic pose, then began to lip sync along with the Duran Duran song. Zen stood at center stage, trying to be a good sport as Corey bumped and grinded against her.

Out of the corner of her eye, Zen saw her Blackberry on the table, lit up. She was missing a call from Ramesh. She was tempted to jump down and grab her phone when Allie snatched the Blackberry and answered the call.

* * * *

Ramesh sank down in his seat at the booth as Riley handed him his beer. "I asked for a Kingfisher," Ramesh said, staring at the strange Hindi label.

"You asked for an Indian beer. This is what the bartender gave me. Look, you can't always get exactly what you want. Personally, I'd rather be at the women's party."

"Me too," Orlando said, slapping Ramesh on the shoulder. "I can't imagine Allie's having much fun at a gay cabaret. If she were with me, she'd be having fun." He finished off his Bertoluccio and signaled the cocktail waitress.

"Hold on," Ramesh said, "I'm trying to make a phone call here." Zen (he assumed) answered. "Oh my God, I can't believe how much I ate at that buffet," he said by way of a greeting.

Allie laughed on the other end of the line. "If I were you, I'd be more worried about what Zen is eating."

"Allie?"

"Ding, ding, ding! Get this man a cigar!"

"What's Zen doing?"

"Standing with her legs apart while Corey crawls on his belly between them," Allie said. "I wish I had a video camera. Hey, do you know how to work the video function on Zen's Blackberry?"

"You tell Corey I'm going to kick his ass next time I see him," Ramesh said.

"She's only having fun, Ramesh. You know she's not doing anything wrong. Oh, wait, she's coming down now. I'll pass the phone over—"

The club on the women's end of the line exploded in raucous laughter, then cheers. When the noise died down a bit, Zen got on the line. "I hear you ate too much at the buffet," she said.

"Oh, God. There were crab legs *and* lobster *and* shrimp. I ate them all, but only after I had a T-bone steak and a baked potato."

"Have you guys done any gambling yet?"

"Of course. There's no point to visiting a casino if you're not going to lose money. I've lost about sixty so far. Orlando's the lucky one; he won five thousand!"

"That's great," Zen said. "Now Allie and Orlando can afford to buy us a really nice wedding present."

Ramesh laughed. "I wish you were here."

"I wish *you* were *here*," she said. "And I wish these drag queens were bare-chested studs with tight pants and six-pack abs."

"They are," Ramesh said. "Look under their skirts."

"No, thanks. That's one mental image I can go to my deathbed without."

Another round of loud whoops and hollers rose from the crowd. Ramesh could barely hear Zen anymore. "What's going on now?" he asked her.

"Kameko and Melissa have completely taken over the show," Zen said. "They're in a chorus line of queens, belting out the classic LaBelle version of 'Lady Marmalade.'"

"You have to record it for me."

She laughed. "Of course. This is going up on the Pagan Spirits page on MySpace. Oh, I've gotta go. I think Allie's about to join them."

The cocktail waitress brought another Bertoluccio for Orlando and another Bud Light for Riley. Ramesh's friends from the biology lab were drinking regular Bud, seemingly by the case. Ramesh had barely touched the mysterious Indian beer, but suddenly he was in the mood for something stronger. "Bring us a shot of Jack Damiels all around," Ramesh told the waitress before she left the table. Returning to the phone call, he said, "Have fun, baby. But not too much fun. And make sure everyone gets home safely."

"We all brought cab fare," she said. "We'll share a ride. And of course, Allie will stay with me." She knew she didn't have to worry about the men, since they'd each booked a room at the casino hotel to sleep off the effects of the bachelor party. "You have fun, too. Within reason."

"Don't worry," he said. "I only have eyes for you."

"Keep 'em that way."

"I promise."

As he hung up, another loud roar issued from the drag show crowd. Ramesh assumed Allie had finally made her way into the chorus line.

Orlando used his casino winnings to buy the guys a limo ride. After a few hours of cruising around Milwaukee, the limo driver left them at their hotel. Orlando made sure Ramesh went to his bed safely.

Chapter Ten

The doorbell chimed, and Zen shot out of her seat on the couch to open it. Allie stood in the hall, a suitcase in each hand. Her long hair was pulled back in a simple ponytail. Zen noticed her wipe the beads of sweat from her forehead. She wore a thin, white cotton summer dress, appropriate to the heat of the day.

Behind her, Orlando stood, balancing Antonio on his hip. She felt warmth, happiness, and anticipation from all three of them. "Ti Ti!" Antonio exclaimed, still using his favorite version of "Auntie." His little hands stretched out toward Zen.

"I can't do this," Zen said. Her eyes met Allie's.

"You can't let us in the door?" Orlando asked.

Zen shook her head and stepped aside to admit her sister's family. Allie set her bags down and took a seat at Zen's breakfast bar. She motioned for Zen to join her on the adjacent bar stool. Meanwhile, Orlando unzipped a pocket on one of the suitcases and began pulling out toys for Antonio to play with. Like handkerchiefs in a magician's act, the toys kept coming.

Zen sat down. "I can't do it, Allie," she repeated.

"You can't do what, Zen?" Allie's tone was nothing but sympathetic. Zen could feel her concern.

"This traditional Hindu wedding ceremony," Zen said. "It's too much pressure! Ramesh's whole extended family and all their friends are coming to judge me! And then there's *this*!"

She rummaged through a pile of papers, most of which were wedding-related. After searching for a couple of minutes, Zen found a photocopy of Ramesh's lengthy, thorough family tree. "It dates back to the mid-century," Zen said, chagrined.

She handed the paper to Allie, who studied it. "What's the problem?" Orlando asked. He knelt in the center of Zen's living room, where he and Antonio were rolling a plastic ball that flashed colored lights back and forth to one another. "Did you find out Ramesh is descended from some infamous serial killer or something?"

"It's not *his* family tree I'm worried about," Zen said. "It's *ours*. Ramesh knows his great-great-grandfather's name, and I don't even know who my father is!"

"Stop freaking out," Allie said gently.

"That's easy for you to say," Zen said. "Have you ever been to a Hindu wedding? From everything I've heard, the whole first part of it consists of me being given away by my father. He's supposed to symbolically accept Ramesh into the family and give Ramesh's family the dowry. Then our family priest and Ramesh's family priest recite this." She took the family tree from Allie's hands. "You're my family priestess, Allie. What are you going to recite? Who's going to give me away?"

"Where are you going to come up with a dowry?" Orlando asked facetiously. The ball flashed yellow and green and came rolling toward him. Allie shot him a look, but Zen sensed a lot of affection behind his remark.

"Because you and I don't have a father doesn't mean we don't have a family," Allie said calmly. "Who says we can't shake up the old phallocentric way of doing things? Auntie Kameko is going to give you away. Face it, she's been a mother *and* a father to us. Plus, she knows her family tree back to the time of the shoguns."

Zen breathed deeply and thought for a moment. Then she said, "Ramesh's mom isn't going to like this."

"She doesn't have to like it," Allie said. "No one has to like the wedding ceremony. The ceremony is a symbol. It's up to you and Ramesh to make the marriage—and enjoy it."

Allie got up from the counter and opened Zen's kitchen cabinets until she discovered where Zen kept the tea. She pulled down a box of soothing mint tea and began boiling water in the kettle on the stove top.

"You're anxious about the details of the ceremony," Allie continued. "It's understandable two weeks before the big day."

"I remember how anxious you were before you married Paul Phillip," Zen said. It felt a little better to recall the jumble of good and bad emotions inside Allie before Allie's first wedding. "You didn't even know he was going to leave you for another man."

Orlando, helping Antonio spread a large number of colorful blocks across Zen's carpet, interjected. "The night before I married Catherine, I spent half the night puking my mother's stuffed cabbage rolls into Catherine's parents' backyard zinnia bed. It wasn't the Bertoluccio that time. It was sheer nerves."

Allie seemed to be ignoring her husband as she patiently waited for the water to boil. "I'll call Kameko yet this evening, when we get back from dinner. She's been hoping for a larger mother-of-the-bride role in the wedding anyway. As for you, Zen, I think we're going to perform a calming spell on you." She shut off the whistling kettle. "Right after you drink this mint tea."

Zen took the tea and sat on the sofa, watching her nephew and brother-in-law play as Allie disappeared into Zen's bedroom. Allie took one of her suitcases with her; Zen guessed it was the one containing Allie's magical supplies. When Allie stuck her head out the bedroom door and said, "I'm ready," Zen got up to follow her sister into her bedroom.

Orlando looked up at Zen. "I had a flashback," he said. "Remember the first time you invited me over here?"

Zen smiled. "That's ancient history now, Orlando."

He nodded. "It's not a history I'd want to revisit. I would never betray your sister. It can be...fascinating to look back in time and remember, though."

"Yeah," Zen said, momentarily feeling a slight twinge of nostalgia.

She found Allie lying on her back across the black sheets on the bed. Zen felt a little embarrassed. She hadn't changed her sheets that morning, and given how hot and sweaty the night before had been, she wondered what impression Allie got of her. If Allie felt uncomfortable, though, Zen couldn't sense it.

"Sit on the floor, at the foot of the bed," Allie guided her.

Zen did as she was told, sitting before the makeshift altar Allie had set up. It was simply a black scarf laid across the floor, with Allie's incense bowl and a small bell sitting on top. The incense bowl smoked, smelling of the unique fragrance of sandalwood.

"Are you comfortable?" Allie asked quietly.

"Yeah, I guess so," Zen said.

"Is your cell phone off?"

Zen laughed. "Hold on." She took the phone out of the holder clipped onto her belt, flipped it open, and turned the phone off. "Okay, I'm ready."

"Ring the bell, and wait for the silence after all vibrations of the sound have faded." Zen rang the bell, then listened for the last echoes of its high, tinny ring. At the same time she realized the room was silent once again, Allie spoke. "Now, the four-count breath. It's one of the oldest and most simple relaxation techniques. Breathe in as you count to four, slowly. Hold your breath for another four count. Breathe out on the next count to four, and then inhale on the next count to four. Do this until your thoughts are empty of everything but your breathing and your counting."

Zen breathed in deeply and began counting to four, hoping she understood Allie's instructions correctly. The sequence seemed to come naturally to her. At first, she noticed Allie breathing along with her. This was a distraction for a moment, but in between feeling Allie's growing sense of calm and her own steady breathing, Zen became lost in the four-count. All other thoughts slowly drifted away, including the feel of the carpet underneath her.

When Allie spoke again, her voice was calm. Its rhythm matched that of Zen's breathing. "Ring the bell again," she said. "This time, as the sound fades, you will repeat to yourself a single word: Om."

Briefly, Zen thought back to the Indian temples she and Ramesh had visited, and how the worshipers seemed to sit perfectly still except for their breathing, focusing on the word "Om." She cleared these thoughts from her mind, though, by bringing her thoughts back to her four-count breathing.

"Say the word," Allie said softly. "Say it as many times as you like, each time drawing the word out as long as possible. Your mind will clear of the last traces of your extraneous thoughts. Then your mind's eye will be ready to see."

Zen pronounced the syllable, finding it seemed to come naturally to her. Her gift of empathy somehow switched itself off; she could no longer sense Allie's emotions. The word, "Om," became all that was real to her. She didn't count how many times the word came out of her mouth, but when she was ready, Allie spoke again.

"Imagine," Allie said. "In your mind's eye, picture Ramesh's mother accepting you, welcoming you into the family. Picture your desire as a ray of light. Imagine the ray of light as a drop in a still, black pond. As the drop of light sinks beneath the placid surface of the water, the light spreads out as ripples. The ripples of light slowly begin to spread until they reach the horizon."

Zen saw it in her mind, exactly the way Allie described. Being loved and accepted by Ramesh's mother felt incredibly beautiful. The feeling filled Zen from the top of her head to the soles of her feet.

Her imaginary ripples of light reached the horizon of her mind just as Allie said, "Ring the bell once more. As the sound concludes, so does the ritual."

Zen opened her eyes as the tinny sound of the bell faded to nothingness. She breathed in deeply once more, this time noticing the scent of the sandalwood incense. In that instant, her gift of empathy returned. She could feel Allie's love and concern for her. Allie came down off the bed and gave Zen a hearty hug.

"Come on," she said. "Let's get ready for dinner. Antonio hasn't had anything but goldfish crackers to eat since Chicago, and I bet he's starting to get cranky."

"Not yet," Zen said, focusing on her nephew's feelings, slightly dampened by being in the other room. "He's having way too much fun throwing everything in my utensil drawer onto the kitchen floor."

Allie cocked her head slightly. "You can sense that?"

"I can hear it," Zen said, laughing.

* * * *

Zen sat on the bed. It was stiflingly hot in the guest bedroom at Nalini and Sadguna's house, though she had opened the window. The iced tea Ramesh made for her sat untouched. Zen was sweating almost as much as the glass of tea. Her nerves made her sweat more than the temperature did.

She had let Hetal do her makeup. Hetal made Zen's eyes with heavy black eyeliner and mascara, topped off with an exotic shade of turquoise eye shadow. The heavy make-up gave Zen a slightly more exotic look. If she hadn't known better, she would almost have believed Hetal was trying to trick the Sudhra family's many relatives, friends, and business associates into thinking Zen had some Asian in her, after all. Hetal told Zen she had dreamed of braiding Zen's hair, until she realized Zen had donated her hair to the gods and goddesses, and it wouldn't be long (or blonde) any time soon.

Zen wished she didn't have to be alone. She would have given anything to have Allie in the bedroom with her. Better still, she wished Gillian were here. Gillian had been at Zen's side, coaching her through her end-of-term nursing exams, spending nights on Zen's couch to quiz Zen on her medical vocabulary and make fresh coffee each time they ran out. She'd been with Zen through the preliminary wedding jitters, that disastrous Sunday dinner with Ramesh's mom, and the more serious doubts that came afterward. Gillian was a rock. She was like granite. She was like...

Zen's thoughts were interrupted by a knock on the door. "Zen, may we come in?" Allie asked.

"Door's unlocked," Zen called back. She sat up a little straighter, adjusting her long, pink satin dress with the long sash over one shoulder. She tried to smile.

The door opened, and Antonio bounced in. "Ti Ti's scared," he said. He put his little hand on Zen's knee and looked up into her eyes. "Don't be afraid, Ti Ti. Mommy's not afraid." He looked up at Allie, who stood behind her son, holding hands with Orlando.

Orlando cocked his head to the side. "Did he just say what I think he said?"

Antonio looked over his shoulder at his father. "Daddy's confused," he said. He added a little giggle and said, "Confused tickles."

Zen nodded. "Yeah, it kinda does at first," she said. "You get used to it after a while."

"Wait a minute," Orlando said. "What's going on here, Zen? What are you and Antonio doing?"

"I can't believe you haven't figured it out already," Allie said.

"Figured what out?"

"He's got it," Zen said. "Antonio has the gift of empathy."

"So, you two can read each others' minds?"

Zen laughed. "Of course not. We can read each others' feelings."

Orlando sat on the edge of the bed beside Zen. "That's actually kind cool. The next time Allie's angry with me but I don't know it, this kid might really come in handy." He picked Antonio up and put him in his lap, giving his son a healthy squeeze.

"By the way, you're only a few minutes away from your grand entrance," Allie said.

Zen took a deep breath. She tried to remember the relaxation technique Allie had taught her two weeks before. She closed her eyes and visualized a drop of light falling into still, black water, with ripples of light spreading out toward the horizon. "Okay," she said.

"We'll go with you," Orlando said. He lifted Antonio onto his shoulders, a good height considering Orlando's size.

"Ti Ti's really scared now," Antonio said. Zen gave up on her ripples of light. Allie took Zen's hand and walked down the back staircase into the kitchen with her.

She was pleasantly surprised to find Kameko and Nalini laughing together, as if they'd been friends since their school days. "Come," Kameko said. "Sit next to me, Zen. Orlando, Allie, Antonio, come sit at the counter." Zen noticed the wedding planner sitting at the counter already. Hetal, wearing a cream-colored dressed infused with threads of gold, stood beside Nalini and Sadguna.

Nalini looked perfect, not a single hair out of place despite the heat. Her dark-blue dress appeared untouched by perspiration, though she glowed from within with warmth and happiness. At her other hand sat a man Zen had never met before, but understood to be the Hindu priest hired by the Sudhra family. He was simply dressed in gray. He greeted Zen with a gesture of welcome.

"You were raised by a wise woman, Zenobia Van Zandt," Nalini said.

Sadguna, also, appeared unphased by the summer heat. He looked cool in a light blue button-down shirt and a matching tie with a repeating pattern. Zen looked closely and noticed the repeated design was a lotus flower.

"Thank you," Zen said. "Allie and I are very proud of her."

"Thank *you*," Kameko said. "And you'll be happy to know, as traditions dictate, I have formally welcomed Ramesh into the Kitatani clan."

Zen was so intensely focused on her would-be in-laws, she'd nearly forgotten about the prospective groom. She turned toward Ramesh, who sat at the head of the table. He looked more handsome than she'd ever seen him before, in a new, white, Indian-style shirt. His long hair was pulled back in a neat ponytail, and if Zen breathed deeply enough, she could smell his cologne. He radiated happiness even more so than his parents. Zen remembered once again why she loved him so much.

"That's great," Zen said. "What happens now?"

"I have to give you away," Kameko said, somewhat sadly.

"I've written out the text of your speech," the Sudhra family priest said, handing an index card to Kameko. "Just fill in Zenobia's name where you see the blank lines."

Kameko took the card and scanned it with an amused smile. "And, of course, I'm to fill in Zenobia's genealogy," she said.

"Of course," Nalini said, smiling. She leaned forward, ready to listen.

"I, Kameko Kitatani, mother of Zenobia Van Zandt, am the daughter of Aiko and Fukiko Kitatani..."

Kameko recited her lengthy geneology, tracing the motherline through her mother's ancestors. When she finished what was written on the index card, the Hindu priest recited the Sudhra family's genealogy.

"It is not only the blood of these ancestors we cherish as we recite these names," the Sudhra family priest said. "It is their spirit that has been passed down from generation to generation. It is their spirit we celebrate today. It is their spirit that grows in these two. We join them together to create a new spirit, a new family, a new future."

He went on with more prayers and rituals. When the ceremony was beginning to seem endless, Ramesh's parents got up from the table. Nalini shook hands with Kameko, and Zen realized the formalities were over.

"Mr. and Mrs. Sudhra, it was so nice to see you both again," Zen said, standing. Slowly she made her way over to Ramesh's side. He looked more handsome than she'd ever seen him before, positively radiant. He looked almost like the primal forest-god of her dream.

Nalini positioned herself directly in between Ramesh and Zen. "If you'll excuse me, I'd like to go freshen my makeup before the second part of the wedding," she said.

"I'll join you," Hetal said. They walked up the back stairs, toward the master bedroom and bath.

Zen threw her arms around Kameko. "Thank you," she said. "I don't know how you got Nalini Sudhra to accept me, but you did it."

"I didn't do anything," Kameko said.

"You're being too modest," Ramesh said. "I saw how the two of you were talking before the wedding."

"I'm not being modest," Kameko insisted. "This was the work of the Goddess. Truly."

The second part of the wedding ceremony took place at the Hindu temple. Zen and Ramesh had been there several times since their trip to India.

But friends and family, including Allie, Orlando, Antonio, and Priya would have to wait until the ceremony was completed to see the happy couple. Inside the temple, the Sudhra's family priest lit the traditional fire. The only witnesses to this ancient practice were Nalini and Sadguna, Hetal, Auntie Kameko, and the bride and groom themselves. Zen and Ramesh sat together underneath a red wedding canopy.

"Fire has a very special meaning in the Hindu tradition," the Sudhra family priest began. "Fire is light, and the light is the truth." He proceeded to read a long, ancient text in Sanskrit. His reading was almost like song, chanted rather than read as a newspaper would be.

He put the book down, picked up another, and read aloud a series of verses in English. When the priest was finished with his tract, it was Kameko's turn to read. Her text was entirely in English, but it was just as long, and also taken from the Hindu sacred texts.

"Zenobia, take the hand of Ramesha," the priest requested when the readings were complete. Zen and Ramesh stood and held hands.

"Now you walk around the fire," the priest explained. The bride and groom made a slow, clockwise circle around the sacred fire, the same way they had paid their respects to the temples in India.

Lastly, the priest explained that Zen should taken seven steps forward. "These are also very symbolic," he said.

"These steps are asking the gods to bless your marriage with prosperity and with children. Honor your ancestors as you step forward now."

Zen stepped forward joyfully. Her new in-laws seemed to be counting her steps with her. When the seven steps were completed, she turned to face her husband. Ramesh's face glowed like sunlight with the radiance of true happiness.

Ramesh then placed a necklace of gold beads around Zen's neck, clasping it for her behind her head. As he did, he leaned in close to Zen and whispered in her ear. "Do you know what this means?"

She shook her head.

"We are now officially, *officially* married," he said. "As soon as the reception is over, we get to go on our honeymoon."

Zen squeezed Ramesh's hand. "Tonight," she said, "and every night for the rest of our lives." She looked into the fire, then down at the lotus-and-jewel ring she proudly wore on her finger, and knew it was true.

ABOUT ERIN O'RIORDAN

Erin O'Riordan lives in the Midwestern United States with her husband and co-author Tit Elingtin. Her erotic stories, essays, and film reviews have been published in numerous magazines and websites. She loves world mythology for both its spirituality and storytelling value and refuses to choose any one faith. The ideal trap for Erin O'Riordan would be baited with dark chocolate, espresso drinks and Christian Bale movies.

Readers can view more of O'Riordan's work, including free samples, at <u>www.aeess.com</u>. *Midsummer Night* is the second in the twelve-part Pagan Spirits series.

If you enjoyed <u>MIDSUMMER NIGHT</u>,
you might also enjoy:

<u>THE SMELL OF GAS</u>
By Erin O'Riordan and Tit Elingtin
April 2011 from Melange Books
<u>http://www.melange-books.com/</u>

Love pulp fiction? Just try putting down *The Smell of Gas*. *TSOG* is full of saints and sinners you'll love to hate. There's Brigid, the high school basketball player and secret heroin addict. Fred, a Catholic lesbian teen, loves Brigid, but doesn't know about her affair with Edward, a married Evangelical preacher. Sex, ethics, religions and mythologies clash as you dig deeper into their connection to the death of a young couple.

Excerpt:

January 2000
In Fred's bright white room, she'd stacked three rows of votive candles in red jars on her dresser. Fred's roommate, Leander, said they reminded him of the cemetery, but Fred used them as a meditation point when she prayed.

She liked the deep blue sheets on her bed. The white-and-blue color scheme matched the dress and cape of the woman in the poster above Fred's bed. The print of Murillo's Immaculate Conception of the Escorial, painted in 1678, portrayed the Virgin, eyes looking up to heaven, surrounded by cherubim and standing on a crescent moon.

Behind the Virgin's head, the cherubim dissolved into an orange haze. In the light of the burning votives, the whole room seemed to glow orange.

Three rows of seven candles before her, she said one Hail Mary for each.

Fred finished saying her twenty-first Hail Mary and got off her knees. She blew out all of the candles except one. The cheap candles smoked, filling Fred's small bedroom with a grayness that reminded her of an underwater scene. She walked over to the bed and lifted the corner of the mattress. She had to grope for a moment to find it, tucked inside the elastic of the blue fitted sheet's corner. She held up the razor to the candlelight. The blood left on it from the last time didn't bother her. It was clean blood, her own.

EMINENT DOMAIN
By Erin O'Riordan and Tit Elingtin

A young couple buys the waterfront home of their dreams. After years of rehab to their home, they find it was all in vain. The government is going to take it from them. Feeling robbed of his liberty, Jeff is left hopeless and is willing to lose it all.

Excerpt:

The phone landed on the floor beside the accelerator, going unnoticed as Jeff stepped on the gas and rocketed through the parking lot. At nine in the morning, the Wednesday before Christmas 2011, few citizens visited city hall. Jeff lucked out: fewer barriers between his Toyota Matrix and what he intended to do.

City hall lay straight ahead.

The glass and steel double doors opened from within, and a woman stepped out. Her sudden, horrified expression as she dashed out of the way meant she'd seen Jeff's car and, in the split second before he hit the building, realized he wasn't stopping. Jeff didn't know whether she made it to safety or not. It didn't matter as the glass came shattering down over the roof of the car and steel scraped the doors with an agonized groan. After the first set of doors, Jeff hit the second set.

Jeff rocked forward in his seat before his seatbelt arrested his momentum. He felt the jolt as his seatbelt tightened and the airbag deployed, slamming into his chest and face. It stung him as it threw his arms clear of the steering wheel. His head slammed into the headrest. His body rocked with the shock wave, but Jeff had no intention of letting the doors slow him down. He floored the gas. The car lurched forward from the wreckage.

It was almost beautiful, like the Fourth of July, the way sparks flew and glass shattered. With the noise of steel scraping against steel, Jeff's entrance put the town's annual fireworks display to shame. Jeff inhaled and the smell of the gas can in the back seat hit his nose.

Look for Eminent Domain *soon on Amazon.com*